Dare to Respect

a novel based on

Wives who Accepted the Challenge

❦

TAMMY OBERG DE LA GARZA

ISBN: 1533558140
ISBN-13: 978-1533558145

DEDICATION

This book is dedicated to my Christian Sisters.
Thank you for standing in the gap and pointing me upward.

ACKNOWLEDGMENTS

Nina Roesner for being faithful and answering God's call to support this book. Thank you for your prayers of protection and wisdom.

Kathy Zawilenski for your tireless editing and encouragement.

Jakee Hanipale for keeping me on track when I was about to lose it.

Debbie Schmidt and Deb Byers for imparting wisdom on Saturday mornings.

Donna Lawrence for challenging me to go down unknown paths.

Oonagh David and Kristina Peterson for spiritual reinforcement.

Reynolds De La Garza for… sharing your life with me.

FOREWARD

When Tammy Oberg De La Garza contacted me about writing this novel, I admit I was intrigued. Here's a piece of "inside baseball" that you won't see anywhere else… I prayed with this then-stranger on the phone about God's will, and then tasked her with listening to Him about who the main characters were going to be. I needed to know she understood the vast array of women out there and their struggles. I needed to know she wasn't just trying to make a buck off our trademark. I mean think about it – she contacted me out of the blue with "I think God's asked me to write a novel about women doing your book." I didn't know her from Adam. So when Tammy presented me with her outline of the women, I knew she not only understood enough of what is going on in marriages in Western culture, but that she was actually following Christ in her actions. I had a piece of paper with the characteristics of the women on it – and she covered every single element. She literally didn't miss anything. So how could I not encourage her?

And when I read the first draft and actually couldn't put it down because I cared about the women, I knew her book had purpose.

I long for each woman who does *The Respect Dare* (Thomas Nelson, 2012) to have a group of women to walk with as they do the journey, however, that doesn't always happen. And unfortunately, when they are alone, sometimes they quit. I realized that Tammy's book could be the way they linked arms with women who also struggle in marriage and are trying to improve their marriages by respecting their husbands.

I recently received this from a reader: *I am so grateful for the Respect Dare challenge. I am on Dare 32. I started this challenge as a 4th year anniversary gift for my husband. Our anniversary is June 22nd. It has brought a sweet level of holiness in my marriage. I have fallen deeply in love with God again and find myself falling in love with my husband more and more each day. I even find myself getting butterflies in my stomach thinking about seeing him when I get home from work. I am kinder to my husband; less controlling of outcomes; more present for my girls. I pray more; I smile often; I am joyful and my laughter has returned. One of my favorite traits about myself is my sweetness. I lost it for a while... It has returned! I love being sweet to my husband. I have seen him fall more in love with me too. He calls me pet names he used to call me when we were dating. He leaves me love notes and flowers. He wants to be by me. He talks to me about what is on his heart. He shows me how much I mean to him.*

I sat back and wondered at what God had done in her life, and I want that for all of you as you consider the insights the women in Tammy's book accrue along the way. I've led enough women through *The Respect Dare* and our ministry's marriage course, *Daughters of Sarah®*, to know that the women you are about to get to know are as real as they come. I feel like I've not only met them, but also interacted with them over their situations. Tammy does a lovely job addressing real issues that real women struggle with. Their solutions may not be the ones God encourages you to pursue, but I'm confident that as you continue to grow in your relationship with Him, you'll find His ways easier and easier. There's real freedom in this journey!

Years of marriage can also bring years of baggage, conflicts resolved poorly, pride taking first seat, and love gone awry. We invite you to join our communities on Facebook and at www.GreaterImpact.org where you'll meet women just like you doing the next right thing in their marriages to bring deeper connections with Him and their husbands. In fact, as the women in *Dare to Respect* discover, what you learn spills over into all of your relationships – and makes them better, too.

Love to you,

Nina Roesner
Author, *The Respect Dare* (Thomas Nelson, 2012)
Executive Director, Greater Impact Ministries

Chapter 1 - A New Season

Alma slammed the trunk closed and hustled into the large Park District building with its silver dome reflecting the hot August sunshine. As soon as she entered the chilly ice arena and her eyes adjusted to the fluorescent lighting, she regretted her selection of shorts, t-shirt, and sandals—almost as much as she regretted the sarcasm in her parting words to her husband before leaving for hockey practice, "Maybe you'd stop being so useless if you turned off that stupid television for five minutes!"

Puffs of visible breath parted as she rushed toward a teenage boy whose hand gestures urged her to move faster. No words passed between the two as a pair of beat-up skates were thrust into his hands. The boy man merely nodded and sauntered coolly into the ice arena, where sharp whistle blows announced the start of hockey practice.

This handoff, reminiscent of a track runner passing the baton in a relay, caught the eye of Joyce, another hockey mom, who smiled appreciatively at Alma and meekly confessed, "My son left his neck guard in the car. Every week it's the same thing—whether it's equipment, asthma inhaler, or a sports drink, something is always left behind and I end up racing back and forth between the rink and home."

Alma joined the small circle of women who were arranged in cold plastic chairs in the lobby. Her dark brown hair fell in soft waves framing her round face. Her petite frame carried evidence of having borne three children and a preference for tacos. In her mid-40s, Alma's eyes were the epicenter for fine lines that spread outward like rays of sunlight, and her strong hands were capable of juggling homework, wiping tears, and conveying comfort to patients at the OB/GYN office where she worked as a nurse. Alma had been married to Marco, an assembly plant manager, for 19 years and together they were raising their teenage children, Alicia, 18, Mateo, 15, and Max, 13.

Today was the first day of another season of ice hockey for the Agitators hockey club. Alma's middle son, Mateo, had been skating since the age of four. At six he had started playing as a Mite with short legs and a tiny helmet. Games consisted of large clumps of 5- and 6-year-olds chasing after a puck as it was pushed around the ice. Unsteady players slipped and shuffled toward an elusive puck, using their sticks for support and balance. In his first game, Mateo had somehow managed to stay vertical long enough to reach the puck before any of the other players. He'd started to skate toward the net, and then stopped suddenly. Unsure of what he was supposed to do, he looked anxiously into the sea of parents' faces until he found who he was looking for—Mamá. Their eyes locked and his head tilted to one side, the way it always did when he asked her a question. Without words the boy asked his mother, "What am I supposed to do?" It only took one heartbeat before she responded, "GOOOOOOOOO!!!" with a roar so loud it surprised the mild-mannered Alma herself.

Mateo had progressed through age-level teams every two years—the Mites, then Squirts, Peewee's, Bantams, and now as a sophomore in high school, Midgets. No longer did Mateo seek out encouragement from his mom in public; in fact her role had been relegated to occasional nods and urgent, mumbled requests for forgotten gear. Alma tried not to dwell on the growing space between mother and son, especially since it was the exact treatment all the other hockey moms received from their sons. The hockey dads, who were as equally involved as the moms, had a different type of interaction with players—typically the fathers barked coaching suggestions for improvement to their kids who usually shrugged silently and looked down to avoid eye contact. It was a different type of relationship there. It was less nurturing and felt rougher to Alma's tender heart and empty arms.

Alma particularly didn't understand the more recent interactions between her husband and their son. Marco, who had always been such a playful and loving father when the kids were young, seemed to confront Mateo frequently with questions about homework completion, criticisms about stick handling, or even the way Mateo cleaned (or didn't clean) his room. At times, Mateo's father seemed downright mean-spirited. Alma also noticed that Marco's treatment of their son had begun to rub off on the way he spoke with all of the members of their family.

She frowned when she thought of how impatient Marco had been with her last night, while telling him about her day at the OB/GYN office. Despite the fact that she tried to condense the summary of a particularly complicated and heart-wrenching case, he gesticulated his hands as if to say, "Yeah, yeah, come on—get to the point already." Hurt and angered, she had stopped talking mid-sentence and stormed from the room. Juggling kids, work, home, and transportation had husband and wife going in opposite directions nearly every day. When they did have a moment together, Alma longed to talk with Marco and share a little bit of herself with him. These days, however, he seemed more interested in movies on his tablet than in meaningful conversations or even pleasant exchanges with his wife.

Joyce interrupted Alma's thoughts, asking, "What's wrong, Alma? Why are you frowning?" Joyce was noticeably older than Alma, and considerably heavier. Her long, limp hair was ashy gray and made her look more tired and worn than her 59 years.

Alma forced a smile and felt her anger burn as she relayed how her husband had dismissed her during their short conversation the night before. "*Y porque*? Why? Because his movie was so important that it commanded all of his attention!"

Joyce snorted loudly, "HA! I know EXACTLY what you're talking about! My husband keeps going out of the house just to avoid talking with me. He interacts more with our mailman than he does with me." Having a flair for drama, she gestured wildly and spoke so loudly that the other women in the lobby turned to listen.

Joyce and her husband, Jim, had been high school sweethearts and married right after graduation. Their 40th wedding anniversary was rapidly approaching, and they were very proud of their three children. Their oldest, Janine was in her mid-thirties, recently married, and expecting her first child. John, a senior in college, was squeezing out the last drops of reckless youth before starting medical school next year. Their youngest child, Justin, was just starting his sophomore year in high school.

Curious, having caught the gist of the husband-bashing session, two more hockey moms, Mona and Anne, scooted their orange and blue plastic chairs closer to Alma and Joyce. The four women had known each other casually for as long as their sons played hockey—some for nearly a decade—yet none had the time or energy to develop their relationships more deeply outside the hockey rink. Although the income brackets of the middle-age women varied, with some more affluent than others, they all were able to shoulder the hefty cost of team membership, equipment, and tournament fees.

It didn't take long before the women started trying to top one another with descriptions of the disgusting behaviors their husbands displayed in private or public. Laughter streamed from the group while their collective stress began to melt away. One of the women was saying, "I don't know how much more I can take of this. . . ." when the team manager, Maxine, emerged from the rink in her smart, corporate suit and heels.

Maxine assessed the group of women seated in the lobby and pulled up a chair. "What's going on, Ladies?"

Mona responded without missing a beat, "The usual—a little husband bashing." With that the women returned to one-upping each other with tales of marital crimes suffered at the hands of their mates. After finishing a long description of her husband's impending birthday depression, Alma sighed, "Sometimes I wish he would just disappear . . . not permanently, but for like 14 or 15 hours a day." The other women rewarded her comment with vigorous nods and roars of laughter that halted unnaturally when they spied Jessica enter the lobby.

The youngest of the hockey moms, Jessica was in her late 20s and buoyantly walked past the circle of women, followed by two little girls in a single file line—much like ducklings waddling behind their mother. Jessica had neatly styled blonde hair with highlights and lowlights. Her smartly rounded nails were a muted pink and her natural makeup accentuated high cheekbones and deep blue eyes. Jessica embodied the healthy, girl-next-door image that stirred feelings of jealousy in the brains and hearts of other wives. Several eyes rolled and Mona frowned as she elbowed Anne seated next to her. "I bet you'd give up your husband's entire paycheck for a month if you could look as perky as she does."

With a smirk Anne shot back, "Ha! No chance. It would only be a waste, because one month into a new school year and hockey season, I'd still look like something left behind in the garbage disposal." Anne was a third-grade public school teacher in Chicago and everyone knew she worked as many hours out of school as she did in the classroom. She frequently lugged a heavy teacher tote filled with papers to the ice arena. The women admired her dedication, but never offered to help grade the stacks of math worksheets or spelling tests.

Joyce, the most senior of the women, only muttered out of the side of her mouth, "I wouldn't mind using my husband's paycheck to buy myself new parts, especially if he was as attentive and good looking as hers." Jessica's husband was fit and handsome. Every time he attended one of his son's games, he was very visibly present with his family—his arm was always wrapped lovingly around Jessica's shoulders and he bought popcorn for his little girls between periods. "No wonder she looks perfect all the time."

Maxine shook her head and placed her hand on Joyce's arm. "Let's not go there, all right? I've got enough to worry about with my own family to start comparing myself to someone else's." At 39, Maxine was a highly accomplished project manager whose daughter was an extraordinarily talented goalie. Cynthia was born to Maxine and Samuwel right after they were married, fresh out of college. Samuwel had stayed home so Maxine could launch a successful marketing career; she worked long hours and moved up the ranks at her software company. She was genuinely shocked four years ago when she discovered she was pregnant with twins. After the boys were born, she had begged Samuwel to quit his job and stay home with their sons. She argued that it would be a waste to throw away all the sacrifices she had made for her career for more than ten years. After several heated negotiations she had convinced Samuwel to return to his role as Mr. Mom so she could continue being the breadwinner. To his credit, Samuwel defied every stereotype of absentee Black father and sent Maxine off to work each morning with a travel thermos of hot coffee and a carefully packed lunch.

Joyce looked pointedly at Maxine, "How did you do it, Maxine? How did you train your husband so well? He cooks, cleans, does laundry, and runs around with your sons all day. When I tell Jim to do something, he disappears like the last brownie at a church potluck—silently and undetected."

Nodding her head, Anne chimed in, "You said it, Joyce! I spend most evenings cleaning up my husband's empty beer bottles and nagging my stepsons to do their homework. Some days I'm a master juggler, but there are days when I feel like I'm hitting my head against a brick wall." She shook her head, shrugged her shoulders and looked up at the ceiling as if calling upon a supernatural power to sustain her.

Mona tightened her lips against her teeth, reached over, and patted Anne's arm, "Well at least YOUR husband is faithful and comes home every day after work. Not like SOME low-life husbands I could name." Her face twisted in an angry expression that made her eyes bulge and her lips pinch into a deeply wrinkled downturned line.

Alma slowly shook her head thinking how many wives were living tumultuous lives because of their husbands. Marco wasn't so bad—he hadn't cheated on her, didn't drink to excess, and loved his kids. Over the past few years his easygoing nature had started to darken with hints of bitterness and anger. A frown crinkled her forehead as she recalled the latest shouting match between Marco and Mateo. It pained her because she knew how deeply Marco's sharp words and ridicule sliced into his son's tender heart. Rather than reprimand her husband in front of the kids, she gritted her teeth and imagined what a peaceful home theirs could be if Marco would just . . . go away. A gloomy, ironic grimace crept across her mouth.

When Alma recovered from her fantasy, Maxine had called the attention of the small circle of women. "My church was just advertising a small group study for women who wish to build healthy and God-pleasing marriage relationships in their homes." Maxine thought for a moment and then continued. "There's some book or devotion they're going to follow—I can't remember exactly, but the title has the word "dare" in it. I don't know what it's about, but one woman at our church who did this study was convinced it saved her marriage." The women were silent for a long while before Alma cautiously spoke up in her soft voice, "I'd be willing to try something that could help my marriage."

Surrounded by cautiously nodding heads, Joyce inquired loudly, "Maxine, can you get more information about this study? I don't know if it will help, but there are a few things I'd like fixed in my husband." She spread her hands open wide to emphasize the magnitude of ways she wanted to change her mate.

With that, Anne pounced, "Yeah, I've got a long list of things I'd like to change in Tony. If there's a book that can show me how to do that, I'm in!" Maxine agreed to investigate further and promised to bring the information to the next practice, Thursday night.

Chapter 2 - Maxine

Maxine carefully slid her laptop into the leather attaché that mirrored the dark, warm tones of her manicured hands. She drove directly to the ice rink, where her daughter was already practicing. At Maxine's request, Anne had driven Cynthia to practice. Their families lived in the same neighborhood, and occasionally carpooled if one unexpectedly was tied up at work.

Maxine made a mental note to reciprocate Anne's kindness by offering to drive her stepson to practice or a game in the near future. Most hockey parents were careful not to rely too heavily on others for transporting their kids to practice. For all practical purposes, the average car or minivan had adequate space to transport one enormous hockey bag and a stick. Doubling the amount of equipment and bodies made the ride uncomfortably cramped and twice as fragrant. The other, subtler motivation related to status. Parents who had flexibility and freedom from their jobs to make early morning, weekend, and late night practices or games generally had attained higher levels of success than those who were locked into a rigid schedule. Without saying a word, hockey families paid attention to who brought each player to practice, and instinctively knew which player's parents took advantage of others' generosity. The only valid exemption to this rule was the multiple-player family with siblings who played on different teams.

Arriving at the rink, Maxine checked on her daughter, who was fully outfitted in the distinctive gear of a goalie: mask, throat guard, chest and arm protectors, goalie-specific jock, pants, knee and leg pads, blocker, catching glove, skates, jersey, and goalie stick. Her bag was twice as large and heavy as her male teammates. As the only girl on the team, Cynthia was relegated to dressing in the women's bathrooms at every hockey venue. Watching her daughter block a volley of slap shots screaming toward her head, Maxine knew everything was as it should be and found a chair in the lobby near the other moms. Before she had a chance to settle herself, Anne's penetrating voice halted all conversations around her. "So Maxine, did you find out more information about that book that's supposedly going to solve all of the problems with our husbands?" Anne folded her arms in a defiant, yet daring pose.

Maxine took a deep breath, "As a matter of fact, I did." She slid a hand into her stylish tote and revealed a ruby red paperback with lace edging the cover. She held up the book briefly and quickly turned it so that the cover was facing her and said, "I had a copy of the book expedited to my office so I could check it out for myself. Apparently the book has good reviews—4½ stars— and is broken down into 40 "Dares" for wives to complete."

Without providing the opportunity for an interruption, she took a quick breath and continued, "It's recommended that the book be shared in small groups, to provide the reader with encouragement and opportunities for discussion. I bought the small-group leader's guide so that we can do this exactly as recommended. I also checked out the author's blog, which starts with, 'Are you wondering how to stop feeling alone in your marriage? How to deal with your husband's unloving behavior against you? What about boundaries?'"

At that, Maxine stopped and looked into the yearning eyes of the other women, who sat slowly nodding their heads. No one spoke as the women considered this image of a healthy marriage, much like a child would consider a fairy tale. Suddenly, thundering sounds and the explosive smell of 19 hockey players fresh from practice filled the lobby and broke the spell. All but Maxine's daughter, Cynthia, stomped through the lobby on heavy skates and pushed through the locker room door to change. Maxine spoke above the din, "Ideally, readers are instructed to take one Dare each day, but the leader's guide suggests that many find success completing three to five Dares per week. Since we're all so busy, I think we should start small with three Dares per week. That way we'll be able to help each other through the tough Dares. We can meet right here at the rink while our kids have practice on Thursday nights. If everyone orders the book tonight, we could read the introduction before next week's practice, and start the first Dare on the following week." Maxine stopped talking and took a quick breath. "So . . . what do you think, Ladies?"

The four women cautiously looked at each other. Joyce was the first to speak up in a strong voice. "Yes. I think this will be a good chance to get my marriage back on track. It's a definitive YES for me." In response to Joyce, Alma and Anne nodded in agreement, but Mona remained uncommitted. Alma looked at Mona and asked gently, "What do you say, Mona? Will you join us?"

Mona, a Palestinian woman, was silent for a moment before warily responding, "Yeah, okay. I'll do this with you. I could use some girlfriends on my side." Then, a little more confidently, "So what's the title of this book anyway, Maxine? Something with Dare?"

Maxine shuffled the book around in her hands before turning it to face Mona and the rest. *"The RESPECT Dare?"* Mona asked incredulously. "Really? That's perfect! It'll be good to finally teach that cheating husband of mine how to a have little respect for me." Maxine had a confused look on her face, but thought it better to not explain the biblical emphasis of respect in marriage until later, once it was too late to turn back.

Chapter 3 – Alma

Alma opened the box that was sitting at her door when she got home from work. It had been a long day caring for the steady stream of pregnant women who fretted over dietary restrictions, high blood pressure, and weight gain. Her back ached and her feet were tired despite the support and flexibility provided by the bright blue gym shoes her kids had given her last Mother's Day. The shoes were only a few months old, yet they already had a worn look that matched Alma's weary face. The strain of her marriage in recent months was aging her, and she was surprised to see that the woman in the mirror looked strikingly similar to her mother. In Mexico and then in the United States, Alma's father and mother had worked tirelessly to earn the meager amount of money necessary to feed their children, and the toll was reflected in their prematurely aging bodies. They frequently reminded her that those sacrifices were made in order to provide her with a better education and life, and it was her responsibility to do everything she could to improve the future of her own children.

With tired hands and a heavy heart, Alma pulled on her reading glasses and considered the book. "*The Respect Dare*: 40 Days to a Deeper Connection with God and Your Husband" she read aloud. Flipping the book over, she read the description on the back that described the journey of storytelling and thought-provoking questions. The book offered hope; assuring the reader that countless marriages had been dramatically impacted through completion of the 40 Dares.

A deep sigh pushed through her mouth as Alma considered the word "hope." She wasn't sure there was any hope left for her marriage. Where had they gone wrong? Something in their union had died . . . or at least needed serious lifesaving intervention.

It wasn't always like this. How deeply she had loved Marco when they were married nearly 20 years ago! His thick, black, curly hair, caramel brown eyes, and quick smile made Alma's breath quicken each time she saw him—not that they saw much of each other during the first few years of marriage. Marco had been laid off from the Post Office right before they married, and he quickly found two part-time jobs to provide a steady income. It wasn't long before Alicia was born, and Alma's mother moved in to help care for the colicky baby while Alma attended night classes at the junior college.

Marco's part-time jobs filled the financial gaps, while Alma stretched every dollar and made economical meals that resembled the cuisine of her northern Mexican ancestors—rice, beans, corn, and love. She didn't care about wealth, resigning herself to a lifetime of watching every penny. Secretly, she thought she would rather live in a cardboard box than a mansion without love. But Marco had surprised her and developed drive and ambition shortly after Alicia was born. He climbed his way up to operations manager at the assembly plant where he worked and was able to leave his other job behind. Instead of a cardboard box, the family was doing well, staying one step ahead of their bills and living in a modest, 3-bedroom home on the northwest edge of Chicago.

Her husband's job was very physical, but he always had energy for their growing family—first Alicia, then Mateo three years later, shortly followed by Max. When the kids were little, Marco would wrestle all three kids to the ground at the same time, allowing their giggles and whoops to smooth over any rough edges caused by his workday. One of their favorite games was Boxing Monkey—a made-up game in which he donned an old Halloween gorilla mask and jumped up and down. With "OOOH OOOH AAAH AAAH" and imitating the gait of a primate, he would chase after each of the kids, sending them squealing with delight to hiding places all over their house.

Alma laughed out loud when she recalled the image of her brood of little monkeys tackling Marco to the ground and climbing on his head, chest, and arms. Her smile faded, however, when she thought of their lives today. The teenage kids still loved and respected their parents, but friends and other interests seemed to occupy more and more of their time. Family dinners found Marco and Alma sitting alone at the kitchen table in silence, eating something she pulled from the freezer and reheated. As the kids poured their energy into sports, social events, and music, it seemed that Marco's vitality noticeably diminished. He wasn't the "fun" parent anymore, no longer indulging in unpredictable and laugh-inducing antics. His behavior over the past year could be characterized as controlling, impatient, and angry. The moodier Marco became, the farther his actions pushed her away. Most days it was easier for Alma and the kids to leave him alone watching soccer games or *las noticias*—news—on the Spanish television channel. The man who once was her partner and playmate had now become the grumpy old man whom everyone avoided.

She was not enthusiastic when considering their future. Of course they would never divorce—no matter how generous the Pope's disposition with divorces—but Alma could only feel lonely despair at the prospect of decades' worth of silent dinners, dreary encounters, and tedious interactions.

She closed her eyes and set the book down on the table, lifting up a silent prayer, "St. Priscilla, patron saint of good marriages, pray for us!"

Chapter 4 – Mona

Mechanically reciting the words of Salat—her prayers in Arabic—Mona quickly got up from her kneeling position and returned to her morning chores. Five times a day, Muslim women and men participated in the ritual of standing, bowing, prostrating, and reflecting upon blessings and the relationship between God and mankind. This custom was supposed to serve as a reminder for Muslims to act righteously and avoid evil.

In Islam, it was believed that women receive the most benefit from Salat inside the home, while men find it outside the home. Mona's mouth twisted to the side and a frown sharpened her features as she snorted, "Sure, men find it outside the home while we're stuck inside. Invisible." Her husband, Aahil, had recently admitted to having an affair with a Kafir, a non-Muslim, at work. Prior to confessing his infidelity to Mona, he had seemed tormented, which his wife had assumed was work-related but never would have dreamt it was sex-at-work related. Aahil, whose Arabic name meant "prince," owned up to his transgression one evening after dinner, wringing his dark hands together and begging her forgiveness. Intercourse, sexual contact, and even flirting outside of marriage was forbidden. He was plagued by guilt for having crossed the firm line established by his religion.

At first Mona thought he was teasing her; trying to arouse her jealousy. During their entire courtship, Aahil had never initiated any physical contact between them. In fact, the two were never together without the accompaniment of a Mahram, a close family friend. There had been a series of carefully arranged meetings with the sole purpose of getting to know each other to determine if they were compatible for marriage. To Mona, whose family could be described as modern Palestinian-American, all of it felt very formal and controlled. But she fell for the shy, thoughtful man whose dark brown eyes embraced her though his arms and hands could not. His funny smile and quick wit brightened her thoughts, and made her laugh in a way that conveyed to Aahil that she saw nobody else but him.

But she saw the shame in his eyes and reluctantly recognized that Aahil was not joking. Mona's disbelief transformed into flashing, fiery explosions in her brain. His disloyalty was as uncharacteristic as it was unacceptable. In Islam, adultery is the ultimate form of betrayal. Condemned by the Qur'an, the Muslim's sacred book, adultery does not have prescribed consequences. The religion's prophet, Muhammad, was quoted in a separate hadith (a body of books that show portions of Muhammad's life) saying that infidelity was one of the justified reasons for killing another person.

In those first moments of learning of Aahil's infidelity, visions of murder had indeed filled Mona's head, while sharp and angry words flew from her mouth and pierced his tormented heart. Thankfully their son had been spending the night at his cousin's house, and didn't witness the hostile scene.

Now Mona experienced the recurrence of fury and resentment flooding her senses as she imagined her husband with another woman. Who was she? What did she offer him that Mona hadn't? Was she younger? Thinner? More beautiful? Did Aahil love this woman, or was it just meaningless sex? As the endless list of unanswered questions punctuated her thoughts, her movements with the vacuum cleaner gradually grew more abrupt and forceful.

Mona's face was freezing into a scowl while unrelenting accusations grated on her tongue and lips. As always, her endless stream of questions led to the opening of the big question, "How could he do this to me?" Sometimes the question took on a more aggressive tone, "How DARE he do this to me?"

She had been so naïve, trusting the words and actions of her husband without a second thought. But never again would she be caught unaware and foolish. She had been severely wounded and was resolved to never allow her husband's disloyalty to happen again. Aahil complied when she had demanded unlimited access to his cell phone, e-mail accounts, and social media platforms. He promised that his transgression would never be repeated, but she checked up on his actions and communications several times throughout each day, oftentimes spending hours following trails that led nowhere. She was both eager and terrified to catch him in an untruth, but for months there had been only professional interactions with colleagues at the firm where he was an accountant.

She had even considered hiring a private detective, but decided against it when she read the stories of vulnerable women being taken advantage of by unscrupulous investigators. The Internet had provided her with an abundance of information about cheating husbands and "ways to keep your man from straying." Legal advice about divorce and retribution was available at her fingertips, and she received emotional support in an online group for victims of cheating partners. Though she was nervous when she first entered the chat room, she soon relaxed as she read stories similar to her own. The women warmly welcomed her into their circle of anonymity and confidentiality, as did the small handful of men whose wives had been unfaithful.

There was one group member, in particular, who had been especially helpful in handling the aching torment following her husband's guilty admission. His name was Stephen and he seemed to be equally raw from learning of his wife's deception. He, like other members, encouraged her to stop holding back her emotions and explore her feelings of pain and shame. Shoving the vacuum cleaner roughly into the closet, Mona considered reaching out to her group.

Ready to unleash the ever-present bubbling resentment, she irritably clicked her way to the Divorce Support Group website and felt the feelings surge through her fingers as they gave expression to her thoughts. After posting, it only took a few moments before responses began to accumulate beneath her wrathful paragraph like an army of soldiers assembling for battle. She read the supportive comments from nameless allies, "You should leave the bastard!" "He doesn't deserve you!" "Make the cheating coward pay!" In addition to the battle cries, there were pop-up links to related articles such as "10 Ways to Catch Him Cheating" and "Getting your Groove On After the Storm." Mona could feel the tension in her forehead easing. The energetic feedback affirmed her fury and justified the anger and resentment that tore at her emotions.

She took a calming breath and allowed her hands to slide from the keyboard. She spied *The Respect Dare* paperback on her desk and snorted when she imagined the other hockey moms joining in sisterhood solidarity against cheating husbands.

Picking up the crisp new book, Mona threw it across the room.

Chapter 5 – Anne

The Respect Dare sailed through the air in a red, blurry line. Anne's 14- and 15-year-old stepsons, Zach and Pete, were playing the literary version of dodge ball with her book. Hoots and teasing rocketed back and forth as the brothers tried to pummel each other with the paperback that splayed open each time it was hurled. "STOP IT!" Anne shrieked in her strongest teacher voice imaginable. With hands on her hips she took a fast gasp of air, "This behavior is inappropriate! I need you to put my book down and start your homework." The boys froze and stared at Anne as she tried to assume an authoritative role with her adolescent stepsons. Pete merely shrugged, wound his arm back, and catapulted the book in the direction of his brother's head. Anne, anticipating disobedience, leaped forward, intercepted the book, and pulled it down to her chest, all while roaring, "NOW!"

Unimpressed, both boys rolled their eyes and trudged toward the stairway to their bedrooms. Behind them, Anne called, "Hey, come back here and pick up your backpacks and shoes from the entryway! And don't forget, you need to do some laundry tonight so you have clean clothes to wear to school tomorrow." Neither boy responded; instead they continued their retreat to the solace of their bedrooms. Anne growled, but bent over and picked up the boys' backpacks and made a mental note to wash a load of socks and underwear because she knew the boys wouldn't.

Agitated and mumbling under her breath, Anne set *The Respect Dare* on her desk in the study with her worn leather teacher tote and briskly walked into the kitchen to begin dinner. Too tired to cook after a long day in the classroom, she pulled out a stack of menus and considered which cuisine the family would enjoy this evening. Staring blankly at the choices, she absently twirled a thick ribbon of her shoulder-length brown hair around her index finger. She'd been married to Tony for almost five years and was grateful for the luxurious lifestyle he provided. They'd met at a friend's wedding, at which Anne, who was approaching her dreaded 30th birthday, had been contemplating her curse of solitude: "always a bridesmaid—never the bride." She was the last of her friends to remain single and experienced pangs of envy with every bridal shower invitation that appeared in her inbox.

Anne was a tenured teacher and was completely unprepared to be swept into an irresistible romance with the owner of a struggling, upstart construction company. They dated every evening for six months and were married downtown at the courthouse. In addition to adjusting to her new role as wife, Anne had to quickly fill the additional role of stepmother. Tony had sole custody of Zach and Pete, and quickly lost contact with their mother who had succumbed to a life of addiction.

The three males in Anne's life were sports fanatics and filled her life with foreign sounds, smells, and ideas. Anne's only connection to the female world remained with her colleagues at the school—every Friday afternoon she and a large group of teachers headed to the local bar to ease the tensions of teaching in Chicago.

Ordering four dinners from a local Chinese restaurant didn't take long, but Anne was agitated and yelled at the man who took her order. She had to repeat her request for extra steamed vegetables each time she ordered another entrée. Eating vegetables was not high on the priority list of any of the males living in their home, but she knew it was best to get everybody into the habit of having a balanced meal if the boys were to continue eating healthy into adulthood.

Slamming her cell phone a little harder onto the sleek,

granite counter than she intended, Anne surveyed the chaos in her kitchen. Remnants of last night's pizza crusts and sports-drink bottles littered the table, as did empty chip bags and energy bar wrappers. She angrily grabbed at the garbage thoughtlessly left behind by boys who were playing music and video games while she cleaned the kitchen. Yelling in her best teacher voice, Anne bellowed "Zach! Pete! Turn down that music and get started on your homework. No screen time until you're finished!"

The boys finally complied after Anne had to bark the same orders three separate times. The kitchen tidied, she lifted the kitchen garbage bag from its stainless steel can and carried it outside. Tossing the bag into the black garbage bin, Anne heard a loud clank of glass that sounded like beer bottles smashing together. Lifting the white bag, she inspected its bottom and sure enough, there were quite a few brown glass bottles jostling in the bag.

Why did her husband do this? she wondered. Rather than recycling the glass as she'd been urging him to do, Tony had shoved the empty bottles into the bottom of the kitchen garbage. Lowering her arm carefully past cold, wet coffee grounds and napkins smeared with pizza sauce, she pulled out the bottles, counting aloud as she did so. "Five, six, seven, eight, nine!" she counted aloud. She shook her head angrily and rinsed the bottles in hot water at the kitchen sink, and then carried them to the recycle bin in the garage, where her eyes grew wide. There, in plain view, was the family's glass-recycling bin, brimming with beer bottles. It served as a visible reminder of the increasingly large role alcohol was playing in Tony's life.

That certainly explained why the empty bottles had been shoved into the bottom of the kitchen garbage can. Tony had been trying to mask the vast quantity of bottles that had amassed in the span of less than a week. She rolled her eyes when she thought of what the neighbors would think when they saw the light blue container overflowing with brown bottles, on display for all to see. Shame besieged her and she changed tacks. Wrapping the offending bottles with old newspapers to keep them from clinking, she carefully reinserted them into the bottom of the kitchen garbage bag.

Plain and simple, Tony's drinking was becoming a

problem. She had tried several different approaches to rid him of the habit. At first she tried appealing sweetly to him, and when that didn't work, she angrily confronted him. Once, she had even threatened to leave him. Returning home after a long weekend in Michigan for a grueling hockey tournament, the reek of cigarette smoke and stale beer had flooded her senses the moment she opened the front door. Normally a functional alcoholic, Tony had spent the entire weekend isolated in their home with the blinds closed, drinking and watching college football, while she dragged herself, two teens, and a load of appallingly putrid hockey gear to five hockey games in 72 hours.

After the long drive home through an ice storm that had rolled in from Lake Michigan, Anne surveyed the living room and shrieked, "What the HELL is going on here? You were supposed to be at the building site all weekend, but from the looks of things, you haven't even left the house!" She continued to heap insults and accusations upon Tony's disheveled head until he unsteadily lifted his hands and admitted that he probably drank too much. He vowed to stop drinking, and was successful for several months—until the Chicago hockey team won the Stanley Cup playoffs. The special occasion had set off a string of weekend benders in which he imbibed with abandon.

Ever since then, Tony went to work every day and met with his construction site supervisors, but made it painfully clear that the weekends and evenings were his to enjoy. He rationalized that because he worked hard, paid his dues, and was nearing the big 50, he deserved a break from the stresses of life.

Looking up at the clock on the professional grade, stainless steel range, Anne guessed her husband must have lost track of time again and texted him, "Where are you? Dinner is on its way and I ordered your favorite, so get here ASAP to enjoy!" She tried not to sound overly demanding in texts, and frequently peppered her demands with compliments, pleases, and smiling emoticons.

The house finally quiet, she stared off into the distance and thought about her marriage. Things had been feeling unsteady for some time, and something was bound to give. She loved Tony and wished she could figure out how to fix whatever was broken within him that caused him to drink so much. Nothing she'd tried was successful, but without a drastic change, their marriage wouldn't last. Her shoulders sagged and her eyelids drooped. Aloud she spoke, "For the boys sake, I hope I can make this *Respect Dare* thing work."

Chapter 6 – Joyce

Joyce scanned the canned vegetables that rode the conveyer belt in Checkout Lane 5 of the grocery store. She smiled at the senior citizen who squinted as she monitored the $.79 price of each can of peas that scrolled down the digital display. The sale had started the previous day, and was a good chance to stock up on canned items she might use in the coming weeks. When Joyce noticed there were two cases of water in the senior's cart, she carefully navigated her bulky frame around the counter and deftly lifted one of the cases and slid it over the scanner.

Joyce had been a checker at the grocery since their youngest son entered first grade. She and Jim had agreed that it was more economical for her to stay home and raise their three kids than sending them to daycare. Once all the kids were in school, she took a part-time job as a checker because it gave her the flexibility of being home when they were. Every day she dragged thousands of food items across the scanner while imagining each of the families that would gather to eat those meals. A basket of organic produce, brown rice, sweet potatoes, and tofu for the peaceful mother whose baby nestled in a sling strapped to her chest. Heavy packages of meat and cases of beer were for the automobile mechanic with black-stained fingernails. Lettuce, carrots, and celery at the beginning of the week for the hopeful, middle-aged woman who returned a couple of days later to purchase a dozen doughnuts, two cartons of ice cream, and a bag of chips all while avoiding eye contact. It was that shopper with whom Joyce felt the most connection.

Joyce peered into the lives of people by seeing the contents of their shopping carts. Sometimes she felt the knowledge was akin to a priest hearing whispered sins in his confessional. She saw frantic late-night purchases of baby diapers and adult diapers. She shared recipes, honored expired coupons, and listened conspiratorially to the new cook who burned dinner and was in a rush to get her salad and hot bar purchases home before her husband arrived home from work. Joyce was solid and reliable. She had been the familiar constant in Register 5 for more than a decade, enabling the store manager to count on the fact that she would always work her scheduled hours.

Today, a woman in her 20s was purchasing a small, heart-shaped birthday cake, a bottle of champagne, raw oysters, and ribbed condoms. Joyce fought to keep her eyebrows from arching high in response to the young woman's low-cut blouse, bright red lips, and romantic merchandise. Joyce steadied her voice when calling, "Have a nice day" after the customer rapidly walked away, her tall stilettos skidding on the highly waxed tile floor. Joyce watched the wake of stunned and staring men whose eyes stuck on the retreating figure as if welded to her bumper.

Disdain filled Joyce's thoughts, followed closely by repulsion, then envy. With her sturdy build and her hair tied up in a practical bun, it had been a long time since any man had been captivated by her walk, or smile, or kiss. Jim still kissed her, but they were brief, friendly pecks that conveyed attachment based on time. Lots of time. Almost four decades, three children, two homes, and five dogs later, the exhilaration in their relationship had softened to fondness. When Jim approached Joyce in the early years of their marriage, her breath would catch, her eyes would sparkle, and her body would tense in anticipation of his feverous displays of love. The last memorable display of Jim's passion had been 16 years ago, which resulted in their bonus child, Justin.

Joyce had been 44, and thought she was well past the days

of fertile eggs—in fact she used to joke with Jim that they didn't need to worry about contraception because all her eggs were fried. Evidently one was still intact. At her yearly physical, Joyce had told the nurse she had entered menopause because she hadn't had her period in nearly six months. She felt her heart in her throat when the doctor confirmed she was five months pregnant. Now Justin was 15 and Joyce was facing major life transitions—John was applying to medical school and Janine was pregnant with Joyce's first grandchild.

Navigating her son's teenage hormones while adjusting to impending grandparenthood was more than most women would care to consider. Between transporting Justin to and from hockey games and practice, helping Janine prepare the baby's room, and occasional parents' weekends at John's out-of-state college, Joyce had little time left to consider her identity. While her job kept her strong and active, Joyce's figure reflected the turbulent middle-age passage from post-baby weight to a complete loss of her waist and a thicker belly. Unlike her first two post-partum experiences, breastfeeding had not made the baby weight disappear—it just shifted from the high front to the padded sides. She cringed when she thought about the state of her sagging breasts.

At first, she had been completely overwhelmed with the baby and her active children, and there was little energy left for lovemaking with Jim. Once she had regained her momentum several years later, she avoided close contact with him in bed, afraid that he would reach for her breasts and instead manipulate her double chin. The distance she put between them in bed swelled into their daily patterns and life. Jim was good-natured and went along with every request or expectation of him; escaping only to golf, bowl, fish, and hunt. There were no fights or resentments between the two, only compatible friendship and caring. She didn't know how they got here, but the relationship had distinctly deteriorated over the years.

Joyce didn't know how or if *The Respect Dare* would help bring a zing back into her marriage, but as she turned to the next customer in line, she knew she wanted Jim to look at her in a way that conveyed his hunger for her again.

Chapter 7 – Small Group Beginnings

And the wife must respect her husband.

Ephesians 5:33 NIV

The first small group meeting of the hockey moms was set for 8:30 during the team's Thursday-night practice. Although the team had practice or conditioning four times a week and games on the weekend, Thursday night was the only time slot that none of the women had other obligations. All five had assembled in the rink's birthday party room. Given the late hour, it was highly unlikely that the space would be reserved. Nervous chatter and chair adjustments were made once everyone was seated.

Although the women knew each other's names and had exchanged pleasantries for several years, it was a shallow friendliness accessorized with smiling veneers. Alma was particularly anxious about being seated with this group of women who seemed very eager to air their dirty marriage laundry in public. She was raised differently. In her family's culture you expressed yourself freely, loudly, and exuberantly at home and only sparingly revealed strong feelings in public.

When she and Mateo left for practice, they were both relieved to escape the harsh, critical observations of Marco. His supervisor had hinted that the company would be eliminating several positions in the coming weeks, and Marco was worried that his job would be phased out. His words at dinner were peppered with curses and sarcasm. Despite the time and care it took Alma to make dinner after a long eight-hour day at the gynecologist's office, eating together was not a pleasant experience for anyone that evening. Despite her misgivings over his negative behaviors and a strong desire to vent her frustration, she hoped that her loyalty toward Marco would prevent her from further publicizing her conflicted feelings of anger, sympathy, resentment, and compassion to these women whom she barely knew.

Maxine drew Alma's attention as she tried to quiet the women in order to start their meeting, "Ladies, before we get started... ." At that moment, the door to the party room swung open smoothly and Jessica strode in, holding the door open for two perfectly dressed toddlers who were following behind. Jessica had tanned skin and soft coral lips. Her teeth had a glow that spoke of laser whitening, and were so perfectly aligned that they could be the "after" shot at the orthodontist's office.

"Sorry I'm late, everybody. I was caught by the 8:25 freight train that actually stopped on the tracks. Can you believe it?" Her voice was light and breezy, sounding more like a pop rock singer than the hockey mom of a high school adolescent. Immediately, the fake smiles reappeared like armor on the faces of nearly all the assembled women.

Maxine was the first to respond, "I was just about to get this group started with introductions." Mona and Anne shot angry, accusatory looks at Maxine, who explained, "I ran into Jessica at my church when I was doing a little more research on *The Respect Dare*. It seems she was interested in joining the small group that met in the sanctuary, but their schedule conflicted with hockey commitments. So I told her about our group and invited her to join us." Jessica was facing the other women so she didn't see the daring, confrontational look on Maxine's face that threatened anyone who would object to Jessica's inclusion in the group. The other women slowly began to nod, and their fake smiles spread even more widely across faces that threatened to cramp from the forced muscle action.

With that, the women took turns introducing themselves. Maxine went first, then Anne, followed by Mona, Alma, Joyce, and finally Jessica, who, when finished speaking, opened a portable cupcake container, releasing the smell of freshly baked, salted-caramel, apple cupcakes. Offering the treats to her acquaintances, who seemed to be warming to her, Jessica alienated each and every one when she added, "I baked these from scratch this afternoon. They're the pride and joy of my hometown in South Carolina. I figured each week we could take turns baking and bringing refreshments." And if that weren't bad enough, she continued with, "We could follow a holiday theme like Spooky Ghost Cookies in October and mini-Gingerbread houses in December. . . . OR since we obviously represent different ethnicities, we could bring treats from our cultural traditions."

Maxine groaned inwardly while Jessica beamed eagerly at the tired, aging women with whom she deeply wanted to connect. "Thanks for thinking of a snack, Jessica. I'm sure they're as delicious as they look." Maxine noticed Jessica's injured look because she hadn't taken one of the calorie-laden, glorious masterpieces that were probably featured on some fancy baker's blog. Maxine could certainly afford the few extra pounds that the treat might provide, but wasn't interested in getting sidetracked from the task at hand. "Now that we've introduced ourselves, let's get to know a little about the author of this book and the reason it was written."

The women were able to relax and ease out of their facades while their minds absorbed the words Maxine read aloud from the book's introduction. It was obvious to Alma and the others that Nina Roesner, the author of *The Respect Dare*, had led hundreds, if not thousands, of other women through challenging or dry patches in their marriages into more satisfying relationships with their husbands. What seemed more difficult to accept was the promotion of the biblical concept of marriage—wives should be respectful and submit to their husbands.

The women stole glances at each other as they considered

the book's logic, which underscored that while a wife's greatest need is to be loved unconditionally by her husband, a man's greatest need is respect. Anne chewed on the inside of her cheek and picked at the chipping polish on her fingernails. Alma's fingers played with the hem of her polyester shirt as she pondered whether her marriage could be transformed by applying this principle. Her patience with Marco was dwindling and she decided she would try anything to change the direction of their relationship. She wondered if the others could do the same.

Mona angrily rolled her eyes at the author's advice about this journey, which hinted at the long and arduous path ahead. She vowed to go along with the Dares only to build a support network. Perhaps she would ask some of these women to serve as character witnesses in her divorce case. Yes, she decided while sitting there with a half-eaten salted-caramel apple cupcake in her hand—she was definitely going to get a powerful attorney, leave Aahil, and make him pay for his betrayal.

When Joyce considered the obstacles she would face in completing the 40 Dares, she, too, was uneasy. As a Lutheran who read her Bible every evening, she was familiar with the "Wives, submit yourselves to your own husbands" reference in the book of Ephesians, chapter 5, verses 22 and 33, but she hadn't really wanted to think about applying it to her own life. In fact, the very idea filled her mind with flashing red lights and loud warning bells like those Jessica encountered waiting for the train to move tonight. No way would she give up her individuality and become a timid wife. Joyce and Jim were equals in this marriage thing and had been since their teens. She would somehow sidestep that principle, but remain faithful to the others. She was certain that their marriage could benefit from some of the other philosophies presented in the book. After all, it was too late for old dogs to learn new tricks.

Sitting next to Jessica, Joyce definitely felt like an old basset hound tonight.

Chapter 8 – The Dares Begin

Expectations For My Progress	*Expectations of my Husband that I will Release*
1. *2.* *3.*	*1.* *2.* *3.*

The first three Dares were launched and readers were asked to examine their expectations of their husbands and themselves. In actuality, Dare #1 required Alma to list three concrete characteristics that would represent her progress in *The Respect Dare*. How would she act differently in a changed marriage? She also needed to write three expectations of her husband that she was prepared to release in order to amend her relationship with Marco.

After the kids and Marco had retreated to their bedrooms with music, movies, or social media, Alma sat at her dining room table and considered this first prompt. She thought about her childhood expectations of Christmas Eve with her family and the presents she'd receive. She remembered her parents' expectant looks at quarterly report cards. Each expectation never measured up on the grand scale she'd envisioned. Christmas gifts broke, and despite the bouquet of "A's," her parents always focused on the thorny B+ in social studies or math.

Alma didn't think she carried many expectations of Marco, so she retrieved a basket of clean laundry and began folding while she considered. What did she expect of her husband? After a neat pile of towels towered on the table, she was surprised to realize that she held a long list of expectations of her spouse. She expected him to be a caring father. She expected him to be generous with their children and raise their sons to be strong and faithful young men, and their daughter to know that her father unconditionally cherished her. Despite her independence and decent salary, Alma counted on Marco's steady income and his company's health insurance for their family. She wanted the easy-going, spontaneous prankster he was when they first met. That wasn't much to ask, she thought. Or was it?

Anne daydreamed about an ideal world in which her husband was a perfect specimen. Tony would no longer sport a beer gut and red-faced complexion. They held hands over the kitchen table while steaming mugs of coffee sat untouched and cell phones lay abandoned. Tony would look into her eyes with a relaxed and accepting gaze that communicated, "I think you're the most amazing woman in the world and I'm fortunate to have found you." Soft guitars would play while a welcoming fire gently danced in the background. A calm and centered Anne would focus only on the present moment. Her complicated day calendar lay neglected on the counter. She would have no need to deliver abrupt reminders or detailed tutorials to Tony about the tasks he needed to complete.

As the fantasy faded, Anne stared at the new crop of empty

bottles on the coffee table. Resisting the urge to clear them away, she opened her journal and began the work of *The Respect Dare*. Creating a neat "T-Chart," she carefully organized her list of behaviors she would possess as a result of this work, and the expectations of her husband that she would try to release.

Guitars also played in the background of Joyce's imagination as she thought about her expectations of Jim to which she clung. Where Anne's guitars had been playing gentle tunes, the music in Joyce's daydream was pulsing and hot. In fact, Spanish guitars thrummed out dramatic chords while Jim tracked and pursued Joyce across a dimly lit dance floor. The distance between the two closed rapidly and he took her roughly and together they stepped the bold moves of the tango. He wasn't passively following her lead in this dance; rather, he took control easily from his woman who accepted his steering. In her fantasy, Joyce's form was curvier, smoother, and more sensual than the shapeless man's robe she wore over gender-neutral flannel pajamas.

Mona sat in front of her computer, long into the night, while echoes of snoring drifted down the stairs of their three-bedroom home. Her son, Samir, came up from behind, and startled her on his way to the kitchen for a late night snack, "Hey, Mom, it's just me. Don't have a heart attack." Kissing her briefly on the cheek, he exited the room, just as she turned around with her arms open in anticipation of a hug. Her smile faded and she reminded him about the leftover kofta in the refrigerator. The minced lamb with a strong onion flavor was his favorite, and was probably the reason Samir emerged from his bedroom at such a late hour. At 15, his growing appetite intensified during hockey season when he played hard on the ice several times a week.

Returning to the computer screen, Mona resumed typing her assignment for the first Respect Dare. Her fingers started slowly, but picked up their pace and intensity as they struck the lettered keys. So intense was her focus on the entry, she didn't hear Samir pass through the living room and up the stairs with his plate of steaming food. She typed and typed and typed until she forgot about the actual prompt of the first three Dares. Her expectations had angrily flowed into words and she realized she had filled an entire page of bulleted expectations of her husband—all of them referring to his fidelity and security. In disgust at her list and having gone a bit off track, she saved the document in a folder entitled "Divorce Case" and clicked the icon that would take her online.

Clicking the Bookmarked tab, Mona immediately went to the infidelity support group site and reviewed the 17 new entries by spouses who had just discovered their marriages were ruined by cheating mates. As she scanned the community's descriptions of discovery, she felt anxiety rise in her chest. Her nausea increased as she read the entries of those who had gone before, who recommended counseling—either individual or marital—and scheduling an appointment with an attorney. Just as she was reading a selection on how to create a detailed timeline of all of the cheating spouse's activities, a personal message appeared in her in-box on the survivor's website. Quickly she clicked on the note and discovered it was from Stephen. She ravenously devoured his words.

> *Hi, Mona, I just wanted to reach out to you and say thanks for helping me through this terrible time. My heart feels as if it's being severed from my chest, and sometimes it hurts so badly I can't breathe. I am so grateful for your kindness to me and don't know how I'd get through this without your friendship. Nobody understands the pain I'm feeling like you do. Your husband was a fool to toss aside your feelings when he cheated on you. He doesn't deserve you.*

Mona stared at the message for several minutes before logging out of the site. Her gaze fell on *The Respect Dare* on her tabletop. She'd been using the book as a mouse pad while she read the personal message from the only man who understood her feelings.

Maxine only had ten minutes between meetings to gather her thoughts. She had asked her administrative assistant to hold all calls in order to squeeze in a few moments to work on *The Respect Dare* homework. The women were scheduled to meet in just two days, yet Maxine hadn't even read the first Dare. She would need to tackle the work quickly if she wanted meet the "three Dares a week" quota she had established for the group. She skimmed the pages rapidly before scribbling a response to all the prompts for the first three Dares. Satisfied with her use of time, she closed the book just as her office door opened for the 4:30 client.

Joyce's head was bowed and her hands folded while her mouth formed silent words in her conversation with God. She read scripture, prayed, and had a dedicated quiet time for meditation every morning after Jim left for work and before her son, Justin, awoke for school. She loved the Lord deeply and after years of turning to Him for guidance, comfort, and wisdom, she craved her time alone with Him. Despite her loving relationship with Jesus, she wasn't ready to joyfully embrace the biblical principles for wives that were established at the beginning of time. She didn't mind doing little activities that demonstrated her love for Jim, but she wasn't interested in becoming weak and submissive to her husband in any form. Certainly God didn't expect wives in the 21st century to obey the same marriage rules that were effective hundreds, if not thousands of years ago!

Joyce's own father had been killed in the 1958 Lebanon crisis in Beirut, and she had no memories of her parents' conversations. Playing the role of both parents for her three daughters, her mother was a strong matriarch who was too busy to pursue any romantic relationships. Joyce never had a role model from which to learn successful interactions between husbands and wives. She was curious, however, and most interested in learning how to show Jim respect without sacrificing her lead role in the home.

Because of her interest, Joyce took her time reading each new chapter. She re-read the Bible verse at the beginning of the Dare and felt the prayers inserted at the end of each Dare helped quiet her mind and focus her thoughts on the task at hand. While at work she found her mind drifting off to the example given in the day's reading. There she'd be, in the middle of ringing up a long grocery order, thinking about how she could respond to the current Dare. Joyce was fully committed to this process and would undertake each Dare to the best of her ability, no matter how frightening.

Jessica put away the dinner dishes. The girls, 18 month-old Kayla and three year-old Ashley, had drifted off to sleep once they'd had two bedtime stories and a lullaby. The house was quiet. Her husband, Bob, a corporate attorney, spent many nights alone in his home office reviewing documents in preparation for important negotiations or court proceedings. She passed by the partially closed door and saw the blue light of the computer shining off of his expanding forehead, and didn't linger at the doorway so she wouldn't interrupt him. Sighing, she made her way to their large master bedroom alone.

Pulling the soft, velvet throw pillows off the embroidered duvet cover, Jessica got ready for bed. She slid between the sumptuous cotton sheets and felt the silky chenille fabric against her cheek. Being surrounded by such luxury had been unfamiliar to her when she and Bob were first married, but favorable circumstances soon become commonplace and she quickly was able to compete in the marathon of maintaining their public persona. She shopped for her daughters' attire at exclusive boutiques; purchased the top-end hockey equipment for her stepson, Bobby Jr.; and used several mobile phone applications to discover, follow, and shop for stylish trends in fashion and beauty. Her lifestyle was a far cry from her humble beginnings. Dare #2 had made her think of her home life, particularly of the marriage role models she observed. She and her brothers and sister grew up in a trailer home. Jessica's mother had been a hairdresser and her father took on odd jobs around the trailer park. He drank too much and dressed in clothes that were torn and covered in paint splatters and oil stains. Despite his lack of grooming, Mom's appearance was meticulous. She spent hours at second-hand stores searching for outfits that demonstrated her dedication to beauty and fashion. Her hair was always perfect—soft waves framing her face and adorning her shoulders like a waterfall cascading over ground swells.

Despite careful attention to her appearance, Jessica's mother was constantly competing with other women for her husband's attention. Before they divorced, his wandering eye constantly scanned the landscape for pretty women, much like the radar in an air traffic controller's tower. When his eyes locked on a pretty female he openly stared at her, seemingly oblivious to everybody around him—including his wife and children.

Jessica recalled her embarrassment at her father's behaviors, and sitting in her mansion 850 miles from her hometown, felt her face blush with shame. She shook her head and pushed her thoughts away to focus on the Respect Dare assignment.

Chapter 9 – Small Group Meeting Dares #1–3

It was the hockey moms' first Respect Dare small group meeting and five of the six women sat anxiously in the plastic orange and blue chairs around a table. Alma sat quietly observing the other women's attempts at small talk, while she considered how "real" she would be in sharing her first week's experiences. She had completed all three of the assigned Dares and was most challenged by the third Dare—the one where she had to consider her childhood experiences with conflicts in relationships.

In her family home, Alma was the youngest of three children and completely unaware of conflicts between the adults in her family. Perhaps her older siblings shielded her, but she honestly could not remember any specific instance when her parents argued. At worst there were prolonged periods of silence between them—at the dinner table, in the car, or engaging in daily tasks. Even watching television was turned into a separate activity for her parents. Her *papá* watched television in his bedroom and her *mamá* watched the small black-and-white in the basement while she ironed and folded laundry.

Alma wasn't sure how thinking back to her childhood could help, but she had done her best and hoped the next Dare would be more applicable to her situation with Marco. She was anxious and wished the meeting would begin soon.

Jessica was the last to arrive and apologized for her tardiness. She motioned to her daughters, who each carried a "busy bag" with toys, books, and stuffed animals. They followed her to another table, where they were hoisted into chairs.

Taking the lead, Maxine cleared her throat and started the meeting. "This week we agreed to tackle the first three Dares. Was this manageable for everyone?"

A nervous silence filled the room before Anne leaned forward. "It was a little weird for me to have homework, considering I'm usually the one teaching the lessons or nagging kids to complete their work. But the reading and tasks were doable for me." With that, heads began to nod, indicating a general acceptance of that perspective.

Maxine acknowledged the assent and continued, "*The Respect Dare Leader's Guide* suggests that before we start each week, I read group guidelines that ensure a safe and productive meeting." After reading through the simple rules that promoted anonymity, confidentiality, and no cross talk, she continued, "Since we have about 90 minutes before the team finishes practice, I think it makes the most sense for each of us to share our experience or something meaningful from each of the questions. It might be too lengthy or personal for each of us to read all of our responses." With that, the tension in the room noticeably decreased. Alma sat back in her chair, Mona unfolded her arms, and Jessica stopped examining the polish on her fingernails.

The women summarized their responses to each of the Dares and the awkward unfamiliarity began to wane as the time passed. When one woman spoke, the rest listened and made eye contact with the speaker. Alma smiled often at speakers as if to communicate her acceptance and caring. Anne and Mona were vigorous head-nodders. Maxine took notes, while Joyce made intense eye contact and frequently looked as if she wanted to pose a question but restrained herself. Jessica's attention waned—when she wasn't redirecting her daughters, she frequently caught herself staring off into the distance, seemingly deep in thought.

When the women had finished talking about their responses, Maxine cut right to the core and asked them to imagine and share a succinct vision for an improved marriage. Joyce was the first to respond, stating bluntly, "I want more intimacy in my marriage."

Anne picked up the thread and quietly said, "I want to stop being responsible for every aspect of our family life. I'd like my husband to carry his share."

Mona was eager to share, "I don't know what more I can do to improve my marriage, since my husband is the one who shattered our marriage when he decided to have sex with another woman." An immediate silence filled the room as the women digested the information Mona shared. After several long moments of awkward tension, Alma hesitatingly offered, "Mona, I'm sorry that happened to you. I'm not sure how I'd feel if Marco was unfaithful to me, but given his attitude lately, I suspect we're entering dangerous territory in that same neighborhood." Alma's mouth twisted and her eyes grew very sad, "I just want to feel the closeness that we shared when the kids were little. We were very busy juggling babies, jobs, schools, and extended family, but we were on the same team. Marco was with me—even when we weren't together. Now we could be in the same room but if feels as if we are miles apart."

Maxine reached out her hand and rested it on Alma's shoulder for comfort. "Sometimes I feel the exact same way, Alma. Except with my husband I feel like he's escaped into a world filled with toys, kiddie meals, and play dates. I come home from work, ready to unwind, and he doesn't stop talking. I get that he's been home all day with the kids and doesn't get to spend a lot of time conversing with other adults, but I just wish he would see things from my perspective for a while. I just want some time and space to myself. So we, too, are on different wavelengths." Where Alma had demonstrated sadness at her marriage revelation, Maxine flicked her hands as if swatting at a pesky insect.

When Maxine finished speaking, she turned toward Jessica, who was absentmindedly stacking blocks on the empty table before her. The other women followed Maxine's gaze and looked expectantly at Jessica. When she looked up, somewhat startled by all of them staring at her, she offered, "Well, Bob and I have only been married four years, so we're in a totally different situation than those of you who have been married forever." Anne and Joyce rolled their eyes and Mona folded her arms across her chest, but

Jessica continued, seemingly unaware of the displeasure her comment had sparked, "Bob is such a thoughtful husband. When he comes home from work, he plays with the girls before dinnertime. Last week he brought home a purebred Maltese puppy for the girls who absolutely squealed with delight, as you can imagine. So if I had to think of something that we could have in an improved marriage, it would be another date night each week. You see, we go out for dinner every Wednesday to the most romantic restaurants. I think it would be really awesome if we could add another date night into the rotation. I'll suggest it to him this week, and I'm sure he'll think it's a fantastic idea." She hadn't stopped playing with the blocks the entire time her narrative unfolded. When she finished talking, her eyes dropped again to the blocks, which she began stacking one on top of the other.

An audible snort of disgust blew from Mona's mouth, while an envious sigh slipped from Alma's. After several moments of uncomfortable silence, an explosion of noise punctuated the quiet, and a bitter odor emanating from hockey players washed over the women. The team crossed the lobby and streamed into the locker room to change out of their wet gear. Maxine took that as the cue to wrap things up, "Okay Ladies, that was really good work. Let's tackle Dares #4, 5, and 6 for next week." The women rose and broke into paired conversations while they drifted away.

As Alma made her way to the exit, she pondered the commonalities between the women's disappointments in their marriages—all but Jessica. Alma thought about the connectedness she'd had with Marco when they'd been married for only four years. Things certainly hadn't been perfect—their fights were filled with as much energy and heat as their lovemaking. Alma pondered this reality, and wondered if things were really as flawless as Jessica wanted them believe.

Chapter 10 – Dare #4: Joyce

"For I know the plans I have for you," declares the LORD, *"plans to prosper you and not to harm you, plans to give you hope and a future."*

Jeremiah 29:11 NIV

Joyce was in the middle of scanning a long grocery order, nearing the end of a 12- hour shift, when her mind drifted to *The Respect Dare*. Her body on autopilot, she thought about what she'd read earlier that morning and considered God's plan or vision for her life. When she was a younger wife, she was solidly aware that God had created her to raise a family, help her friends, and serve at her church. She found affirmation in a busy schedule filled with hockey practices, soccer games, and ballet recitals. She produced a generation of family mealtimes that, except for sickness, nobody missed. Even taking care of her ailing parents had fallen into a regular routine, in which she knew her role and responsibility.

Uncovering her place in this new phase of life was less certain. Her older two children were out of the home. Although

Justin's hockey team had a full roster of games and practices, the demand for her expertise and attention had considerably dwindled. Justin was taking Driver's Education this year, and after he got his license, would probably spend far less time with his mother. As it was now, the most quality time she had with her son was in the car before and after hockey. Next year he would likely be driving himself or riding with friends. It was startling to recognize that she had one year left before Justin would think he was independent—just needing mom and dad for the occasional loan, meal, or new outfit.

Janine's growing belly was the visual reminder to Joyce that her time of being at the center of the mothering tornado was coming to a close and she was entering an age to which she had never given much thought. Medicare, retirement, and AARP were regular conversations among her friends, and she noticed with irritation that each of those topics were of growing interest to her. Early-bird dinners were beckoning; perhaps she needed to start thinking of herself as an elderly woman. Didn't she? She was too old to wear her hair in shocking bold colors as she had in her youth, but too young to allow the greys to go on full display. She received the 15% senior citizen discount at her local diner, but didn't qualify for handicapped parking.

If God had a plan for her—a vision for who she should be—couldn't He give her a clue of who she was supposed to be at 59? If Joyce couldn't identify herself, how could she redefine her marriage? She had mercilessly teased Jim when he went through his mid-life crisis. How she laughed when he considered the purchase of a red convertible, sported a diamond earring, and even attempted extreme skydiving (which ended prematurely with a sudden case of vertigo and airsickness). If this was her mid-life crisis, it was no laughing matter. Why couldn't she just get back on solid ground again?

"Lord, You're gonna have to help me see what You see, because I've got no clue," Joyce prayed. Then she heard a voice, "Joyce . . . Joyce . . . do you hear me? Hello?" Joyce focused her attention on the voice and realized it wasn't the voice of God; rather, it was Jessica from her small group. She was standing in front of her, smiling in a way that showed off her perfectly straight white teeth.

Joyce straightened and forced a polite grin, pushing her lips closed so that they covered her own coffee-stained teeth. Jessica greeted her while unloading a grocery cart neatly organized with items that were stacked around two little girls who beamed like cherubs. Behind her stood a very good-looking man in his late 40s or early 50s. His blue-green eyes and dark hair immediately drew Joyce's attention.

Following her gaze, Jessica introduced her husband, Bob. Joyce found herself stammering like a nervous adolescent, struggling for something clever to say to the confident man in his expensive suit. He listened attentively to Jessica's description of how the two women knew each other, and when she finished, he lovingly circled her shoulders with his arm. His smile was as dazzling as hers, and Joyce noticed the sleek gold watch on his wrist as he reached for the credit card to pay for their groceries. She couldn't help contrasting his clean, perfectly shaped fingernails with her husband's, which were stubby from years of biting them. As the happy family wheeled their cart toward the exit, Joyce noted that Bob's arm had found its natural place resting on Jessica's shoulders as they looked lovingly at their daughters and each other. Joyce could practically hear the romantic music playing in the background as the perfect family floated out the door.

Watching their retreating figures, Joyce allowed the choking fingers of jealousy to pull at her heart because she felt frumpier than ever before.

Chapter 11 – Dare #5: Alma, Anne

Everyone should be quick to listen, slow to speak, and slow to become angry.

James 1:19 NIV

Alma read the words of Dare #5, which challenged wives to operate on a different timeline, specifically her husband's. The chapter suggested a woman might see a solution to a dispute before her husband. Rather than voicing anger and launching into a quickly constructed tutorial, the wife should give her husband time to process and verbalize his own resolution—which may, or may not, be parallel to hers. Quick to listen, slow to speak, and slow to become angry. In short, Alma was being asked to wait while God taught her husband the lessons he needed to learn. While waiting, she would need to refrain from lecturing, yelling or trying to teach the lesson to Marco herself.

Alma tried to think of the last time she and Marco had fought. There had been very few blowouts in nearly two decades of marriage. Her pattern of dealing with disagreements was to explode with a barrage of accusations in Spanish and then storm from the room. Marco's tactic was more passive—he never brought up an issue that bothered him. Rather, he would stew in solitude, avoiding whomever transgressed against his sense of right and wrong. Having grown up in a volatile home, he had no intention of repeating the mistakes of his father and always took a mild, if not passive, approach to handling conflicts.

Alma smiled in recollection of one of their more vigorous arguments. Their oldest, Alicia had been only a baby and Alma stayed at home while Marco juggled responsibilities at two full-time jobs. She no longer remembered the issue of contention, but she did recall his docile and noncommittal response to the volley of accusations that were aimed in his direction. Rather than engage in combat, he simply continued to shave in front of the bathroom mirror, careful not to get any shaving cream on his uniform. This simple action had infuriated her beyond comprehension and perhaps to get his attention, or demonstrate the degree of her anger, she impulsively grabbed the plastic storage bowl of sweet potatoes she had cooked for a large batch of baby food, and flung the entirety of its contents at his stunned face. She was dumbfounded as she witnessed the orange potato blobs splatter against his uniform shirt, his cleanly shaven face, and the shower curtain behind him. Instantly bracing herself for a violent response, she was doubly astounded when he leaned over and very calmly closed the bathroom door.

Alma chuckled to herself at the very memory. Many years later, they jokingly referred to it as the Sweet Potato Event of 1998. Thinking back, she recalled the fear that had surged through her veins when he closed that door. She was certain that after he had cleaned his face, he would storm out of the bathroom in a rage. Without contemplation, she had grabbed the baby bag, stuffed little Alicia in her car seat, and ran out the door so that she didn't have to face the music. After spending the entire day at her sister's home, Alma returned and found the bathroom had been cleaned of all incriminating orange evidence. When Marco came home late that night, he never said a word—never reprimanded or shamed her as her papá would have done to her mamá—he just curled up behind her in bed and lovingly wrapped his arm around her middle, where the twisted knots in her stomach unwound at his touch. That night she discovered a new definition of kindness and gentleness.

Her appreciation and love for him grew past boundaries she never knew existed. She entwined her fingers with his as they rested on her waist. No words passed between the two—she pressed his hand in a silent request for forgiveness, and he returned a gentle squeeze to signify it had been granted.

After reading Dare #5, Alma vowed she would watch for a time when her instinct was to erupt or correct her husband and respond differently. She didn't expect that her chance to practice extending grace would present itself that very evening. Marco came home from work and draped his worn tie and wrinkled white shirt over the chair that was already heavily burdened with numerous layers of shirts, pants, and sweaters. This habit of heaping mounds of clothing on chairs instead of returning it to a hanger in the closet, drove her crazy—especially as there were few chairs in their home that weren't adorned with an article of his clothing.

She took a sharp breath in preparation for her typical reprimand that hanging up his outfit properly in the closet would only take a few additional seconds—then caught herself. It felt as if a thick board was lodged in her chest as she stifled the rant that threatened to escape. She slowed her breathing in hopes that it would slow her thinking and the quick temper that was flaring within. When no sound came, Marco turned around, surprised to find her still in the room, yet silent. He shrugged his shoulders and returned to the task of making his daily fashion deposit on the growing pile. Finished, he pulled on a sweatshirt and jeans and left the bedroom without a single word in her direction.

Alma's heart pounded and anger heated her ears. Hearing him searching the pantry for a snack, she knew it was safe to release some of the tension. Her eyes rolled up and her hands gestured heavenward as if to ask "WHY does he do this every time?" Her lips moved silently and her face changed and twisted quickly to reflect the path of her moods—first questioning, then angry, next frustrated, and finally disgusted. Exasperated, she took a deep breath and began reciting the rosary aloud in Spanish, "*Dios te salve María, llena eres de Gracia…*"

When finished, Alma sighed deeply and reached for the journal and pen she kept with *The Respect Dare* book. She knew this journey wouldn't be easy and couldn't help but imagine how difficult it would be for some of the other women in the small group to complete this Dare.

Anne laid her pen down on the large ancient desk in her classroom and adjusted her position in the hard wooden chair. It was Open House night at her school, and with very few parents coming to meet her, she was able to complete her *Respect Dare* homework. She had just finished her fourth journal entry and was beginning to read the next chapter. Absentmindedly fingering the edge of the bookmark, she felt her heart seize as the words of Dare #5 reached her consciousness, "Remain silent while Tony figures things out for himself? Oh, this ought to be interesting . . . and take forever! Who has time for that?" Spending her days in a classroom jammed with 30-plus students all day, where each minute was precious and jam-packed with learning opportunities, she operated at a brisk pace. Some called her abrupt, but she liked to think of herself as efficient. She was constantly being pulled in three directions at once.

It's not that Anne didn't think Tony was intelligent. He made daily decisions about building plans, contractors, and permits that made her head spin. There were just some areas in which she was the master, and the rest of her family only needed to heed her directions. Her education and experience with students enabled her to orchestrate her stepsons' academics, extracurricular activities, and behavior management. She wielded her knowledge like a sword, slashing a clear path for her family to follow.

Anne instinctively knew that remaining silent and listening to Tony couldn't end well. "Humph, I wondered how long it would be before we were asked to become doormats for our husbands. I just didn't think it would happen this early in the process!" She was determined to remain assertive in her relationship with him and wouldn't subvert her power to anybody. She felt justified in veering from the book's recommended template, particularly with this dare. After all, the problems in their marriage stemmed entirely from his drinking problem.

Chapter 12 – Dare #6: Maxine, Mona

Do everything without grumbling or arguing.

Philippians 2:14 NIV

Maxine checked her phone while she stood at the front door waiting for Cynthia to shove her scattered hockey gear into the large goalie bag with the team logo. "Dad, where are my gloves?" Cynthia called to Samuwel who was serving dinner to the twins in the kitchen. He patiently responded, "They're on the drying rack in the basement."

While Cynthia dashed down the stairs to retrieve her equipment, Maxine looked across the living room into the home's large, open kitchen and quipped, "Great job, Dad, it's lucky she thought of the gloves before we got all the way to the rink." A deep crevice divided Samuwel's forehead and a tinge of sarcasm filled his voice. "SO sorry, Maxine. From now on, I'll make sure I carefully pack each and every hockey accessory into our HIGH SCHOOL daughter's hockey bag after washing them—so it doesn't inconvenience you." Their four-year-old boys simultaneously looked up from their plates and watched the interaction of their parents across two separate rooms.

Maxine lowered her phone, looked up, and with mockery in her voice said, "Thank you SO much. It's good to know that I can count on you to take care of all the little things at home while I manage million dollar projects at the office."

Samuwel's face smoothed and his voice lowered, "It's good that we all know our place then, Ms. High-Powered Executive..." Before he could continue, Cynthia bounded up the stairs, kissed him, and dashed out the door.

Maxine slowly pulled the door closed behind her and got the final word. Spoken just loudly enough so that Samuwel could hear from the kitchen, she said, "I'm fortunate to have such a loyal employee who takes care of all my needs." After the door clicked closed, she muttered, "He's lucky he still has a job."

Following her daughter to the car, Maxine could feel the tension rising in her chest and adrenaline shooting down to her fists. Less than an hour ago she had been calmly considering Dare #6—to do one act of kindness toward Samuwel. She planned on taking the boys with her to Cynthia's practice so Samuwel could have the evening to relax, but in the stress of driving home from work and last-minute rush to get Cynthia and her equipment organized, she faltered. Getting behind the wheel of the car, she gritted her teeth and inwardly berated herself for mindlessly slipping into familiar patterns of warfare against her husband. She sighed and wished for an easier Dare tomorrow.

Mona was having a bad week. She had picked up the first cold virus of a long hockey season. Spending so much time in ice rinks and transporting players to late night games and practices creates the perfect environment for the lingering upper respiratory infections that are common markers of hockey parents. Despite the fact that it was only late September and the leaves were just beginning to color, the Chicagoland weather had already turned cold and rainy; feeling more like November than the beginning of autumn.

A hot cup of tea warmed Mona's hands while she huddled

in her car. She didn't have the energy to wait in the rink while Samir practiced tonight, plus her red nose and watery eyes were less than appealing. Parked in the illumination of a large floodlight in the parking lot, Mona was able to read *The Respect Dare* and complete some of the writing exercises. Though she was tired from trying unsuccessfully to sleep with a cough and a stuffy nose, she read the text with less resistance and cynicism than she usually did. She had already completed Dare #4 and was considering Dares #5 and 6. Arguing and yelling loudly at her husband had become her go-to form of communication over the weeks since learning of his affair. She was rightfully angry over his betrayal, and in her tired state accepted that her interactions with Aahil were exhausting and drained her of energy and hope.

The group's next meeting was in a couple of days, and Mona decided she would attempt to hold back from speaking quickly and expressing anger in her next interaction with Aahil. Even though she believed that he deserved every angry word and outburst, she rationalized that it was better to do the Dares so she had something to share with the other women in the group. Perhaps she would just ignore him during the next couple of days so that she wouldn't have the occasion to explode.

Her phone chirped, indicating a text. "Are you still at hockey practice?" came from Stephen.

Mona smiled and responded, "Yes, but it's almost over."

Several moments passed and her phone chirped again. "I hope you aren't sitting in the car with your cold."

She smiled again. "I am, but I've got a hot drink and a tissue box keeping me company."

After several minutes another text arrived. "I'd bring you chicken soup if I could. I've got a great recipe that uses spices that would knock every germ from your body."

Over the last week Mona had little energy for cleaning so she spent extra time online. Stephen was experiencing a new wave of pain and jealousy over the discovery of recent receipts for intimate wear that his wife had never worn—at least not in his bed. When he admitted embarrassment over his blindness to the situation, Mona had suggested they chat privately to alleviate the public scrutiny he was experiencing. From the group forum to a private chat room, to texts, their friendship had progressed rapidly and she found comfort in sharing her anger and pain with someone who could relate.

The two texted back and forth until Samir opened the car door and wedged his large hockey bag in the back seat, laying his hockey stick diagonally so that it would fit in the car. "Who are you texting?" he asked as Mona hastily shoved the phone in her coat pocket.

Mona was dismissive, "Just your Khalah."

Samir didn't miss a beat. "Why is Aunt Jana texting you this late at night?"

Mona paused for a moment, and then said, "She isn't. Jana sent me a message earlier in the day, but I was napping and missed it until now. I'm sure she's in bed and won't even see my text until morning." The muffled notification chimed in Mona's pocket and Samir shot his mother a questioning look. "I'll read it when we get home. It's late and you still have homework to finish after your shower." With that, she turned on the radio and backed out of her parking space, hoping that the nasal sounds of the Palestinian violin would mask any additional notification alerts from her cell phone.

To change the subject, Mona asked her son about practice and he made a thorough commentary on each drill they completed and every goal he scored. Having successfully redirected Samir's focus, she was relieved and went into automatic response mode as she made occasional noises that demonstrated she was listening. After several minutes, her attention wandered and although she continued to nod and insert the occasional hmmm, her mind drifted to something Stephen had said in a text, "You never really know someone until you see what he or she does when nobody's looking." How true that statement was. She thought she knew her husband well after so many years together, yet she never could have imagined he would have cheated on her. Maybe there were more things about Aahil of which she was unaware. She would think about that tomorrow and perhaps Stephen could help.

Chapter 13 – Small Group Meeting—Dares #4–6

All of the women had arrived before the agreed-upon time, including Jessica, whose daughters were noticeably absent. The women chatted with each other and the energy in the room was more robust than it had been at their previous meeting. Alma and Joyce sat near each other and were discussing the team's new jerseys, while Anne and Mona shared tissues and swapped cold remedies. Maxine, efficiently organizing her her books and journal, was seated next to Jessica who had made another attempt at bringing snacks for the group. "Hey, Ladies, I brought something new to share tonight. Bob came home early from work today and took the girls to their toddler tumbling class so I had a little extra time to myself. Instead of sweet, I went for savory this time—high rollers with imported Havarti cheese, roasted turkey breast, and homemade spinach flour wraps. They're a fun finger food." Like the fur rising on the back of a cat, Mona and Anne's animosity was aimed directly at the young, pretty woman who was perfect in every way.

Despite any hostile feelings, the women each took a high roller from the travel platter as they passed it around the circle. Maxine took two because she had rushed from work and hadn't time to eat the meal Samuwel had prepared for the family. After consuming the tasty snack, Maxine wished she had taken a little more time and eaten dinner with the boys—or at least packed a to-go box to take with her. Reminding the participants of the group guidelines, Maxine opened the meeting and each responded to the task of Dare #4. The women shared visions of themselves in a harmonious marriage. There was a distinct sense of longing that came from them as they described dreams of being peaceful wives who encouraged instead of nagged their husbands and were confident that they were loved and accepted exactly as they were.

Anne's answers were short and sounded more like bullet points—happy, healthy, and loved. Mona's answers described someone who was independent, healthy, and strong; sounding more like someone who was single rather than in a committed relationship. When Jessica described herself, Alma thought she could hear romantic violins playing in the background. Her flowery description reminded Alma of a scene from her favorite novella, a Spanish soap opera that ran for several seasons.

Maxine's description was a list of characteristics for a better husband. "I must have misunderstood this Dare, because I wrote how Samuwel would act if we had the perfect marriage." She had the look of an executive in a board meeting—that is to say somewhat arrogant and unwilling to shift positions. She looked straight at the women, as if daring them to suggest she try to brainstorm her own characteristics in an improved marriage. Each woman avoided Maxine's intense glare by looking down, fiddling with pens, or sketching shapes on journal pages.

Breaking the uncomfortable silence, Maxine suggested they move on to Dare #5 and discuss the different ways each had kept from having a shouting match with their husbands. Anne was the first to speak, "I did a really good job with this Dare, Girls. Listen to this." She described how she held her tongue when Tony announced they were going to remodel their master bathroom. "This has been a very sore spot between us in the past. Tony wants to just tear everything out and upgrade it all. You know, travertine tile in the bath, multiple shower jets with a large rain showerhead, granite countertop—the whole works." She paused and looked at Joyce and Mona, who weren't as wealthy as some of the other women in the group. "The problem that I see, but he doesn't, is that he wants to do all the work himself. He says that he puts up high-end bathrooms in buildings and clients' homes, and now he needs one for himself." Anne realized the women were all looking at her with expressions that indicated they saw no problem with the situation. She explained, "But Tony is *always* working. He comes home late every evening and works at construction sites all weekend. He doesn't have the time to remodel our bathroom, and I'll be forced to share a bathroom with my stinky, adolescent step-sons." Smiles of acknowledgement appeared, as each of the hockey moms were all too familiar with the smells, sounds, and filth associated with teenage boys' bathrooms. She continued, "When he started talking about his plans to start demo this week, I listened. It was hard, but I listened. The changes he described do sound pretty cool—I think heated floors and towel warmers would be a nice addition." She paused again and glanced at the others to gauge their responses. "In the end, he told me that the project would launch this weekend." She finished with a weak smile, "We'll see what happens. I don't think it's going to be as smooth as he says, so I'll get a lot of practice holding my tongue over the next couple of weeks." There were smiles and nods. Alma wondered how nice it would be to have that particular burden in her marriage. Their own bathroom was covered in pink tiles reminiscent of the 1960s.

"Does anybody want to share their responses to Dare #6?" Maxine prompted.

Joyce, who was fully committed to this process eagerly leaned forward, "Yes, I'd like to share my experience with this Dare. Jim and I have been married for almost 40 years. During that time, I've done a million favors for him that he's simply taken for granted. Like, making his favorite dinner—BBQ baby back ribs—even though I can't stand it. Or washing his clothes and folding his socks in the crazy rolled way he likes. Not to mention coming home after working in a grocery store all day long, only to spend an hour in the kitchen assembling a meal which gets inhaled in seven minutes flat! Every single night since we've been married I've given my husband a thorough narrative of all of the things I did for him or our family that day. I was always looking for some grand expression of gratitude, but he usually just offered a monotone 'thank you.' On top of that, it just sounded like I forced it out of him." Her pained expression communicated four decades of frustration over the lack of affirmation. She thought for a moment and her face softened noticeably. "But this week was different. At the end of the day, instead of telling him that I took his car for a carwash and filled the gas tank, I kept my mouth shut. Then something crazy happened. No, he didn't begin to sing praises to me for the favors I'd done," Joyce paused and let the anticipation build for dramatic effect. "I felt *God's* approval! Don't ask me how, but in place of Jim's pat on the head, I felt like God was proud of me. I know it may sound weird, but this week when I did things for my family, I acknowledged God and offered each task completion to Him. I did it to honor God. So when Jim didn't say anything about his car, it didn't bother me. I held my silence for days. On the third night, he reached across the couch for my hand, gave it a squeeze, and thanked me for being such a good wife! I was so shocked I was absolutely giddy! I could feel waves of happiness reverberating through my whole body, but all I did was smile at him." At this point in her narrative, Joyce stood up and simulated the powerful moment—shaking her arms and torso so wildly that she reminded Mona of a retired belly dancer. Joyce stopped shaking, and catching her breath, gasped, "And that was it. There was no profound expression of undying love, no passionate sex in the living room." She took a few deep breaths before concluding, "Just a moment of honest and real appreciation. It was awesome!" Joyce's eyes were wide and sparkly, her countenance animated, and the smile that crept across her face was enchanting.

Alma respected the group guidelines of no cross talk, but couldn't suppress the urge to clap her hands. After she concluded her applause, she began to speak in her slow and thoughtful manner, "My experience with this Dare was a little different." Alma smiled at Joyce, and then lowered her eyes for a moment to her journal. Looking up, she continued. "As you know, I've been struggling with Marco's recent lack of kindness. Because of this, I guess I've been withdrawing from him. In fact, when I read Dare #6, I realized that it's been a long time since I'd done even a minor errand to help make his day a little easier. So, even though I really wasn't enthusiastic about doing a task for him without expectations, I tackled a pile of his clothes that had been accumulating on a chair near his closet. I hung the clothes neatly in the closet and pushed the chair back where it belonged in the room. I admit that at first I was pretty grumpy about the whole thing and had to pray for a spirit of willingness. But when it was finished, I felt differently. I was proud of the job I'd done and was happy with the result. I don't even know if Marco noticed, but it didn't bother me." She thought a moment while her finger traced the edges of her journal. "If I had done this act of kindness a couple of weeks ago, I sure would have felt angry at him for not acknowledging my favor, and stupid for wasting my time. Instead, I experienced a calm and joyful feeling from completing this Dare—without a thank you from Marco."

Mona listened to Joyce and Alma with more than a little cynicism, and inwardly questioned how women could feel valued by their god and find fulfillment in helping their husbands even if they don't acknowledge their wives' efforts. Could women really feel joy just from adjusting their perspective through a conversation with Jesus? She wondered what she would have felt if she had found the opportune time to complete Dares #5 and 6. She remembered reading the chapters, but didn't recall why she hadn't put even a half-hearted attempt into completing the tasks. When her turn to share arrived, Mona covered her journal and explained her illness prevented her full attention on the Dares. "But," she promised, "I'll complete them this week and catch up to the rest of you."

Chapter 14 – Dare #7: Anne, Mona

Do not let any unwholesome talk come out of your mouths, but only what is helpful for building others up according to their needs, that it may benefit those who listen.

Ephesians 4:29 NIV

Anne read the words of Dare #7 and felt convicted. "Oh crap. I mean, darn. I mean shucks. I mean bummer." Dare #7 opened with a vignette of married friends talking about their husbands, and the conversation was not flattering. She thought how the example given was a pretty accurate portrayal of the conversations she'd exchanged with family, friends, and even casual co-workers. Faultfinding and grumbling about husbands were typical of the culture—certainly men complained about their wives all the time.

Dare #7, however, suggested that "husband-bashing" with friends did not have a positive influence on the marriage. Anne thought about this notion and realized that when she was first married to Tony she thought the world of him. She only mimicked her friends' bitter comments about their husbands to better fit in with her peers. She didn't really believe the derogatory things she was saying, but over time those false criticisms transformed into truths to which she added a whole new repertoire of grievances. Now with less than five years of marriage under her belt, she spoke poorly of Tony all the time. How could she bridle her tongue to honor the admonition of keeping her comments positive and uplifting? She thought it was going to be tough, then impossible when she read the next challenge—to ask Tony about a time when something she had said or done made him feel diminished. "Oh crap . . . darn, shucks . . . CRAP!"

Up until now, participating in the Respect Dares had only required Anne to think and act in isolation. This Dare, however, was going to be a humbling activity. She agonized over asking Tony this question. She told herself, "Don't think about it. Just do it. If you think about it too much, you'll never be able to carry out this task. Put on your big-girl pants and talk to him." With that, she took a deep breath and dialed his cell phone number.

Mona had been very busy trying to catch up with the other women in the Respect Dare small group. If she tackled one Dare per day, she'd be able to complete Dare #9 in time for the next meeting. She found Dare #5 pretty easy to complete, because prior to learning of Aahil's infidelity, she had never spoken against her husband's decisions. She was in the habit of listening, rather than reacting. For the next Dare, she cooked his favorite meal for dinner, roasted lamb and spiced rice with toasted nuts. She was still unsure about the connection to God, but while she cooked she thought over how encouraging the women of her small group had been for her to catch up with them and complete the missed Dares. Anticipating their approval brought pleasure to Mona as she prepared the food and gave little thought to the man who would consume it.

When Aahil came home from work and saw a meal that was typically reserved for special occasions, he seemed pleased—initially. His smile was quickly replaced by a somber expression. "What is the special occasion?" he tentatively inquired.

Mona tried to dismiss his apprehension with a nonchalant response, "There was a special on lamb at the market." Together Mona, Aahil, and Samir sat for dinner. The conversation was carried entirely by their son, whose name in Arabic aptly meant talented entertainer. Listening to Samir's tale of comedy from the morning's chemistry class, she was transported to a simpler time when she trusted everything her husband said and she didn't wrestle with images of him in another woman's embrace.

Her smile faded into a frown and she looked up to see Aahil smiling gently at her, his eyes warm and kind as they had been so many weeks ago. Being pulled into his visual embrace, she felt her resistance slipping away. To break the spell, she stood abruptly from the table and removed her plate despite the fact that there was a good deal of food remaining. Samir protested, "Aw, Mom, don't go, I'm about to get to the good part!" Aahil didn't protest, but indicated his acceptance of the situation with a small nod and sad smile. Without waiting for a response, Samir continued his story, and she followed the narration from the kitchen where she scraped the remains from her plate into the garbage and broke into tears.

Rushing to her room, Mona locked the door and sat down heavily on the bed. On her bedside table stood her journal and her cell phone, with a flashing blue light that notified her a text was waiting. Feeling torn between checking the message and completing her journal writing, she turned her phone face down and diligently opened her notebook. She reflected on her experience of cooking the special dinner for Aahil but didn't write about the torment she felt during the meal. When she had finished writing, her curiosity pulled her gaze toward the blinking light that seemed to be calling, "read me, read me, read me." She reached for the phone, and in doing so knocked her book on the floor.

The text was from Stephen and spelled out "CALL ME" in capital letters. Mona wondered what painful new discovery he had made about his unfaithful wife and pushed the CALL button. He answered on the first ring and spoke loudly. "Mona! I'm so glad you called. I don't think I can handle this much pain for much longer." He didn't even wait for her answer before starting a drawn-out description of the latest encounter with his wife. Mona's mind drifted from Stephen's sarcastic voice back to Aahil's quiet countenance and sad smile. She became aware that he hadn't begged her forgiveness in a while, or made any grand gestures of reconciliation. He seemed to be patiently waiting for her to make the next move in their relationship. "Can you believe after all the pain she has caused me she wants me to forgive her? Mona, are you there?"

Mona was jolted back into the present conversation on the phone. "Hmm? You say she is asking to be forgiven?"

"Yes! Can you believe it? She's just like your husband, begging pardon for unpunished crimes. Let's face it, neither one deserves mercy. Your husband keeps you living from paycheck to paycheck, and from what you've said, he isn't winning any awards for strength and stamina in the bedroom." Thrown off balance by Stephen's unexpected words, Mona flushed a bright red.

In an attempt at changing the subject, she asked, "Where are you right now? Everything is so loud in the background, I can hardly hear you."

Stephen's voice grew even louder and Mona thought she detected a distinct slur in his words, "I had to get out of the house. I'm a couple of blocks from home in a pub and grill. You know what it's like when you just need to get away?"

Mona did know how it felt. "Yes, I know exactly how that feels, Stephen. There are some days I think I might throw a sharp object at my husband's head if I didn't have to leave the house for hockey practice or games."

Stephen's loud laugh flooded from her phone and permeated every inch of her quiet bedroom. She cupped her hand around the phone, pressed tightly to her ear in an effort to prevent anybody from hearing his voice. When he was finished laughing, Stephen confessed, "Mona, you understand me. I wouldn't be able to bear any of this pain if it weren't for you. I don't know what I'd do without you in my life." At that moment, it was Mona's face that held a sad smile. She was happy that they'd developed a friendship and had been able to help each other through painful moments, but something about their relationship was beginning to shift and it brought confusion for her. Stephen's voice sank low, "You're just lucky there is a state line between us, Mona, or I would show you just how grateful I am." Her ears flushed warmly and her eyes grew wide with surprise. At that moment there was a knock on the door and she quickly disconnected the call without explanation and turned off all sounds on the phone.

She rushed to the door and unlocked it to find Aahil patiently standing outside. She pulled back to allow him to enter the room and watched as he calmly sat down on his side of the bed. Facing her husband, Mona took the plunge into Dare #7 and asked simply, "Aahil, has there ever been a time in our marriage that I said or did something that made you feel less than respected?"

He looked sharply up at her with a quizzical look on his face. Recognizing that she wasn't goading him or being sarcastic, his gaze drifted as he considered her question. After several long moments, his words were calm and gentle, "There was only one time, Mona. In all our years of marriage, you were demeaning to me only once. It was after you'd learned of my . . . indiscretion. You were hurt and talking on the phone with your sister, I suppose. Samir and I had just come home from a hockey game, but you were so upset you didn't hear us enter the house. As we stood in the entryway, you said things about me that made me feel like a disgraceful child who didn't deserve redemption. I was humiliated because you were right and also because Samir heard your words. Out of embarrassment, we each retreated to our own bedrooms without a sound so that you didn't realize we'd heard everything. That was the only time you ever degraded me."

His sad smile had crumpled into the miserable expression of a wounded man. His shoulders slumped and his head drooped, heavy with guilt. Despite the fact that she was justified in feeling betrayed, Mona felt remorseful for the grief her words had inflicted upon him. Unable to move forward or reach out to her husband, she could only verbalize an earnest, "I'm sorry for doing that, Aahil. I never meant for Samir to know any of that." For the second time that evening, huge tears swelled in Mona's eyes and she fled from her husband to hide the guilt and shame.

Chapter 15 – Dare #8: Alma, Jessica

So God created mankind in His own image, in the image of God
He created him; male and female He created them.

Genesis 1:27 NIV

Alma was stuck. She sat alone at the kitchen table one evening, trying to consider why she married her husband. Dare #8 asked her to recall the positive qualities that had attracted her to Marco, and sadly she could not. The man to whom she was married today was nothing like the beautiful man who was completely enchanting in her early 20s. Marco's recent moods clouded every interaction, including those with complete strangers. Last week he went to the grocery store with Mateo to pick up some French bread and eggs, but when they returned, Mateo had a strange look on his face and disappeared up to his bedroom. Marco stormed into the kitchen and slammed the eggs so hard on the counter that Alma was certain she heard the distinct crunching sounds of eggshells shattering. "What's wrong, Marco?"

Marco had thrown the bread onto the kitchen table and complained about the proximity of another customer in line. "You know how people at the fruit market stand too close to you? Well,

I'm trying to take out my wallet to pay for the food, and this stupid woman was standing so close to me, she actually bumped me twice. I was getting ready for her to grab my wallet or maybe climb up on my shoulders. What's wrong with these people? Don't they have any manners or education?" He had stormed out of the kitchen, with the occasional sound of slamming doors or flying objects thumping behind.

His behaviors and overreactions were not attractive; in fact they were beginning to embarrass not only her, but also the kids. Last weekend, Max replayed an unfriendly scene between Marco and the priest after confession. It seemed no one was immune to the storm that followed her husband. But he hadn't always been like this. One of the first things that attracted Alma to Marco was his unbelievable generosity of spirit—he sought out the good in every situation and every person. Unlike all of the angry and unforgiving male role models in Alma's childhood, Marco demonstrated kindness. He had been playful and provided unexpected moments of craziness. One night, when the two were dancing at a nightclub, he suddenly did a backflip, much to the surprise and delight of the other dancers.

Another endearing quality that he possessed was his generosity and devotion to his mother. Although at times it interfered with her plans, Alma instinctively knew that if a woman wants to know how a man would treat her in the future, observe carefully how he treats his mother. A man who demonstrates love and fondness for his mother will certainly display similar affections for his wife.

While it was relatively easy for Alma to recall all of his positive qualities, what she found incredibly difficult was reconciling the Marco of the past with the man of the present.

The second part of Dare #8 required Maxine to share the list of Samuwel's positive qualities with him. She had rushed through the creation of her list and was in no mood to take the time to have a lengthy discussion with him about it. In a spirit of generosity, she compromised and decided to text Samuwel the list on her way down from her office. By the time the elevator had traveled from the 23rd floor to the lobby, she had typed in all of the characteristics she found charming when first meeting Samuwel. Before sending, she punched out a quick PS—"and you've still got it." There. That should keep him happy for a while.

Lately it felt as if she were carrying all the responsibility for the well-being of her family, including doing these Dares to keep her husband happy. The rushed readings and writing assignments were getting on her nerves, and Maxine began to resent the time she felt she was wasting with the other women in their small group meetings. This was time she should be using to catch up on work emails that had come in after hours. Maxine wasn't sure how much longer she would be able to lead this marriage ministry.

Jessica's flowery handwriting filled the pages of her journal with equally lofty sentiments. She was delighted to be asked to write a list of Bob's positive qualities, and despite the fact that she was only required to cover five characteristics; she had just finished composing a seven-page tribute to her husband. Because they'd only been married four years, it was easy to remember how Bob had attracted and conquered her heart forever. It started with his great looks and good manners. He knew how to secure the approval and command the attention of those around him. His words, eloquent as if they'd been written by a master playwright, flowed easily from his lips. He was a leader with his colleagues in the law firm and an elder at their large church, which could accommodate as many as 10,000 worshipers. Bob was dynamic and quick to show his appreciation for things he deemed superior.

Jessica knew she was fortunate to have captured his adoration and did everything in her power to complete the image of the perfect family her husband expected. Even in their infancy, their two precious daughters were well behaved and Jessica dressed them in outfits that reflected her husband's elevated social status. Bob frequently encouraged her to spend whatever it took for her to look the part of a successful attorney's wife.

She reread her words, stopping occasionally to correct a grammatical error or revise a thought. Once it was absolutely perfect, she glanced at her reflection in the mirror and smoothed her hair before rising from the dressing table. Walking out of her bedroom she peeked at her sleeping babies in the nursery and walked down the marble stairs that led to Bob's office.

Deciding to surprise him, Jessica entered the office without knocking. She was eager to share her responses to Dare #8 with him and imagined the two would spend the rest of the evening wrapped in each other's arms. The door swung smoothly on its hinges and she saw Bob facing the computer, its bluish light glowing from the screen. His face looked strange—jaw tensed, lips curled inward, and eyes staring forward. He didn't even notice Jessica enter the room until she was directly in front of him. There was a shiny layer of moisture on his forehead and just as his mouth opened and eyes began to roll back, he saw his wife.

Chapter 16 – Dare #9: Maxine, Joyce

A fool shows his annoyance at once, but a prudent man overlooks an insult.

Proverbs 12:16 NIV

Maxine drummed her bright fingernails on the large desktop in her office. After admittedly rushing through the previous Dare, she felt somewhat guilty for not putting as much effort into this process as she was encouraging the members of her small group to do. Setting the timer on her phone for a solid 20 minutes to complete this new Dare would ease her conscience. As she began to read Dare #9, she noticed that the chapter was a little longer than the others had been and was glad she had allotted such a large chunk of her workday to tackle this assignment.

Maxine's eyes skimmed the words and she processed the author's encouragement to overlook an insult or verbal assault that might come her way from her spouse. The vignette that was presented as evidence of the benefits of employing this tactic was of a grown woman and her teenage stepson. The woman was patient when responding to a curt comment thrown at her by the adolescent and responded with kindness. The upshot was that the boy's anger melted and their relationship evolved to a new level that very day.

Maxine's eyes narrowed at the words on the page as she neared the end of the chapter. Anticipating the Dare that was about to be launched, her fingers instinctively tightened around the book. She continued reading, skipping over the questions and the suggestions for prayer. She stopped reading when she processed the suggestion that set her anger ablaze—to overlook the next instance when Samuwel insulted her. "That's it! I knew this was coming. This is the portion of the experiment where the women are told to subvert their self-esteem and identity and bow down to the man of the house! Arrgh! I HATE this part of the church world. Why can't women be strong and powerful and successful AND married? What is it about saying 'I do' that suddenly makes a women defer to her husband and say 'I can't' when she is fully capable?"

She had felt it coming for several days, but now was certain the moment had arrived. She opened the top drawer of her desk and slapped the book onto a pile of folders and in a very low voice growled, "I quit!"

"Jim, does this outfit look okay?" Joyce turned in a slow circle for inspection for her husband. In the silence that followed, she smiled inwardly at the awkward situation in which Jim found himself. She had completed the reading and writing assignment portion of Dare #9 earlier in the day, and wanted to test her ability to overlook a hurtful comment. She felt somewhat devilish for having set up her husband—she had pulled one of her least favorite dresses from the dusty portion of her closet and modeled it in the living room. Not only was the dress too snug in the stomach, it accentuated parts of her anatomy that drooped below the darts that were supposed to give shape to the garment, particularly in the bust area.

To amplify the invitation for an insult, Joyce stood squarely between her husband and a baseball game—one in which Chicago was fighting for a place in the playoffs. Jim's lips started forming words, then stopped. He looked up at the ceiling and back to his wife. He seemed to stutter. He scratched his ear then folded his arms. If Joyce hadn't been fishing for a small piece of rudeness, she certainly would have burst out laughing over his obvious discomfort.

"Well, Honey," he began tentatively, "I think you make that outfit look as good as it ever could right about now." When Jim finished speaking, he took in a deep breath and anxiously awaited an explosive reaction. Joyce was completely stunned. Was this the most offensive comment he could muster over her deliberately unflattering getup? There were no cutting remarks, no cruel laughter. He had danced carefully across a minefield, seemingly incapable of causing intentional pain to his wife. He'd sidestepped a situation that would hurt her feelings, even if it meant a careful feat of word-crafting.

Disappointed that he hadn't delivered an uncomplimentary remark of her outfit selection, Joyce shrugged and wordlessly returned to their bedroom. Jim hadn't been authentically truthful with her about the awful clothes she wore, but he did it to protect her, and that was completely endearing.

She changed her clothes and came back out into the living room in her favorite jeans and a faded sweatshirt – the one their son John had left behind when he returned to his dorm on campus. Walking past Jim's line of vision into the kitchen, she stopped dead in her tracks when she heard him call out after her, "I liked your first outfit better. It didn't' give you 'long butt' like these mom jeans do." He smiled, seemingly pleased with his cultural knowledge of the phrase "mom jeans" that had surfaced quite a few years ago.

Now Joyce was mad. She wasn't expecting an insult to be thrown at one of her favorite outfits. Her jeans were worn smooth in all the right places and more comfortable than sweat pants. Topped off with her son's old college sweatshirt, she had thought she might remind Jim of their high school days and reignite some of the passion from their glory years. Embarrassed that her revised appearance drew criticism, she took a quick breath and was about to launch her own verbal arsenal. In a flash, she remembered Dare #9 and her deep desire to reawaken the connection in her marriage.

Allowing the air to escape slowly from her unappealing chest, she reached into the refrigerator for two cold beers and composed a calmer response,

"These jeans may not make my butt look hot, but they're comfortable and something I'd wear to a ballgame—which is what I'm about to do with my husband on the couch." She extended her arm, offering one of the beers to him and took her place next to the aging man on their lumpy couch.

Opening both of their glass bottles, Jim smiled and said, "Thanks, Hon," and resumed watching the baseball game.

Chapter 17 – Small Group Meeting Dares #7–9

Bear one another's burdens, and so fulfill the law of Christ.
Galatians 6:3 ESV

The clock on the brown paneled wall in the chilly room read 8:45 p.m., a full 15 minutes later than the agreed-upon start time, and only four of the six women had assembled. Those in attendance were discussing last week's hockey tournament in Madison, Wisconsin. The Agitators had suffered humiliating losses game after game, but more embarrassing was the uncouth behavior of their new coach. He had stood on the bench yelling obscenities at the referees, the other coaches, and between periods could be heard clear across the ice yelling viciously at the players themselves.

The coach's actions even drew criticism from the opposing team's parents, who spoke loudly amongst themselves as they filed out of the rink, "Where'd they find THIS guy?" or "Glad I send my son to a Catholic high school, so he doesn't have to listen to foul language all season," and "At least we know why their team mascot is an Agitator."

The general consensus was that the coach had to go, but the hockey moms in particular were distressed. "This kind of behavior is completely inexcusable," Anne declared in her most authoritative teacher's voice. "I don't think it's a good idea for our kids to be subjected to that kind of environment."

"I agree," added Alma. "I thought the coach was a little rough around the edges in the first few games of the season, but the tournament was more intense. My husband stormed out of the rink even before the game ended." She paused and then confessed, "I even think Mateo is beginning to dislike hockey. At first I thought it was just high school pressures, but after last weekend's display I believe it's the coach." Mona and Joyce both nodded their heads in agreement.

Anne interjected, "Earlier this week, I made a call to the high school principal, and the district superintendent. The coach isn't a district employee, and there's a chance he can be released from his contract."

"I'm all for that." Joyce offered, "Jim and I don't pay all this money each year to expose Justin to abuse. Plus, it's going to be a very long season if we don't do something fast. We could be stuck with this moron for the next six months!"

"Speaking of time," Alma interposed, "isn't it getting late? Where's our fearless leader?"

"And her sidekick, Jessica." Anne added.

As if on cue, the door to the room swung open and Jessica rushed in with her daughters in tow. "I am so late! I'm terribly sorry. Bob was going to pick up the girls from dance class, but then had to stay late at the office at the last minute, so I had to drive clear across town to pick them up before coming here." Each of the girls was dressed in pink tights, leotards, and a lightweight jacket. Alma noted with surprise Jessica's daughters clutched a kid's meal from the local hamburger hut. She also noticed that Jessica's hair was the tiniest bit disheveled. As if reading Alma's thoughts, Jessica reached for a comb and smoothed down her perfectly highlighted mane.

Mona nudged Anne when Jessica had turned her back to settle the girls at the small kiddie table and whispered, "What? No special homemade snacks for us tonight? Is that a crack that I'm seeing in her perfect veneer?" Alma cleared her throat loudly, uncomfortable with the comment that passed between the others, and hoped that the uncharacteristically frazzled mother hadn't heard it.

Jessica turned back to the group of women, "I'm really sorry, Ladies. I'll make up for it next time with a new recipe for you to try." Anne leaned into Mona with a look on her face that conveyed superiority.

Alma patted the empty chair to her left, "Don't worry about it, Jessica. These things happen—we've all been there." She shot a pointed look at Anne and Mona who sobered considerably at her implied admonition. "Besides, Maxine hasn't arrived, so we hadn't even started yet."

"Oh. That." Jessica pulled a cell phone from her designer purse. "I received a text from her as I was pulling out of the parking lot at the dance studio." She slid her finger across the screen, pushed buttons, and read, "Please inform the women that I will no longer be able to participate in the Dares with them. Too many obligations and not enough time." Jessica stopped reading and put down the phone to look at the women who stared blankly at each other.

Alma wondered if Maxine's sudden departure from the Respect Dare small group had anything to do with the nature of the Dares. As soon as she had read Dare #9, she had thought specifically of Maxine and wondered how she would interpret the challenge to overlook a sharp word from her husband. It was a difficult thing to do with friends or strangers, but nearly impossible to do with a spouse. Alma knew just how hard it was, because she had been bearing Marco's loaded comments and argumentative confrontations for weeks.

She understood that on some level Marco was dealing with deep insecurities and the vulnerability that accompanied the male aging process. She also knew that to fire back at him or engage in battle would only intensify his pain, thus prolonging this phase of male development. Like childhood stages—"the terrible twos" or the "tumultuous teens"—when an individual goes through a trying period of social development characterized by defiant or unruly outbursts, Alma felt Marco's mid-life crisis was another stage of development through which men had to travel. Or at least that's what the books on male mid-life crisis had suggested. She was holding on to the promise that once her husband emerged from this unruly behavior, he would go back to being the calm, joyful, and kind man he had always been.

"Does that mean she's giving up on us?" Mona asked apprehensively.

"I think it means she's not ready to try something different in order to get different results," Joyce said. "This week's Dares were very difficult. Each one brought me to a place where I was vulnerable and felt very exposed in front of my husband. Asking him to tell me when I'd ever made him feel degraded was so uncomfortable! If it weren't for the vignettes of other women's experiences and the thoughtful rationale for each Dare, I would never have had the guts to do it. I was so nervous, that I brought home a bottle of wine that was on clearance at the grocery store that evening. The wine was disgusting, so I'd only had a sip before facing the music." The women all laughed in response to Joyce's frankness.

Anne patted Joyce's shoulder. "I know exactly what you mean. I had a hard time monitoring how I speak negatively about Tony. I caught myself saying something derogatory about him three times in the teacher's lounge . . . and that was just in one lunch period! To prevent myself from continuing down that path, I ate lunch in my classroom for the rest of the week, and didn't join my colleagues for our usual Friday evening cocktails!" The small group was silent at first, and then stifled giggles started to ripple in the circle, growing in volume and frequency until all five women were roaring in laughter.

Mona was the first to regain her composure. "Thanks, Anne for sharing your struggle with us. I, for one, needed to laugh. I completed five Dares this week because I had missed two from last week, so I've been very focused on my marriage and the possibility that I have some responsibility for the damage in our relationship." With that admission, the entire room grew still. Up until that moment, Mona had denied any culpability for the rift in her marriage, placing all of the blame on Aahil, but her sentence demonstrated a slight turn of perspective. "I'm not ready to forgive him, but this week I was reminded of his positive qualities and his patient nature. When I tried to recall something hurtful he'd done this week to me, there was not one instance. In fact I couldn't even remember a time when his words were insulting toward me." Mona paused as if flipping through memories trying to locate a snapshot that didn't exist. She looked down at the floor and traced the tile pattern with the toe of her shoe, "I discovered that there was a time when my own words caused deep pain for my husband, and he was too kind to even make me aware of the hurt I'd inflicted on him." With that final statement, she broke into sobs, covering her face with both hands. As she cried, Jessica searched her purse for a tissue while Anne reached over to reassuringly pat Mona's shoulder.

Mona's tears splashed down on the journal that lay open on the table. "I'm not a good wife," she sputtered between large gasps of breath. Alma watched as Jessica handed Mona a package of tissues, and thought Mona's reaction was bigger than her transgression. "Don't worry, Mona, it wasn't that bad. I'm sure your husband will forgive you." At that, another sob escaped Mona's chest and the intensity of her cries escalated once again. It was almost as if she were sorry for a crime larger than a sharp tongue.

Chapter 18 – Dare #10: Anne, Joyce

Do not judge, and you will not be judged. Do not condemn, and you will not be condemned. Forgive, and you will be forgiven.

Luke 6:37 NIV

Early Saturday morning Anne was awakened by the sound of men's voices and the slam of the front door. Confused, she thought she could hear the clank of metal tools and the thuds of heavy work boots growing louder. After a few moments, she discerned Tony's voice issuing orders about bathroom demolition and it dawned on her that construction on the master bath was about to begin. Sitting up with a start, she realized the men were climbing the stairs and heading her way.

Anne barely had enough time to pull on a bathrobe and bolt out of the room before Tony and his two-man crew invaded her peaceful sanctuary. She was embarrassed by the bras that hung over the tub and the unopened box of tampons on the European towel shelf. Couldn't Tony have warned her of his plans ahead of time? She shot him the dirtiest look she could manage as they crossed paths in the hallway.

As Anne walked down the stairs and headed to the kitchen for some coffee, her husband's stiff Spanish echoed loudly in their spacious bathroom. Several minutes of loud hammering triggered shouts from her stepsons' bedrooms and the irritating sound of slamming doors. Fuming, she constructed all the complaints she would unload on Tony the moment he entered the kitchen. She predicted his response would involve a plea of innocence. Surely he would defend himself by reminding her of their discussion last week, and contend that her lack of protest indicated acceptance. Even though she was alone in the kitchen, she growled, "I knew this Respect Dare would bite me in the butt." She thought about the loud noise, construction dust, and lack of privacy that lay ahead of her in the weeks or possibly months to come. Just thinking of it made her tired.

In a low voice she promised, "Tony is going to be sorry he crossed me." Satisfied, Anne stirred cream into her coffee and stared out the window, wondering what upgrades Tony had in mind for the bathroom. The bitterness in her heart seemed to have reached her tongue because the coffee tasted acrid and unpleasant. Leaving her coffee cup in the sink, she wandered to the kitchen table, making a mental list of several specific changes she would recommend.

An enormous crash came from upstairs, accompanied by the sound of shattering glass. Anne sat down with a grunt and dropped her forehead on the kitchen table. After a few moments of bracing her nerves, she felt something pressing sharply into her eyebrows. Lifting her head, she saw it was the edge of her *Respect Dare* book. Opening to the bookmarked page at Dare #10, she began to read. After several minutes, an ironic smile snaked across her face. This was going to be a very long day.

Joyce vacuumed another creampuff into her mouth. Ever since Jim had made that "mom jeans" comment, she doubted she would ever feel attractive again, and decided to give in to her comfort food cravings. Abandoning all self-control, she swallowed the cream puff and then reached for a mini-chocolate bar specially packaged for Halloween.

Joyce had occasionally glimpsed desperate people eating food in the parking lot of the grocery store, but she had vowed that no matter how stressful her job became, she would never sink to the depths of those lonely bingers. Today she admitted defeat and joined their ranks. It was her lunch break and she didn't want to be seen eating like this in the employee lounge. Looking down at the pastry box on the empty passenger seat, she was trying to decide if she wanted another cream puff or open the bag of peanut butter cups. Suddenly, someone was standing outside her opened car window. "Joyce! I thought that was you." A shriek escaped Joyce's throat as her head whipped around to see who had shattered her solitude.

"Alma?" Joyce turned her head momentarily and closed the pastry box while casually wiping her lips to remove any traces of whipped cream. Praying that Alma hadn't witnessed her food fest or the mound of empty candy wrappers in the front seat, Joyce tried to redirect the focus, "What are you doing? Why are you outside my car?"

Alma paused for a moment, "Oh . . . um, I'm here picking up a baby shower cake for a co-worker. We're going to surprise her at the end of the day when we close the office." Alma crouched forward so that she was eye level with Joyce and noticed the open package of candy and the pastry crumbs on the front of Joyce's cashier apron. "You work at this store?"

Joyce followed Alma's gaze and gestured to her sugary contraband. "Yeah I work here—for the past 10 years. I came out to my car on my 'lunch' break." Joyce's hands made quotes around the word lunch, acknowledging Alma's notice of the junk foods in her front seat. "I turn to food for comfort. Usually sweets help me settle down. This Respect Dare is throwing me off balance! I started off strong and confident, eager to tackle each Dare head-on. I figured since my marriage wasn't that bad, I'd be able to cruise through the entire book without much difficulty." She looked out the front window and traced the edge of her keychain, "But last week, the Dares got tough for me. Maybe they're helping the other women with their relationships, but Jim isn't exactly responding with love songs and rainbows." Her sheepish smile communicated volumes to Alma, who rested her hand on Joyce's arm.

"Oh, Joyce. This work is really hard for me too," Alma admitted. "I can't always express myself fully in our meetings, but sometimes I feel like I'm all alone in my marriage." Seeing compassion in Joyce's eyes encouraged her to continue, "I don't know if things will ever improve, but going through this book helps me realize that God is the only one equipped to meet all my needs. He promised to take care of me."

"And we just need to trust that He'll keep his word, Alma."

"Yeah, we need to keep walking on this path He's laid in front of us—no matter how dark or difficult it may seem. We just have to keep trudging forward."

Joyce smiled bitterly. "Yeah, I get it . . . just keep swimming, just keep swimming!" Her reference to a popular animated movie about a lost fish made Alma smile. Taking a deep breath, Joyce pushed the button that closed her window, stepped out of the car, and straightened her apron, "Thanks, Alma, I needed that encouragement."

Alma, sensing a new closeness with Joyce, opened her arms and the two women hugged briefly. After a moment, Alma pulled back suddenly, "*Ay, Dios mío*! I've got to get that cake and go back to work!" Together, they laughed, and side-by-side, they entered the grocery store.

Chapter 19 — Dare #11: Anne, Mona, Jessica

Finally, brothers, whatever is true, whatever is noble, whatever is right, whatever is pure, whatever is lovely, whatever is admirable—if anything is excellent or praiseworthy—think about such things.

Philippians 4:8 NIV

Anne sneezed again. The fine, white, construction dust lay on every horizontal surface of her home. She'd been sneezing all day and started to wonder about the damage this invasive powder must be doing to her lungs. Breathing in all the fumes and dust had made her nauseated all day. Her stepsons, Zach and Pete, constantly poked around the worksite, tracking white, dusty footprints into nearly every room of the house.

Tony's work crew had been in her home for five consecutive days. He left her in charge while he was downtown getting a permit for the extensive plumbing work that needed to be done. The first four days of the project had gone relatively smoothly. Anne had not blasted him for starting the project against her wishes. She resisted the urge to say, "I told you so" when on

87

the fourth day the crew ran into a problem with the plumbing and discovered they would have to alter existing pipe configurations.

She recalled Tony's frustrated expression and the urgency with which he grabbed a beer out of the refrigerator. Sitting down heavily at the kitchen island, he looked across the room at Anne, who sat at the kitchen table grading papers. Sensing his gaze, she looked up from her grade book and locked eyes with him. She wanted to discuss the bathroom plans with him and help him fix the current challenge threatening the progress of the project.

Tony's intense stare held for several moments and it took all of her discipline not to break the silence and dive into a grand conversation. She started counting silently to herself, a tactic she often did when she needed to restrain herself from verbal attack on her stepsons when they were out of line. She made it all the way to 13 before he cracked. His voice was loud and angry tones, "I can't believe this! The current pipes that run along the bathroom wall don't extend far enough to reach the new Jacuzzi and steam shower. The idiots that laid out the bathroom didn't take any remodeling into consideration when they drew up the plans, and now I have to go downtown for a building permit. The guys have another project next week, so now it's going to take twice as long to complete." Anne didn't know why Tony hadn't anticipated delays and bumps in the road. There was always something in every construction project that extended the timeline. He should know better—after all, he did this for a living!

Every cell in Anne's brain was begging for permission to release a barrage of sarcastic insults and complaints. Her Dare work had challenged her to be a confidante rather than a critic, and she was getting more than enough practice with this bathroom remodel. Tony continued, "All I want to do is replace the soaker tub with a Jacuzzi and a steam shower. The plan was to reconfigure the toilet, sink, and tubs, but now everything has to be changed. This isn't going to work. How can this work?"

He paused and Anne knew she should use this moment to encourage him, to reassure him that his talent and expertise in this area would enable him to figure out a new plan. She thought about all the ways she'd been encouraging him at every bump and turn in this evolving troubled adventure for the past four days. She reminded herself of the satisfaction she felt when avoiding the temptation to belittle or demean his plans.

She pushed aside thoughts of the momentary pleasure that an explosion of sharp and pointy words would offer. Instead, she mentally constructed a positive encouragement that would garner the approval of the women in her small group. She was about to verbalize a carefully worded response when Tony abruptly rose from the island with his empty beer bottle. He removed two more from the fridge and stormed out of the kitchen, tossing the empty beer bottle into the recycle can with such force that she was certain it would shatter. In his absence, Anne knew she had safely averted a backslide.

Mona had been a jumbled mass of emotions, and today was no exception. Working with the other hockey moms on *The Respect Dare* was more difficult than she had anticipated. She had joined the group because of the pain she was feeling in response to her husband's affair. Mona longed for a place to air her frustration, anger, and sadness. She didn't nurture any hopes of restoring her marriage; in fact, she had been fully prepared to divorce Aahil, getting her revenge by taking as much money and property as possible.

She had joined the online support group with the same purpose, but now that was only adding to her confusion. During his last two calls, Stephen had become overly friendly, which made Mona feel unbalanced. In their most recent conversation, he'd announced that he and his wife were getting a divorce. Mona had tried to reassure him, but her words no longer conveyed the certainty she once felt.

She looked at the clock on her dashboard and realized Samir wouldn't be getting out of practice for another half hour. To pass the time, she reached for *The Respect Dare* in her purse. She read through the chapter and answered the questions easily. Getting to the end of the chapter, she was challenged to pray for openness in seeing the positive and focusing on the good. This also confused her. When Muslims pray, there are obligatory rituals in specified positions—from standing, to bowing, then prostrating, and finally, kneeling. Their prayers had a format, beginning with a recitation of the first chapter of the Quran and ending with an oration of the prayers for peace. In their religion, there were never informal conversations with their god. There were no impromptu requests or joyful praises. Perhaps it was because she had been raised in a more Americanized fashion, but Mona certainly didn't feel love for her god the way that Alma had expressed in their last meeting. Alma described a relationship with Jesus Christ that sustained her during her husband's dark phase of isolation. Even though he seemed to ignore her, insult her, and deliberately try to engage her in battle, she spoke of how much God loved her. The tears in her eyes were of joy and hope.

Mona couldn't fathom joy or hope in a marriage with a man who treated her like Alma's husband was treating her. Aahil was present, caring, and never raised his voice in anger, yet she had little optimism for her situation with him. Thoughts swirled in her head about gods and prayer and husbands and goodness. Just when Mona's uncertainty reached a crescendo, the light on her cell phone flashed and a blip notified her of an incoming message. It was a text from Stephen. Mona pushed aside her unsettled feelings and reached for the phone.

Jessica was on her knees. It was late and she was praying that God would step in and give her the strength to focus on the positive qualities of her husband. As she wrestled in prayer, she asked God to push away lingering dark thoughts and protect her.

Walking in on Bob several days ago had shattered her perfect image of him. When she entered his office without knocking, his attention had been consumed with the images on the computer screen and he hadn't even noticed his wife standing in clear view. Her husband, an elder of their church, was sitting at his desk with his pants open and masturbating. He was enraptured by images of women that had wormed their way into Jessica's disturbed nightmares.

Horrified by the scenario on the screen, Jessica had been unable to move or speak for several minutes. While she was seemingly frozen, Bob tried to cover his embarrassment by taking the offensive, "Knock it off, Jessica, you look like the village idiot standing there with your eyes and your mouth wide open." All she could do in response was blink repeatedly and slowly will her jaw to close. Bewildered, she didn't know if she should yell and scream, or get her daughters and leave the house.

Bob continued, "Don't look at me like that, Jessica. There's nothing wrong with what I'm doing." Seeing that she wasn't going to react for a bit, he pushed forward, "This isn't what it seems. I just wanted to relieve some stress. You don't know what it's like. I'm under constant pressure at the firm. I come home and bear the strain of taking care of you and the kids. Then to top it off I have a have a ton of church problems to resolve. I never have time to myself and this just helps me relax."

The frown that rippled across Jessica's tight young forehead eased a fraction and she considered his defense. Sensing the opportunity to close the case, Bob added, "Baby, I'd much rather look at you, but you're so busy with the kids and taking Bobby Jr. to hockey all the time. What I'm doing is completely anonymous and doesn't hurt anybody. I don't want to hear a word about it." With that he snapped off the computer monitor and pushed past her and left her standing in the dark office alone.

Chapter 20 – Dare #12: Alma, Joyce, Maxine

She speaks with wisdom, and faithful instruction is on her tongue.
Proverbs 31:26 NIV

Alma stood in the kitchen mixing ingredients of the *Tres Leches* cake for her husband's birthday. The Three Milks cake was Marco's favorite and even if it took longer to make than other cakes, Alma wanted his *pastel de cumpleaños* to be homemade. Her oldest child, Alicia, kept her company talking about the college applications she had submitted. Driven, Alicia planned on obtaining her MBA and volunteering at an organization that was devoted to mentoring kids who needed role models. Having two younger brothers at home helped unite Alicia and her mother when the male vibe became too strong.

"Mamá, why is Papá acting so weird lately? He's so mean sometimes I don't even want to spend time with him." Alicia's expression bordered between anger and sadness.

"Papá is facing a lot of changes at work, and he's having a hard time staying positive. He's worried that his position might be eliminated." Alma folded the white meringue into the wet cake batter.

"But that doesn't give him the right to be so hard on us. The other day he ordered us to clean the house—he even nagged us how to do it. He's got no right." Alicia buttered and floured the sides of the baking pan while she spoke.

Alma sighed. Every thought in her head was parallel to Alicia's observations and opinion. Now that Alicia was technically an adult, their conversations had taken on a more familiar and friendly tone, and it was hard not to use Alicia's words as a springboard toward voicing her hurt feelings. Alma had been getting a lot of practice at refraining from speaking negatively about her husband, and whenever she took her eyes off Jesus, she felt the need to vent her frustrations on any eager recipient. Alicia certainly recognized the unfair behaviors that Marco had been demonstrating, and as much as Alma was tempted to add her own two cents, she gently rebuked her daughter, "*Mija*, despite the fact that Papá is not himself, we will still show respect and love him through this difficult phase in his life. He loves us, but has some kind of turmoil swirling around in his soul right now." Setting the rubber spatula down in the bowl, Alma wrapped her arms around Alicia's shoulders, careful to keep her sticky hands in the air, away from Alicia's long hair.

Alicia pouted, "I know, but it's not fair."

Alma considered, "No, it's not. But grace never is. Remember all the wonderful ways he has been loving and funny and patient with you during your 18 years on the Earth. Try to give him grace. Hang in there, Sweet Girl. He'll come back to us." Alma scraped the fluffy cake batter into the pan and slid it into the oven, adding, "God will take care of us—of this I'm sure. He didn't promise it would be easy, but He did promise that He would give us what we need to make it through difficult times."

"I don't know how you have so much patience with him, Mamá." Alicia looked to Alma for any indication of disapproval, "I think if I was married to him, I would have bailed already."

Her words stung Alma's heart, and she answered honestly, "Honey, it *is* hard for me. I miss your papá very much, and in my loneliness, I'm finding myself in conversation with God quite frequently. I ask for patience and strength to do what He wants me to do. Even though I would never have asked God to give me this difficult situation, there are good things at work—my relationship with God is getting stronger."

Together the two women cleaned the kitchen in silence, both thinking about the ways God was showing up in their lives. Alma checked on the bubbling pot of beans simmering on the stove and chopped the tomatoes, onions, jalapenos, and cilantro for a fresh *pico de gallo* to accompany the meat Marco traditionally grilled for his birthday meal. As the cake baked, the sweet smell of vanilla and sugar filled the kitchen and quietly spread until it permeated every room of their home, eventually drawing Marco from his bedroom.

"What's in the oven?" he asked Alma bluntly.

Alma put a smile on her face and answered, "I am making a *Tres Leches* cake for your birthday."

"Oh." Marco didn't even try to hide his disgust; his simple response was radiating sarcasm.

"What's wrong? This is your favorite cake." Alma's voice was tight and her face was beginning to match.

"I wanted to go out for my birthday." Marco frowned and put his hands on his hips. "I don't want to stay home. I'm not one of the kids, Alma. I'd like to go out and celebrate my birthday like a grown man." Having finished speaking, he reached for his keys hanging on the key rack and stomped out the door. Alicia took in Alma's stunned face and tear-filled eyes. "Well, Mamá, I guess you've got another opportunity to spend some time talking with God."

Joyce peeled the cellophane wrapper from her fourth snack-size licorice twist this afternoon. She had been crocheting a baby blanket for the imminent arrival of her first grandchild, but eventually gave up because of the way her sticky fingers pulled at the fuzzy yarn. She turned on a cooking show and pulled several more candies out of Justin's trick-or-treat bag. Her ego was still smarting from her husband's comment about her long butt in the mom jeans; and she had avoided his line of vision as carefully as possible ever since.

At Janine's baby shower yesterday, Joyce noticed that her own girth took up almost as much space as Janine's petite frame, swollen with 9 months of pregnancy. Joyce didn't want to consider how it was possible that her strong, active body would house a stomach with similar proportions as a woman nearing the birthing stage. Pushing the unpleasant thoughts from her mind, she stared dully at the screen and allowed the numb sugar buzz to wash over her face and chest, arms and legs.

In her buzzed state, Joyce hadn't noticed Jim enter the living room, and was embarrassed by the spread of food packaging that publicized her private binge. His face communicated confusion and disbelief, "What the hell are you doing, Joyce?"

"Hmm? Oh. I'm . . . uh . . . I don't know, Jim, what does it *look* like I'm doing?" She didn't want Jim to see her food fest, much less engage in a conversation about it. She stood up quickly, swiping at the evidence of her guilt. "Ooh." Perhaps rising from the couch that quickly after consuming so much sugar wasn't a good idea. She felt lightheaded and her ears plugged painfully. Her reading glasses fell from her head and her feet stumbled over each other. Swaying she reached out to the arm of the couch to recover her balance. Jim watched in silence as she collected her faculties and made a hasty exit from the room, humiliated.

At that moment, Joyce was the antithesis of grace and beauty. It was no wonder Jim had lost interest in her physically. Stumbling to her bedroom, she shut the door and began to cry in earnest, locking the door so Jim wouldn't be able to witness her distress.

It was late Sunday evening and the malls were closed. Maxine was surrounded by shopping bags filled with new outfits for the kids' school pictures tomorrow. She could hear them chatting happily in the kitchen over their takeout from the Japanese noodle restaurant across the street from the mall. Smiling, she collected the bags and began to head in the direction of the bedrooms. Maxine halted when she saw Samuwel standing in the hallway with his hands on both hips, looking directly at her. The scowl on his face left no questions about his feelings, "Where have you been all afternoon?" he shouted at Maxine, instantly silencing the cheerful sounds from the kitchen.

"Shopping with the kids, who have picture day tomorrow by the way," Maxine spit at him.

"Why didn't you check with me first?" he began.

Before Samuwel could even finish his sentence, Maxine interrupted, "Oh, now I'm supposed to run everything by you before I do anything? Should I have gotten your permission to go to the store?" The sarcasm left an icy trail over each word that chilled the air around them.

"Yeah, it would have been nice to let me know where you were going before disappearing all day. I would have told you that the kids have new outfits already. I would have also reminded you that we had tickets to the circus this afternoon for the whole family. But, I guess you know better than I do." At the mention of forgotten circus tickets, all three kids objected in a chorus of "*What?*"

"Oh sure, make me the villain. Maybe if you had joined us at church this morning, I would have been able to have a conversation with you. Why didn't you at least have the decency to call or text me? I didn't hear from you all day." Maxine's voice was becoming louder and shriller as the battle gained momentum.

Samuwel's voice also grew in intensity, "Don't you think I did? Why don't you check your phone? Did somebody forget the turn the ringer back on after church?" Maxine didn't give him the satisfaction of looking at her phone. She knew the phone had been set to silent all day. She deliberately did not turn the volume up after church because she didn't want to deal with Samuwel's nagging. She had genuinely forgotten about their circus plans, but it was just as well because she wasn't in the mood for jovial clowns and brightly colored entertainment.

Instead of lingering over her memory lapse, Maxine changed tactics. "If you wanted to go to the circus so badly, why didn't you just call Miss Andréa and take her?" Andréa was the student teacher at the twins' preschool and very enthusiastic about helping the boys' verbal skills catch up to their peers. Maxine noticed the numerous notes coming home were addressed solely to her husband. She also didn't like the way Andréa had smiled so eagerly at Samuwel at the open house last month. Ignoring his discomfort, Maxine had pushed through the crowd of parents and forcibly introduced herself to the perky student teacher, who seemed genuinely surprised to learn he had a wife. Hoping to intimidate her rival, Maxine cast a critical glance at the young teacher's budget attire and purposely smoothed her silk lined, crepe wool business jacket. She launched into a calculated monologue that dazed the young teacher, who was no match for the power and confidence that Maxine exuded. Satisfied with the effect, she had excused herself and exited the room before her adversary could regain her bearings and adequately formulate a response.

Samuwel stared in disbelief at Maxine's unspoken accusation. Interpreting his silence as weakness, she delivered the final blow, "In fact, why don't you call her right now? The two of you can go to dinner someplace suited to her taste—perhaps a bowling alley or an indoor play land?" Her haughty smile conveyed her contempt and plainly mocked him all at the same time.

Samuwel's voice was low and steady, "Maxine, I'm your husband—your spouse. Stop treating me like a kid or one of your employees. I married you for better or worse, but lately all you've been is worse." He paused and she angrily turned her face away, as if to deflect the impact of his words. "You might want to ask yourself why our sons' preschool teacher pays more attention to me than you do. At least Miss Andréa treats me like a man."

At that Maxine looked up defiantly at Samuwel's face and noticed he was no longer looking at her. She followed his gaze to the sad faces of their three children standing in the doorway with tears spilling from their eyes.

Chapter 21 – Small Group Meeting Dares #10–12

Alma entered the ice arena, followed by Mateo, whose progress was slowed by the cumbersome equipment bag, hockey stick, and team water bottle carrier that swung and bumped with each step he took. He merged left toward the locker rooms and Alma made a sharp right into the party room where she was eager to join in tonight's small group discussion. Entering the brightly lit room, she was surprised to see Jessica and her daughters carefully arranging what looked like bite-size pies on a serving tray, next to matching dessert plates and napkins with a floral border pattern.

Jessica looked up and smiled brightly in Alma's direction. "Hi there, Alma. It's good to see you. Come on in and enjoy a refreshment. Tonight I brought mango tartlets for you all." Alma looked down at the pretty desserts and wondered how anybody could eat anything so beautiful. The petite pastry shell was the width of a quarter and filled with a light orange-colored cream, topped with a long, thin strip of mango spiraled to resemble a rose. Each tartlet was garnished with a tiny sprig of mint. It was something that belonged in the pages of a wedding magazine and looked out of place in the bleak miscellaneous room.

"You made these?" Alma's admiration was evident.

"Yes. It wasn't that hard, either. Once I got a system going, things went pretty smoothly," Jessica offered modestly.

"What went smoothly?" was Anne's question as she walked into the room mid-conversation.

Alma responded, "Jessica made these mango desserts for us tonight. Aren't they gorgeous?" One by one the women arrived and the tartlets were discussed, admired, and daintily consumed by everyone except Joyce, who wrapped two in a napkin to save for later.

Once the topic of food had been exhausted, the conversation turned toward the embarrassing behaviors of their coach. After several complaints were aired, the women looked to Anne, who had promised to lodge a grievance with the school superintendent. Anne's facial expression conveyed disappointment. "I spoke at length with the administration about the unsportsmanlike conduct of Coach Rick. Despite their appreciation for our frustration and unsettled feelings, I was told that we're stuck with him for the remainder of the season, but they will explore changes for next season." A collective groan rose from the circle of women.

Continuing, Anne pulled out a folded sheet of paper from her *Respect Dare* book. "In addition to communicating with school personnel this week, I came across some *Respect Dare* resources to support us as we move forward without a leader." She glanced over the words on the page. "It seems that the author has a blog where she discusses all different matters dealing with tricky marriages. I thought it would be helpful if I shared this website with you." From her purse, she pulled out several index cards on which the online address of the *Respect Dare* blog was neatly printed.

While the women looked appreciatively at their index cards, Anne launched the meeting discussion with a reflection on her progress with the Dares. "This week was a monumental experiment in perseverance for me. I had to practice the art of speaking positively over and over and over!" She told the women about the demolition and obstacles involved with the unwanted bathroom remodel project. The women gave nods of sympathy for her difficult position, particularly when she shared, "On top of the noise and the mess, the entire house is coated in a fine layer of dust—drywall particles actually, which are finding their way into my nose, eyes, and esophagus. Every time I take a deep breath, I feel like puking just to rid myself of the pile of construction debris that is probably accumulating in my lungs!"

Joyce patted Anne's arm. "Well, Anne, I appreciate your leadership and thank you for the extra information to help us on our journeys. I don't know about the rest of you, but this week was a killer for me." Joyce looked down and noticed the large, oblong-shaped grease stain darkening the front of her shirt, which was probably the result of resting that king-size order of French fries on her ample chest while watching television earlier in the day. Embarrassed, she crossed her arms in a vain attempt to cover up the evidence of her food folly and tried to focus on her words instead of guessing what each woman thought about her slovenly appearance. "I hosted a baby shower for my daughter Janine who, by the way, is about to pop any day now. It was a lovely affair, but I couldn't relate to any of the things her friends were discussing—designer C-sections, dolphin-assisted births, live tweets of the delivery details? I don't even want to consider the Lotus birth—leaving the placenta and umbilical cord attached to the infant until it naturally falls off." Every woman—including Jessica's little girls—seemed to gasp inwardly at Joyce's revelation. Silence filled the room and the mood shifted. Covering her eyes with both hands, Joyce dismally shook her head. "I just can't believe I am going to be a grandmother." Her voice cracked in a candid portrayal of emotions.

Sniffing loudly, Joyce divulged her greatest fear. "I'm not going to be the momma anymore." True to the group meeting guidelines, none of the women spoke. Despite the anxiety caused by watching a friend in distress, they allowed Joyce the time and freedom to fully express her thoughts and emotions without cross talk or interruption. Their silence communicated reverence of the pain she was experiencing and appreciation for her transparency in confronting this difficult work. "As if that wasn't enough, I learned that, according to Jim, my favorite pair of jeans make my buttocks appear longer, larger, and flatter—characteristics of what everybody calls mom jeans." Her lips contorted in a miserable grimace, "Sometimes I wish that the world would just open up and swallow me whole." With that, the 59-year old woman crumpled in her chair and thunderous wails echoed off the cement floor.

After several long moments, Joyce quieted down and found a tissue in her purse. She shrugged her shoulders humbly and said, "Well, that's all I've got. Thank you for listening."

"Thanks for sharing, Joyce." Jessica offered. The familiar, picture-perfect smile that was absent at last week's small group meeting had returned and was firmly affixed to Jessica's face. "This week was a challenge for me also. There were a couple of times I was tempted to speak negatively to Bob, but with the help of God, I was able to redirect my focus on Jesus." In addition to the reappearance of Jessica's tidy appearance, her verbal contributions once again had the familiar ring of the perfect church lady. The other women waited for her to share more, but her silence served as a clear message to them that she wasn't ready to explore sensitive subjects yet.

Continuing with the elusive, if not superficial tone Jessica had set, Mona's narrative about her progress in the Dares was evasive—particularly since she had promised to complete the previous week's missed Dares. "It's like I'm on a teeter-totter at home, balancing between going one way or the other." She was referring to trying to decide whether to divorce Aahil or stay in the marriage. She was not alluding to the precarious balancing act she was simultaneously experiencing in her relationship with Stephen. They had been in contact every day last week; mostly texting, but there had been a couple of covert phone calls. Despite the fact that she had been completely alone in the middle of the day during one of their talks, she was terrified that someone would overhear her talking with a man who was divorcing his wife.

Unable to restrain her curiosity, Joyce leaned forward inquiring, "What two directions are you considering, Mona?" Alma put a hand on Joyce's arm; subtly shaking her head as a reminder of their group guidelines of no cross talk. Remembering their modus operandi, Joyce immediately pulled back. "Oh, I'm sorry, Mona, I shouldn't have interrupted your thought process, especially after you have all been so patient and gracious with me tonight. Please forgive me."

Mona automatically reassured the group. "It's okay, Joyce. I don't mind your question." But there it was again . . . another request for forgiveness, which was the very foundation of Mona's conundrum. She sighed. "It's just the whole notion of forgiveness is a little confusing to me." She made eye contact with Joyce and allowed a slight smile of acceptance to communicate that there were no hard feelings. She continued, " I understand that forgiving somebody is the right thing to do—which I do when Samir wakes me up from a nap to ask me what time we are leaving for the hockey game. I also forgive my sister when she forgets to call on my birthday. I even forgive my neighbors when they blast their music until the wee hours of the morning in the summertime with their windows open." Mona frowned slightly when she made the reference to her neighbors, causing Alma to wonder if Mona was harboring a bit of resentment toward her neighbors. "Those things are easy to understand and overlook. I just don't know why or how to forgive something that hurts so badly. During the day, I keep busy and can almost forget about his betrayal. But at night, when my body slows down, the pain comes creeping back into my heart. Sometimes it aches so badly that I forget to breathe." Mona folded her hands and stared down at the gold bracelet on her wrist. Looking up she addressed the group directly, "Why *should* I forgive Aahil? In my religion, adultery is punishable by death. But your God asks you to forgive. Are you going to tell me that Aahil deserves to be forgiven?"

At that question, Joyce leaned forward, straining to answer Mona's questions, but again, Alma gently rested her hand on Joyce's arm to steady her. Joyce willed herself to relax and sat back in her chair. Mona hadn't even noticed Joyce wrestling within herself and finished, "I don't know, maybe I should just leave him and get it over with. There's no reason I've stuck around this long. I've got the name of several lawyers who are eager to take my case and lighten Aahil's asset column. I guess I could flip a coin." She glanced up and searched the face of each woman in the circle. Alma's eyes were soft and filled with compassion, and Jessica's eyes had pooled with tears to overflowing. Suddenly realizing she had perhaps shared too much, Mona abruptly closed her share time sheepishly. "Well, that's all I've got for tonight." She had received no answers or feedback from the women, other than a strange sense of acceptance of where she was right at that moment. Mona didn't regret sharing her true feelings, or worry that the women would reject her friendship. With that, she experienced a twinge she hadn't felt in a long time—hope.

Chapter 22 – Dare #13: Joyce, Anne

She watches over the affairs of her household and does not eat the bread of idleness.

Proverbs 31:27 NIV

In the third period of the hockey game, the Agitators were ahead 2–1. The season was half over and they had only won two of their 12 games. As the final minutes ticked down, parents were reaching heights of near-giddiness over the prospect of going home winners. Surely they could hold the score for 35 seconds. The opposing team, the Chiefs, won the face-off and the puck bounce-bounced toward their right wing. The Agitator's defenseman stepped in front of the pass and touched it with the blade of his skate. The bobbling puck bounced over his boot and wobbled over the red line, past the goalie, Cynthia, and into the Agitator's net.

Only nine seconds had passed as the dejected Agitators trudged back to center ice for another faceoff. In the remaining 26 seconds, possession of the puck passed four times from one team to the other, causing the parents of each respective team to gasp, then cheer, and then gasp again. The Agitator's highest scoring player stole the puck from his opponent and stopped dead in the middle of the rink. Standing motionless, he confused both fans and players. After what seemed like minutes, but in actuality had only been three seconds, the final buzzer sounded and the game ended in a tie.

The team rallied around Cynthia, much like some of the parents who consoled Cynthia's mother, Maxine, in the stands. No matter how much a loss hurt, the hard-core hockey fans always said that ending the game in a tie was as satisfying as "kissing your sister." There was no honor in a tied score, and for some, no bright side to "at least we didn't lose."

Joyce, who was hoarse after so much cheering and heckling the referees, cautiously approached Maxine, "Hi Maxine, we miss you in our small group. I know you must be very busy, but if you ever decide to resume your work in *The Respect Dare*, we'd be delighted to welcome you back to the fold." Joyce's reference to the biblical story of a shepherd who celebrates over the return of one missing sheep was not lost on Maxine.

"Thanks, Joyce, for your support. I wish I could continue my work with you, but I'm so busy at work I wasn't able to put my whole heart and time into the Dare homework. If things change, I'll be sure to let you know." Maxine smiled in a way that translated into "thanks but no-thanks" and "this conversation is over." Joyce could sense the walls of isolation that Maxine had erected around herself. Her noncommittal response was similar to that of someone who asks, "how are you?" without really caring about the answer.

Joyce barely had time to call out "goodbye" as Maxine turned and made a quick exit from the stands. Instead of milling around the concession stand with coffees or hot chocolates, Maxine made a beeline for the door in order to avoid further conversations. She drove her shiny new SUV up to the front entrance so Cynthia wouldn't have to carry her hockey gear that weighed nearly twice as much as the other players' equipment.

Somewhat dejected, Joyce felt as if Maxine had rejected her invitation for friendship despite the status of her membership in the Respect Dare small group. Joyce made her way to the parking lot and estimated that she had about 20 minutes of alone time in the car before Justin made his way out of the rink. Her older son,

John, had played hockey before going away to college, and she knew from experience that the testosterone-charged chaos that ensued in the locker room often distracted the young men from their task of showering, changing, and repacking every piece of hockey equipment into their bags.

Joyce started her engine and turned on the heater to take off the chill in her knees and hips, which were starting to show signs of advancing arthritis. Sitting in the car, she pulled out a bag of Halloween candy from under the passenger seat. Weeding out candy from Justin's Halloween bag was a delicate maneuver now that he was older. Each day Joyce would skim a little off the top, being careful to take only one or two of each kind of candy at a time. Although Justin's bag had been quite large this year, she had already worked her way through all of the chocolate peanut butter cups, chocolate caramel bars, and the nutty bars. Today she moved into the fruit flavored, chewy, bite-size balls with a colorful candy shell. At first she ate the candy one at a time, savoring the fruity flavor of each. Then she made flavor combinations of two and three candies. By the time she had emptied six bags, she was pouring the contents of an entire bag into her palm and popping the whole handful into her mouth.

Feeling a little buzzed on the sugar rush that helped Joyce forget about the sting of Maxine's rejection, she reached into her purse for her *Respect Dare* and began reading Dare #13. The author challenged the reader to ask her husband if there was a minor task she could perform that would make his day a little brighter. Joyce considered how unpredictable the consequences of accepting this Dare could be. Saying "yes" to Jim when he asked her to do something this week sounded like a dollar store grab bag gift—you could strike gold or end up with a lemon. She thought about a memorable Christmas favor Jim had asked of her ten years ago and scrunched up her nose. He had requested a traditional Norwegian Christmas meal of lutefisk—an extraordinarily stinky fish that sent all three of their children running from the house seeking relief from the odors. The family had joked for years about that infamous meal, and she wondered what special task she would be completing this week in response to this Dare. Just to be safe, she would stock up on frozen pizzas for a backup plan.

After hitting the snooze button on her alarm clock four times, Anne dragged herself out of bed at 4:50 a.m. Deciding she was too tired from the previous evening's late practice, she had stayed in bed and skipped her morning workout. Listening to Tony's heavy snores bouncing off the walls of their empty, gutted bathroom, she fumbled with her slippers and clumsily plodded down the stairs in pursuit of relief in the downstairs bathroom. Grumbling inwardly about the inconvenience, she nearly tripped over an unopened carton of bathroom tiles that lay in the hallway near the front entrance.

She flipped on the lights of the small powder room and groaned. The sour smell of hockey equipment filled her senses and it was all she could do to keep from retching before turning on the exhaust fan and making a speedy exit. Escaping to the kitchen, the scent of lemon hit her nostrils and the sight of a clean kitchen and an empty kitchen sink gave her great pleasure. Looking at the boys' chore organizer on the refrigerator, she made a mental note to compliment Zach for keeping the kitchen clean while Pete was at practice last night.

After several minutes of waiting for the coffee pot to finish its task, Anne sat down at the kitchen island with a steaming mug of strong coffee. She recalled the heavy emotions that were expressed at last night's Respect Dare meeting. It was oddly comforting that the other women were struggling with their Dare challenges just as much (if not more) as she was. Anne wondered where this week's Dares would take her and her fellow hockey mothers.

Reading Dare #13, Anne wanted to scream. Talking aloud in an acid tone, she muttered, "First I go along with Tony's plans to destroy the peace and order in our house with his bathroom project. Now I'm supposed to add a favor for my husband to my growing list of responsibilities?" She thought about her incredibly filled daily obligations and couldn't imagine where she would find the time to squeeze one more task. Looking at her day planner, she felt tired just thinking about her Friday schedule:

7:00 a.m.	Drive kids to school
7:25	Pick up bakery items for Coffee And
7:55	Set up Teachers' Lounge for Coffee And
3:00 p.m.	After–School (meet with Becky's parents)
3:15	PTA meeting
4:00	TGIF—Teacher Meetup @ Connors Pub
5:30	Hockey Practice (groceries, dry–cleaning)
8:30	Drinks w/ Tony's new client ???

     She drummed her pen loudly on her kitchen table. The past couple of weeks had been very trying on her patience. With the exception of last night, Tony's sons were constantly leaving dirty plates and silverware all over the house, her students were especially needy this year, and her principal had instituted a new battery of teacher observations and evaluations. Learning to be slow to speak and quick to listen was proving to be most difficult for Anne. Each time she bit back a verbal assault, an irritating little voice in her head provided a bitter monologue that relieved some of the pressure that seemed to constantly build no matter the situation.

     Anne wasn't sure if it was the coffee or her resentment but she could feel acid rising in her throat at what she was being asked to do. It was an injustice to have to offer to do a task for her husband who could not only find time in his schedule to have a beer with the boys every day after work, but who also slept long after she had dragged herself out of bed and gotten her day started. Unfortunately for Tony, he picked that very moment to enter the kitchen with a relaxed smile on his face. He approached his wife at the island from behind and rubbed her shoulders suggestively. "Hey, Annie, why don't you leave this work for later and come back to bed and keep me warm?" Anne knew that was Tony's code for being intimate, and the embers that had been glowing warmly in her chest combusted violently.

     Anne turned fiercely to face her husband. "Really? Is there ANY place in this house where I can just have a minute to myself?" Her face turned red and the heat in her voice began to rise. "I know . . . I can relax in my master bathroom! NO, that's right, it no longer exists! I must share my bathroom space with disgusting hockey gear that seems to stink up every room in this house!" The look on Tony's face was disbelieving and wounded. This only incensed Anne further. "Oh, poor Tony . . . you have NOTHING to do with any of this, right? Wrong! You were the one who started this mess. YOU are the one who wanted the boys to be in sports. YOU are the one with all the big ideas, but I'm the one who has to do all the work!"

The smile on Tony's face remained, as though she had just offered to make him breakfast and serve it in bed. His passive reaction exasperated her and caused her voice to raise an octave, "I run around every day juggling work, students, hockey, groceries, cooking, cleaning, and raising your boys! Now I'm supposed to ask you how I can do a little something extra to make your life a little easier? Sure, let me squeeze that in right between scrubbing the toilets and . . . ." Abruptly, Anne stopped yelling. Her eyes flashed open widely and she ran from the kitchen. Flinging open the bathroom door, she ran smack into the foul-smelling wall of rotting testosterone that was emanating from the mound of wet hockey gear piled in the bathtub. Before she could even cross the three feet to the toilet, she heaved profusely onto the marble floor.

Chapter 23 – Dare #14: Alma, Mona

She brings him good, not harm, all the days of her life.

Proverbs 31:12 NIV

Alma was still sensitive about the way Marco's birthday had unfolded. After he had left the house, she and Alicia had finished baking and frosting the *Tres Leches* cake. Figuring he would be home in a few hours, Alicia had spent the remainder of her afternoon chopping tomatoes, onions, peppers, and cilantro for the *pico de gallo* salsa. By early evening, Mateo and his younger brother, Max, had come into the kitchen, lured by the inviting smell of fresh tortillas, and begged Alma to make a couple of tacos to hold them while they waited for Marco's return.

Alma held them off until 8 o'clock, when the boys had convinced her that by then, Papá had probably eaten dinner in a restaurant. The sizzle from the grill pan had attracted Alicia into the kitchen to join her brothers. Listening to her three teenage children laugh and talk with each other had filled Alma with melancholy. This would have been a beautiful memory if only she weren't so concerned with Marco's absence. The kids asked her about it several times, but her answers were noncommittal and she assured them that everything was fine. In the end, it was well past midnight when Marco returned home, slipped into bed, and almost immediately fell asleep.

It was several days after his birthday, but Marco still hadn't offered an explanation for his disappearing act. Alma had tried to discuss her feelings of hurt with him a couple of times, but each attempt was thwarted by an interruption of one of their kids. Determined, she entered their bedroom one evening where Marco lay in bed watching television. Standing in front of the screen, with her hands on her hips, Alma was able to crack open the pressure cooker that had been building steam since the birthday fiasco. "Would you like to explain where you were all afternoon and evening on your birthday?" Marco's blank stare indicated no desire to answer. Where could he have gone that night? Alma's mind ran through the list of possibilities—a short list of family, an even shorter list of friends, and the nearby stores were all unlikely—but the one possibility that nagged at Alma most strongly was the threat of another woman.

Alma took another approach, "Do you know that Alicia helped make your favorite cake for your birthday? Do you know how upset the kids were that you didn't show up for dinner? They were excited to spend time with you and give you their gift, but you didn't even bother to call and let us know you were okay. Did you even consider how worried we must have been?"

Marco's eyes looked into hers. "You didn't even notice I was gone. When I came home for dinner, I heard everybody having such a great time eating and laughing in the kitchen, I figured you didn't need me, so I left again."

Surprise registered in Alma's face. "You didn't come home until after midnight!"

Marco looked away from Alma back at the blocked television screen. "Yes, I did. I came home and could hear you all in the kitchen having a party without me. It was obvious that you had already served dinner and probably had even cut into my so-called birthday cake."

Surprise was replaced by guilt and then hurt. "Marco, we waited for you a very long time. The boys were hungry. What were we supposed to do? Sit at the table all night, waiting for you to come home whenever you felt like it? I didn't know you came home, or else I would have fed you, too."

"Oh right. You could give me the leftovers after everyone finished. No thanks. I went somewhere else for dinner, where I didn't have to beg for scraps. Don't worry about it, Alma. My birthday was great. Now move so I can watch my program." The dullness of his voice both hurt Alma and intensified her concerns. A jealous fury leapt into Alma's chest and the sudden urge to throw something at her husband rose sharply. Instinctively Alma considered the heavy lamp on her dresser and the folding chair next to the bed. Not wanting to test her husband's reaction to a modern version of the Sweet Potato Event of 1998, Alma made a hasty exit from the room and nearly ran smack into Alicia, who was standing in the hallway, listening to her parents argue.

Mona got off the Internet, where she had just read several days' worth of entries on the Infidelity support group forum. She hadn't visited the site recently due to the one-on-one support she was getting from Stephen. In his last text message, he had asked her to send him a picture. She had refused, texting back that it was too late for her to start hunting for a photo she could send him. In the end, Stephen had convinced Mona to snap a selfie and send it to him. Accepting his request, she checked the lock on her bedroom door before taking the self-portrait and sending it to him.

He texted, "WOW, what a beauty!"

She responded, "Oh please. LOL"

He objected, "Stop it. You are attractive. How could your husband be unfaithful to someone as good-looking as you?"

She was startled for a moment by his unexpected flattery. "Don't be silly." She started to type all the reasons she wasn't attractive—wrinkles, a few extra pounds, gray hair—but then deleted them. Instead she typed, "You are just being kind."

"No, Mona. Your eyes are exquisite and your lips are sensuous."

A ripple of pleasure flooded Mona's body. Before she could respond, another text from Stephen arrived, "…and I will be distracted for the rest of the day thinking about those lips." Caught up in the flattery, she smiled and then puckered her "sensuous" lips in an imaginary kiss. She giggled and steadied the phone to type a clever response when a knock at the bedroom door jolted her into reality. Shoving the phone under her pillow, she got off the bed and unlocked the door. Standing in the doorway was Samir with a concerned look on his face.

A frown arched his eyebrows. "What are you doing, Mom? Texting someone?"

"No. Why would you say that?" A muffled text notification chimed under her pillow. The sound registered on Samir's face and hoping to recover control of the situation, Mona put her hands on the boy's shoulders and quickly explained, "If you must know, I am texting your aunt who wants some advice on buying your birthday present."

Distracted by his strong desire for a car, Samir's frown morphed into a giant self-assured smile, "Tell her my favorite colors are silver and black!" Mona smiled in response, turned Samir in the direction of his bedroom and patted his back, "I will. Now let's just forget we had this conversation." Her son was easily distracted, but this encounter snapped her sense of reason. She retrieved her phone and turned it to vibrate before slipping it into the pocket of one of her jackets hanging in the closet.

Spying *The Respect Dare* on the closet floor, Mona reluctantly picked it up and feeling a wave of guilt, opened it to Dare #14. Reading this chapter reminded her of all of the responsibilities in the household that she had recently been neglecting. Trying to reassure herself it was due to a hectic hockey schedule and not her recent misuse of time spent texting and Internet surfing, she wrapped an apron over her active wear and decided to tackle the thankless task of washing the floor.

Chapter 24 – Dare #15: Jessica, Anne

Keep your lives free from the love of money and be content with what you have, because God has said, "Never will I leave you; never will I forsake you."

Hebrews 13:5 NIV

Jessica stood at the checkout counter of her favorite designer boutique. One of the Dares this week challenged her to recognize her blessings and be thankful for the myriad of ways Bob provided for their family. All of the zeros on the receipt she signed helped her acknowledge the expanse of resources that were readily accessible to her.

Jessica and her younger sister, Marilee, were spending the afternoon shopping on Michigan Avenue. Jessica's mother had stayed home to spend quality time with her only granddaughters, Kayla and Ashley. Unable to afford the expense of traveling over the holidays, Jessica's mother and sister made the long drive from South Carolina to Chicago each year in early November. During that precious week, the three women told stories, laughed, and gossiped about all the missed events, celebrations, and scandals that had taken place in the trailer park over the previous year.

Jessica adored her younger sister and admired the confidence she demonstrated when speaking with sales associates in the downtown shops. Marilee spoke her mind spontaneously and never stifled her boisterous laugh, which captured the attention of startled shoppers and judgmental shop girls. Despite the fact that Marilee couldn't even afford a pair of socks, her self-assured presence filled the tiny boutique.

As the sisters exited the store toting elegant shopping bags, Marilee quipped in a brassy stage whisper, "Well, how about those uppity clerks? Their noses were turned up so high, you'd think *they* were the mega-rich designers instead of minimum-wage sales girls."

Jessica's eyes widened in horror at the volume of her sister's comment, and she prayed it hadn't been overheard. "Hush, Marilee. Why would you say something like that? What if they heard you?"

"So what if they did? Maybe they'd treat you with a little more respect if you didn't tiptoe around like you were walking on eggshells." Marilee stopped walking in the middle of the sidewalk. It took several moments before Jessica noticed her sister's absence and walked back to where she was standing. "Seriously, Jess. Why have you become so mild-mannered? It's like my vivacious sister has been turned into a timid little church mouse!" Marilee raised both arms for emphasis. "What's happened to you?" She looked at Jessica with pleading, yet searching eyes.

Jessica's face flushed a bright cherry red. Recovering quickly, she pulled her sister forward by the elbow. Rushing down the crowded sidewalk, they maneuvered their way around the shoppers who were in no hurry. In a terse, low voice Jessica hissed, "Nothing's happened to me. I'm the same person I've always been. The only difference is that instead of buying you a tube of lipstick at the dollar store, I'm charging thousands of dollars on my husband's credit card, as freely as everybody else on Michigan Avenue." Jessica gestured toward a woman dressed in a similar thigh-length fur coat, leather boots, and designer sunglasses. Her voice took on a softer tone, "I'm just trying to fit in with my surroundings." Jessica's pace slowed and her sister easily matched her gait. "This is a completely different culture than the one I used to live in, Marilee. You don't know what it's like to be suddenly thrust into a world of different values, mannerisms, and rules." Jessica turned and slowed her pace to a crawl while her eyes searched those of her sister for understanding. "I've had to adapt in order to be the woman that Bob expects."

Marilee's eyes grew wide and she stopped walking. This time, she grabbed Jessica's arm to prevent her escape. "Finally, we get to the heart of the problem." Marilee's eyes narrowed and she read the fearful expression on her sister's face. "This is all about Bob. Isn't it, Jess?" Seeing Jessica's mouth open in protest, Marilee quickly went on, "You're so busy trying to please your perfect husband, that you've completely lost yourself."

Jessica broke free from Marilee's grasp and briskly marched through the throngs of shoppers and tourists, her sister trailing close behind. "Slow down, Jessica. Wait up!" Catching up to her sister, Marilee fell in step with Jessica's pace; step by angry step the two sisters stomped their way past the famous Water Tower, the Wrigley Building, and over the Chicago River Bridge. Finally out of breath, Jessica slowed her pace and stopped. Facing her sister, the streak from a stray tear marked a trail down Jessica's right cheek. "Bob is a wonderful provider for our family. He works hard to make sure the girls and Bobby Jr. have everything they need. He's generous with my shopping allowance and encourages me to be the best person I can be. I'm lucky to have him for a husband. I just need a little more time to get used to all the new roles I'm filling—wife, household manager, mother, and stepmother." Her voice had softened over the span of her defensive monologue and she concluded with, "Just give me a break, okay, Marilee? Cut me a little slack."

Despite turbulent feelings that were gaining intensity, Marilee feigned acceptance and smiled at her big sister. "Sure, Jessica. Just don't forget where you came from . . . and that we've always got your back." The two women looked directly into each other's eyes. "And for the record, your Mr. Perfect isn't that perfect."

Anne organized the financial records of her husband's construction company to pay bills, cut checks, and report taxes. She made a mental note of gratitude for all the financial resources Tony supplied for their family. He drank too much, but somehow managed to supervise multiple construction sites and keep the business profitable. "If only he didn't drink so much," she thought aloud, "our lives would be perfect." The boys would be going off to college in a few years, leaving her and Tony free to travel and develop new hobbies. She fantasized how their lives would be so much easier without the constant stress and strain of the boys' needs for transportation, constructive redirection, or food. She shuddered at the vast amount of resources spent meeting the growing adolescents' endless consumption of food.

Anne was so preoccupied with the bathroom remodel project that she was behind on running the company's third-quarter report, which ended on September 30. Sitting behind the computer at the large desk in their home office, she counted backward on the calendar and cringed with guilt when she realized the statement was almost six weeks late. She had never been this far behind schedule before, but attributed it to an unusually stressful hockey season and her constant state of exhaustion the past few weeks. She didn't know why, but she had never felt so tired in her entire life. She thought aloud, "What's going on with me? I'm having trouble staying on top of things at home and in the classroom." It only took one glance at the teacher bag overflowing with essays that needed to be graded to confirm her statement. Anne thought for a long moment, then squinted at the calendar and began counting backward again. The quarter had ended six weeks ago, but it had been almost three months since her last period. Stunned, Anne whispered in a weak voice that only she could hear, "I'm pregnant."

Chapter 25 – Small Group Meeting Dares #13–15

Therefore encourage one another and build one another up, just as you are doing.

1 Thessalonians 5:11 ESV

While Alma waited for all the women to assemble at their regular Thursday night small group meeting, she watched one of the Park District employees take down the Halloween decorations and replace them with Thanksgiving turkeys and cornucopias. She loved the fall season above all others, but this fall had been bittersweet. In addition to the difficulties in her marriage, Alma had a growing awareness of the fact that next fall Alicia would be away at college, leaving her alone in a house full of males.

Alicia was smart and had ambitious plans of becoming a successful entrepreneur. Alma was so proud of her daughter, and while she knew that Alicia would thrive as an undergraduate, She also knew her own heart would certainly be taxed with the grief of separating from her.

As Mona, Anne, and Joyce assembled at their table, each quietly noticed Alma's sad expression. Gone was the usual lighthearted banter among the women; rather, they spoke in hushed tones out of respect for Alma's reverie. Typically the last to arrive, Jessica entered exactly at 8:30 p.m., carrying her celebrated dessert tote. Not two steps behind were little Kayla and Ashley. The women had grown accustomed to Jessica's presence, the weekly refreshments, and her juvenile entourage. For her part, Jessica seemed to accept the fact that there would be no rotation of bringing snacks. The other women all seemed too busy to even consider baking.

Once the meeting began, Anne asked if anybody had pressing issues they wanted to share before addressing the specific Dare responses. All the women remained silent, but each casually glanced in Alma's direction, given her austere expression. Alma looked up and realized the women sensed her pain and spoke. "Things at home aren't getting any better with Marco. I'm lonely even when we're in the same room. To make matters worse, Alicia started receiving acceptance letters from universities this week." At that the women smiled and Joyce even began to applaud, until they saw that this information was painful for Alma. "I'm happy for her. I am. It's just that she's my girl. My heart is wrapped up with hers in a way that only exists between a mother and her daughter. I accept the fact that she's ready to face college life and beyond. The only problem is that I'm not ready to say goodbye." Anguish filled Alma's face and she began to cry. Her sobs not only filled the room but also the heart of each woman at the table. Jessica, in particular, seemed to struggle and she covered her own face to hide her feelings and the tears that curled around her fingers.

Alma let herself relax in the silent acceptance of the group and permitted sound to escape her throat as she grieved the inevitable release of her baby girl. After several moments, she chuckled. "And besides, who will I talk to once she leaves?" At that, the mothers and stepmothers of teenage boys playfully snickered, each acutely aware of the limited topics that existed during this phase of life—food, hockey, and pop culture.

After several long moments of reflective quiet, Anne recognized that Alma's composure was restored and indicated they would begin sharing their work on the Dares. As the women took a few moments to retrieve their notebooks and indulge in Jessica's turkey-shaped, cranberry-almond oatmeal cookies, Joyce leaned into Alma and whispered, "You can talk to me, Alma. I'll be there for you, just like you've been there for me." Alma looked appreciatively at Joyce and gave her a quick hug.

The women took their turns sharing their thoughts and experiences with the Dares that had been assigned the previous week. There were humorous, self-deprecating anecdotes and prayer requests. After Alma's emotionally heavy share, the laughter and general playfulness were a welcome relief. When it was Anne's turn to share, she started to read from her journal, but then stopped. A comical look spread across her face, reminding Mona of a caricature. Everyone looked at Anne, surprised by her uncharacteristic silence.

"So this week when I was paying attention to the ways that Tony provides for me and our household, I discovered a whole new blessing that's been entrusted to us." Anne paused for only a moment. "I am, in fact, pregnant." Mona gasped and Joyce's eyes grew wide before a knowing smile spread across her face. Anne continued, "I didn't think this was going to be part of my life experience. Sure, I'm a stepmother to Zach and Pete, but a mother-mother? A 'real' mother?" As the magnitude of this concept dawned on her, a worried look replaced her smile. "I don't know how to be a mother! This wasn't supposed to happen so late in life. How did this happen?"

Joyce snorted, "Well, if you don't know, there's probably a special film the 5th-grade teacher at your school may be able to loan you." The women tried to suppress giggles and smiles.

"No, I *know* how it happened, but . . . *how did this happen?*"

Alma was the second one to break the no-cross-talk agreement. "Anne, I see this all the time at the OB/GYN's office. Women think they're past the child-bearing age, and become lax on birth control."

Joyce cut in, "Don't I know it! I was 44 when I discovered myself in a similar situation."

Mona jumped into the rogue conversation. "My aunt was in her 50s when she had her last child, so you've got plenty of time for lots of babies!" Together the women laughed and reached out to touch Anne's hand or arm for reassurance. Mona continued,

"Anne, it's a great blessing to have a child. You'll find that it's the most beautiful and most difficult job you'll ever face in your lifetime." Anne thought about Mona's words for several moments and a smile slowly bloomed on her face. A muffled phone alarm beeped for several seconds until Joyce barked out a loud gasp and clumsily dug through the contents of her purse. Pulling out an ancient paging device, Joyce yelled, "BABY!"

Alma looked uncomfortable at Joyce's loud outburst, "Yes, Joyce. A baby. Anne is having a baby."

Joyce's face went pale then her ears flushed bright red, "BABY! Baby, baby, baby!" Each of the women grew uncomfortable at the spectacle Joyce was making, particularly as she stood and started stomping and pumping her arms up and down, "Baby! My baby is having a baby! Janine is in labor and just sent me the special signal that she's on her way to the hospital." Joyce gathered the scattered contents on the table in front of her and shoved them back into her purse. She wrestled with the plastic chair to free her coat and ran out the door shouting, "I'm going to be a Granny! Or a Nana . . . or an Oma . . . Oh who cares? My baby is having a baby! WAHOO!"

Chapter 26 – Dare #16: Maxine

Pleasant words are a honeycomb, sweet to the soul and healing to the bones.

Proverbs 16:24 NIV

Maxine's company was hosting a cocktail reception for clients at an upscale hotel with fantastic views of Lake Michigan. As a division manager, she had been responsible for organizing the event and was quite proud of her efforts. The ultra-chic candles that smoldered inside crystal globes mirrored the lights twinkling in the celebrated Chicago skyline. A jazz trio played background music and set a sophisticated ambiance. Bite-size crostini, canapés, crab cakes, stuffed mushrooms, shrimp skewers, and pumpkin herb tartlets were circulated by the wait staff, who were attired in double-breasted jackets and white gloves.

Walking the perimeter of the room and then making methodical inroads to each cluster of senior managers, Maxine was careful to network with associates from each of the organization's big contracts. She was confident that this event would be the tipping point for the senior associates to offer her the Vice

President of Marketing position she'd been eying for several months. Prudently refusing the event's signature dry martini all evening, Maxine knew full well that the buzz she was feeling was pure adrenaline and elation over her professional triumph. Scanning the room for any overlooked executives, she spotted a couple apart from the epicenter of activity and moved in their direction. The man wore an expensive suit and, even from behind, Maxine could tell his shoes were made of costly Italian leather. The woman's sleek, fitted suit accentuated her curves and her suggestive smile was easily deciphered, even from across the room.

Not wishing to miss an opportunity to meet a potential client or colleague, Maxine strode toward the pair with purpose. They were so engrossed that neither one sensed her approach until she was within an acceptable distance for exchanging business cards. The man tilted back his head and laughed at something the woman said. Stopping abruptly, Maxine's shoes made grinding contact with a wooden skewer that had fallen to the floor. Her foot rolled forward and her body tipped backward before the elegantly attired man reacted instinctively, catching her arm before she tumbled to the floor. When the hero looked at his damsel in distress, his face registered surprise and then flushed with a tinge of guilt. Maxine's champion, the attractive man exchanging intimate quips with his attractive companion, was none other than Samuwel.

Chapter 27 – Dares# 17 & 18

Maxine, Mona, Alma

Do not let any unwholesome talk come out of your mouths, but only what is helpful for building others up according to their needs, that it may benefit those who listen.

Ephesians 4:29 NIV

The car ride home was a blur. Maxine clutched the steering wheel tightly with her leather driving gloves and imagined how it would feel to wrap her hands around Samuwel's throat. She hadn't said anything at the cocktail reception, but now that she was out of the professional setting, her words punctured the air like hard jabs and uppercuts. She wasn't inclined to sacrifice her reputation or career over an ugly scene with her errant spouse. Samuwel tried multiple times to defend himself from her attack, but realizing that Maxine wasn't listening to him, he resisted further attempts to convince her he was blameless.

In stark contrast to Samuwel's self-control, Maxine's filters were completely shredded. Her bitter allegations were stained with hatred. After openly accusing him of infidelity, her verbal assault against her husband pushed him up against the ropes. "I suppose you had nothing to do with the voracious way she was looking at you. No, of course not. You're the perfect husband who is always the victim—first the martyr at home and now being forced into a corner by a predator. If I hadn't interrupted your intimate moment, she might have kissed you against your will, too." Maxine could feel the adrenaline surging through her body. She was aware of a twisting and rolling in the pit of her stomach that sent mild tremors down her arms. Despite the physical distress, she continued the barrage, "You poor, poor man. Oh wait . . . did I say man? I meant to say mouse! If you were a real man you would have found a way to discourage her behavior long before it became an embarrassment to me!" Maxine's heart was thumping in her chest and her mouth had gone so dry, the words were beginning to stick on her tongue. She managed to spit out one last accusation; "You made a fool out of me in front of all my colleagues, the entire department, and all our clients. You are pathetic."

Time stood still, or perhaps it increased its speed, but inside the car, there was no sense of direction, speed, or surroundings. There was only the pounding of two hearts that were ravaged and on the verge of becoming permanently damaged. Silence surrounded the two, but their minds were numb, over-stimulated by the wayward events of the evening and the dangling insults that still hung in the air. The car rolled up the long brick driveway and nestled in one of the three spaces available in the garage. Without a word, Maxine left a dazed Samuwel alone in the car. She entered the house and stomped upstairs into her bedroom, locking the door behind her.

Mona had been paying close attention to the words that came out of her mouth during every interaction she had during the past few days. She noticed sweet words with her sister, loving words with her son, and supportive words for Stephen. Mona had no desire, however, to speak nicely to Aahil, but after several days of monitoring her tone with others, she couldn't help but notice the aggressive and negative words she heaped on her husband.

Perhaps it was residual guilt over receiving numerous texts from Stephen on a daily basis, but Mona felt convicted that she should make an attempt at softening her interactions with Aahil, if for no other reason than to set a better example for her son. She heard the front door open and turning her cell phone on silent, took a deep breath and went to greet her husband with a forced smile.

Alma was tired. She was weary from a long day of work, but even more worn-out from the emotional swings that were taking their toll. Her feelings shifted between deep sorrow over her daughter's impending college departure and increasing irritation at her husband's negativity. Her body ached so deeply she didn't know how she mustered enough energy to chew her food at dinner. Spirits sagging, Alma crawled in bed shortly after the leftovers were distributed for lunches the next day. In bed, she curled away from Marco, who was surly and silently watched a hockey game on the television in their bedroom. While Marco hurled the occasional groan or insult at the Chicago team, Alma prayed.

Closing her eyes tightly and clenching her fists together, her words did not follow the rhythmic pattern of the Catholic prayers she normally recited. Tonight, she eliminated the formalities and pleaded with God directly. "Lord, please help me. I'm weak and getting weaker. Help me to understand my husband better. Give me the strength to display the love of Your son, Jesus. I need Your words to encourage Marco, because I feel like I've tried everything and am failing. Please keep my eyes on You, so that no matter what happens in my family I'm always certain that You love me and will never leave me. Lord I can do all things through Christ who strengthens me, but please hurry, because I am not sure I can hang on much longer." Hot tears slid silently down her cheeks and wetted her pillow as she prayed. She didn't have an end to her prayer, and there was no "Amen" because she fell asleep in the warm embrace of God the Father.

Chapter 28 – Small Group Meeting Dares #16–18

A gentle answer turns away wrath, but a harsh word stirs up anger.

Proverbs 15:1 NIV

It was the week before Thanksgiving, and the women seemed too occupied with other things to start the meeting on time. Joyce hadn't yet arrived, and Anne was fielding questions about morning sickness. The topic of conversation turned to Thanksgiving holiday celebrations. As was the tradition, the Agitators hockey team was scheduled to play in the Chicago Turkey Puck Thanksgiving Tournament, and veteran hockey moms were savvy about preparing their turkey dinners around scheduled games that started Wednesday evening and ran through Sunday night. Who planned on hosting this year? Who was going to make dinner reservations? Did anybody want to team up for Black Friday shopping at midnight?

The general atmosphere was merry, and eventually the women became engrossed with Jessica's description of a mouthwatering stuffing recipe with apples, cranberries, and pork sausage. While Anne listened to the list of ingredients, she couldn't decide if it made her queasy or hungry. Never having been pregnant, Anne was tentative about her emotional responses and curious about each new feeling she experienced.

Tony's feelings, on the other hand, were not ambiguous. He was ecstatic. When Anne told him the news in the kitchen, he laughed and boomed so loudly one of the plumbers came rushing down from the bathroom to see if there was an emergency. Tony's cheers had reverberated off the stainless steel appliances as he clapped the back of a very bewildered plumber and shoved a beer into each of his hands.

Ever the teacher, Anne narrowed her eyes in a disapproving stare at Tony and, after repossessing both beer bottles, motioned for the plumber to head back upstairs. When she turned back to face Tony, she noticed he had two beers in each hand and was making rapid strides out of the kitchen and up the stairs to their master bath. Rolling her eyes, she called after him, "Things are going to have to change when we bring a baby into this house." In response Tony just shrugged his shoulders and disappeared into their bedroom; proposing a boisterous toast to his own virility.

Compelled to do everything perfectly, Anne had ordered a slew of parenting books that covered every topic on the care and treatment of children from conception all the way through college. Sitting in the party room chairs, she was thankful for the support that poured freely from these women who were starting to play a larger role in her life.

Interrupting Anne's thoughts, Joyce burst into the room, her face flushed and her winter jacket askew. "Sorry I'm late, but I just came from Janine's house and I have pictures of the new baby, Sophia Joy!" The women crowded Joyce and passed around photos and asked her questions about the delivery.

Mona thought a moment about the baby's name, "Hey, Joyce, your daughter named the baby after you!"

The smile that radiated from Joyce's face pushed light into the heart of every woman present. "Yes. Yes, she did, and I couldn't be more in love with little Sophia Joy. I didn't think it was possible, but I love her just as much as I love my own children!" Wiping a tear away, Joyce explained, "I was so wrapped up with worry about losing my role as a mother, that I'd never really considered the prestigious position of Grandma—OR the benefits. I get to cuddle my granddaughter as much as I want AND get a full night's sleep!" Alma smiled wistfully at Joyce's elation and wished that she, too, had something in her life about which she could be exultant.

Suddenly aware of how much time had passed, Anne suggested the women get down to business in sharing their Dare experiences with one another. With only 30 minutes left in hockey practice, the women wasted no time and used plain language to describe their experiences with speaking positively and providing affirmations to their husbands.

Jessica confidently divulged, "I wrote a positive affirmation for my husband on a sticky note and stuck it inside his briefcase." What she didn't have the courage to reveal was the trepidation she felt upon entering a space that was entirely Bob's. She feared she would see something in his attaché case that would turn her stomach as violently as the images on his computer had.

Mona admitted her new newfound awareness about how negatively she spoke to her husband on a regular basis. She admitted that the lone compliment she offered Aahil, "You look nice today," was about as generous as a rich dog trainer who tossed a worn, rawhide chew to a starving dog. Mona would never admit to the other hockey moms just how many supportive encouragements she had sent Stephen in various texts throughout the week. Nor would she reveal the paltry effort she was investing in the Dares.

Anne closed the meeting in prayer and reminded the women their next meeting would be in two weeks, since the following Thursday was Thanksgiving. Just as the women were stashing their books and reaching for coats, the door to the rink's party room swung open and Maxine stepped forward. "Hi Ladies, sorry to interrupt, but I thought since practice was ending, you might be done." All of the women looked inquiringly at Maxine, "But I can come back later. . ."

Joyce disrupted Maxine's retreat. "Not at all, Maxine. Come on in. We were just finishing." The women's nods confirmed Joyce's invitation.

Maxine hesitatingly entered the room and closed the door behind her. "I just wanted to see how things were going with your

Respect Dare group work." The worried frown on her face conveyed a deeper reason for her presence tonight.

Ignoring Maxine's inquiry, Joyce continued, "How are you, Maxine?" The four-word sentence was all it took to break through any pretense Maxine might have given for visiting the group.

"I'm . . . he . . . we . . . ." Her voice cracked and the pain that was threatening to escape rushed forward and filled the room. "Things are a total mess. I can't make sense of any of it. I feel like I'm drowning." Desperation wrinkled her smooth forehead. "I caught Samuwel with another woman at my work event, and blew up at him." Maxine raked her fingers through her black curls. "I knew he wasn't involved with her, but I was humiliated that my husband was jammed in a corner with the saucepot of my whole department." As Maxine's monologue gained momentum, her voice grew louder and higher-pitched. "I was pissed off at his disloyalty to me, especially in front of my co-workers, and so I poked around his social media account. Lo and behold, right there on our boys' preschool group page is this young blonde mother— who absolutely gushes each time he posts something to the board." Maxine used a little girl voice to mimic the other woman's comments. "'Samuwel, I agree completely!' or 'What a great idea.'" Returning to her normal voice, Maxine went on. "UGH! His responses to her aren't suggestive or anything, but they certainly don't discourage her from pursuing him." Her eyes shone fiercely and her breathing was noticeably accelerated. "Apparently they're on the Preschool Christmas production committee together. From their messages to each other about the play, it's apparent that he enjoys conversing with her. I've seen her profile picture, and she isn't stunning or sophisticated. What could he possibly be getting from her that . . . .?" Maxine stopped short and an expression of pure anguish slowly crept across the smooth skin of her features. "What is she giving him that he doesn't get at home?" Total silence filled the thoughts of the women as Maxine considered why her husband would enjoy attention from another woman, no matter how plain her appearance.

Alma easily heard several of the hockey players emerging from the locker room, but she made no move. The noise in the lobby grew louder; still no one rose from their seat. The pensive expression on Maxine's face clearly indicated she was working hard. "I am a strong, successful Black woman. I know how to get ahead in this world by following the rules and knowing when to break them. Strength and control are the keys to success and yet . . . ." She looked up and seemed surprised to see the faces of five women staring tenderly back at her. "Something is definitely out of whack in my marriage."

Then something happened that would change the trajectory of Maxine's life from that moment forward. She surrendered.

Chapter 29 – Dare #19: Joyce, Jessica, Maxine

For God is not a God of disorder but of peace.
1 Corinthians 14:33 NIV

It was the day after Thanksgiving, and Joyce wanted to veg out in front of the television with a thick slice of pumpkin cheesecake. Every Thanksgiving for the past ten years, Joyce followed the same routine: first a long and chaotic Wednesday shift at the grocery store, followed by a late-night hockey game. Then first-thing Thursday morning, Joyce held court for a turkey and all of his side-dish companions. Years ago, she and Jim had come to the agreement that he would shoulder the responsibility for taking Justin to the hockey tournament games after Thanksgiving. While others celebrated Black Friday with frantic shopping missions, Joyce remained at home with Epsom salts, the television remote, and a pair of well-worn slippers.

It was comforting to know that the kitchen was filled with the family's favorite dishes that only needed reheating to comprise a tasty meal. Like the chiming noise on a grandfather clock, the beep of the microwave sounded at regular intervals throughout the day as Jim and the boys each returned for another fill-up. This year she had sent Janine home with a shopping bag packed with enough leftovers to last the long weekend. Janine and her husband were as afflicted with sleep deprivation as they were enraptured by Sophia Joy. After the meal, all three had fallen asleep on the couch. Joyce was amazed at their ability to remain asleep, surrounded by overzealous football fans who were watching the Chicago versus Green Bay rivalry on television and yelling at the referees.

Because of the busyness of her life leading up to Thanksgiving, Joyce was thankful for the week hiatus from the Respect Dare small group. Taking advantage of a quiet house on Friday morning, she retrieved her book and journal to tackle a new week of marriage Dares. After reading the short chapter, Joyce decided that she'd save the television marathon and cheesecake binge for later, and tackled the new Dare challenge of "getting your house in order" by pulling out the Christmas decorations and eliminating items that held no sentimental value.

Two hours later, she had reduced the inventory of ornaments, lights, duplicate wreaths—and what could only have been miles of wrapping paper—by half. There was still an excess of decorations, but Joyce was pleased with her progress, and strangely filled with energy. Jim and the boys returned from a hockey game and stared at the piles of boxes that filled the entire living room.

Jim's reaction conveyed surprise mixed with a hint of fear, "What's going on, Hon? Are we moving?"

"Ha! You'd think so, by all the boxes here, but I'm just going through our inventory of Christmas paraphernalia and getting rid of things we no longer use or need." Joyce stood up and motioned to the large mound near the entryway. "Would you mind taking these boxes to the thrift store? I'm sure a young couple just starting out could use some of these things."

Jim, who had been lugging the same boxes up and down the stairs for decades, moved quickly before she could change her mind. "Yup. I'll do it right now. The boys can help me load the SUV after Justin unpacks his hockey gear." After witnessing Justin's disagreeable face, Jim playfully put his son in a loose headlock. "Come on, son, let's see if your muscles are good for anything other than checking an opponent." The three easily lifted the carefully packed boxes and after numerous trips back and forth to the car, Jim drove away with the product of Joyce's Operation Unclutter away.

Jessica read Dare #19 and immediately resonated with the Dare to put things in order—particularly her closet. When she and Bob were first married, she brought only one suitcase into her new home. Its contents represented all of her worldly possessions. Bob had laughed when he saw the few items hanging in the oversize walk-in closet that was designed specifically for a woman—compartments to display a large collection of shoes, special drawers for intimate wear, and yard after yard of empty rack space. He had given her a platinum credit card with specific instructions to buy clothing for herself that reflected his status.

In those early days of married life, spending large sums of money on fashion made Jessica queasy, so Bob sent his immaculately dressed paralegal to take his wife shopping for tasteful outfits. The paralegal's vast knowledge of fashion, styling, and beauty services overwhelmed and intimidated Jessica. After their first day of shopping, Bob's assistant had authoritatively entered Jessica's closet and discarded every single item Jessica had brought from home. She'd organized a regime of beauty services with specific details for the stylists without consulting Jessica—haircut, color, high/low lights, eyebrow shaping, eyelash extensions, and personal waxing. Even the color of nail polish used in the manicure/pedicure had been prescribed. It seemed Bob's assistant knew precisely how to create an image that appealed to Bob.

After spending several unsettling days with her fashion tutor—who hadn't yielded on a single directive—Jessica decided it was time for her to find her own way in this new world of status. She became a dedicated student of fashion and after a short period of time had been ready to take retail by storm. Bypassing the high-end retailers at the mall, Jessica leapt directly into the arms of designers and tailors who made sure everything she wore was perfectly suited to her frame and features. Steadily, the cavernous closet filled with sophisticated, tasteful, playful, and expensive clothing, shoes, and accessories. So efficient was Jessica at shopping that it wasn't long before the stainless steel hanger racks were overloaded and she had to store items in other rooms of the house. She frequently stood in her closet, searching for the elusive satisfaction of being surrounded by everything money could buy, but always went away feeling empty.

After reading the latest Dare that challenged the reader to put her house in order, Jessica reluctantly admitted that the one area that was increasingly out of control was her wardrobe. Looking around her closet, she felt a pressure in her chest as she considered how to reduce the items around her. Perhaps it would be easier if she removed duplicate items first. Taking a deep breath, she wrestled with questions, volleying between, "Do I really need to get rid of these?" and "Why would I have three pairs of the same pants?" or "What if I need these some day?" As she worked through her closet, it became less difficult to pull an item from its hanger and carefully fold it before bagging the item for charity. Some of the items she donated were those she purchased with Bob's paralegal and filled Jessica with shame over her lack of savvy. Other items still had tags on them. By the time the baby monitor let her know the girls were waking from their naps, she had gone through her entire closet and dresser drawers. She felt accomplished, having filled eight large bags for donation and noted that there was still an abundance of items she could sift through tomorrow.

Maxine closed her office door, programmed her phone to voicemail, and turned off her cell phone. It was the day after Thanksgiving and while most of the company was celebrating the holiday weekend by overeating and overspending, Maxine was at the office. She wasn't there to work on a project, however. She planned on spending the day reading *The Respect Dare*, journaling, and reading her Bible. Her marriage was in a shambles and needed to be put back in order.

Maxine was well versed in modern society's approach to relationships between men and women—one-night hookups, friends with benefits, take what you can, and always be the one in control. Media aimed at women negatively shaped the way they perceived themselves and their value. Maxine could almost recite from memory the variety of ways to please a man, train a husband, and tighten her abs in less than eight minutes a day. Wives today were encouraged to either find complete fulfillment in their marriages or move on to find someone better suited to meet all their needs.

The Respect Dares were challenging Maxine to try a different approach to marriage, one Dare at a time. For 39 years, she had rejected theological principles that positioned men at the head of their households, and women in the helper role. She had deliberately sidestepped the scriptural passages that outlined specific wifely behaviors that were considered critical for sustaining a harmonious marriage. Throughout her relationship with Samuwel, Maxine adhered faithfully to feminist principles.

Despite the uncertainty of her relationship with Samuwel, Maxine recognized that the road she'd chosen hadn't been effective in building a healthy marriage. With nothing to lose, she decided to try a different approach—the biblical vision for wives. Given modern day adversity toward Christianity, she was acutely aware that the new path ran counter to popular culture. At this point, however, she was willing to try anything that could break the curse that ruined marriages.

Chapter 30 – Dare #20: Anne, Alma

Do nothing out of selfish ambition or vain conceit. Rather, in humility value others above yourselves, not looking to your own interests but each of you to the interests of the others
                                                            Philippians 2:3–4 NIV

Bright and early the morning after Black Friday, Anne was hyper-alert and prepared for a major overhaul of the house in preparation for Christmas. With a clipboard in one hand and a broom in the other, she banged on the doors to the boys' bedrooms and yelled, "Zach, Pete, it's time to get up and get out of bed! We have LOTS to accomplish today and you've already spent enough time sleeping." Groans from the boys indicated they weren't eager to become Anne's Christmas elves. She barged into each room, pulling open the room-darkening blinds, and snatching the comforter from a slumbering adolescent, much like a magician would from an elegant table setting.

"You've got exactly five minutes to get up, go to the bathroom, put on some clothes, and come downstairs to help me, or I'm going to come up here with a bucket of ice water." The boys knew she meant business and began to drag themselves out from the comfort of their warm pillows. "And don't forget to brush your teeth."

As she turned from Pete's room, she could see Zach was already sitting up and reaching for a t-shirt. Smiling, Anne checked on Tony, who was conferring with the men laying drywall in their bathroom. "Tony, when you're done in here, can you come downstairs and give me a hand?"

Tony looked up sharply at Anne's interruption, frowned, and nodded his head dismissively before continuing his discussion with the contractors. Carrying a heavy box of Christmas lights, Anne carefully descended two flights of stairs in order to begin decorating the lower-level recreation room. The disarray that greeted her rooted her to the floor. There were beer bottles littering end tables, pillows scattered around the room, and every lamp in the room was lying on the floor. The sour smell of dirty hockey socks mixed with the pungent odor of stale beer. The muted television was still on and video game controllers stretched their cables at odd angles from the game console to separate places on the couch. A sports drink bottle was lying open on the cream-colored rug, its red liquid pooled like blood at a crime scene.

Anne felt her breathing halt, and a tsunami of anger washed over her. Fists clenched, her body interpreted the scene as a physical attack. Adrenaline pulsed through her arms and legs as she tossed aside the box of pre-lit evergreen garlands and lunged toward the disorder, restoring furniture and lamps to their proper positions. Her heart was pounding and she made furious grabs at bottles and food containers. On her way upstairs to retrieve cleaning supplies, she ran into the boys standing solidly in the stairwell—watching her clean.

"How many times do I have to tell you that you need to pick up after yourselves? I don't mind if you guys have a good time in here, but you cannot leave this place looking like a pigsty." Anne had to stop lecturing for only a moment to catch her breath, before continuing in an increasingly louder tone. "Your father and I work hard all week, and it isn't fair that you destroy the house and I have to clean up after you all weekend." She felt tired and she didn't know if she was going to amp up the volume on her rant or burst into tears. When she saw Tony appear behind the boys with a scowl on his face, another surge of anger made the decision for her. Her voice reached a fevered, shrill pitch, "And YOU! Have you seen this room? Obviously you must have, because you've left, three, four, five six, SEVEN empty beer bottles laying all over the room! I thought we talked about making some drastic changes around here before . . . ."

Anne and Tony hadn't told the boys about her pregnancy, but that wasn't what stopped her mid-sentence. An enormous spasm ripped through her lower midsection and demanded all of her attention. Dropping the glass bottles onto the marble-tiled floor, she folded forward and cried out in pain. Tony pushed past his immobile sons and rushed to cradle his wife in his arms. "Anne, what is it? Are you okay? What should we do?"

After several long moments of silence, Anne put out her arm and pointed to the phone. "Call my doctor."

It was getting close to lunchtime when Alma overheard the nurse practitioner asking tense questions of a new patient whose husband had rushed her to the office for severe cramping and bleeding. Between irregular answers she could hear a man's voice repeatedly pleading, "Is my wife going to be okay? Will she be all right?" Alma always hated to see a pregnant woman in distress, but it made her heart doubly sick when she witnessed such desperation from her husband. No longer thinking about her meal getting cold in the microwave, Alma had no intention of leaving the office, in case the obstetrician needed something.

In time, the woman's breathing became less jagged and her words became audible. Alma thought the voice sounded familiar. Just then the doctor approached Alma requesting assistance in the examination room. Alma followed the doctor, and was surprised to see Anne on the exam table with a large man standing by her side, presumably her husband, Tony. He looked up expectantly at the doctor and his booming voice filled the cramped exam room. "Thank goodness you're here, Doc. My wife is having some problems." His facial features, etched in anxiety, were transforming from pale to crimson. He continued rapidly, "We don't know what caused it, but she was pretty upset this morning at me and my boys. We left the living room a mess—she's always telling us to pick up after ourselves, but we don't learn. It's not fair, really, she works hard all week with those germy, demanding little kids in her classroom and then has to come home to more work . . . ."

The doctor raised her hand to silence the nervous father's monologue and refocused her attention on Anne. As she began speaking in a soothing voice, Alma steered Tony toward the door and spoke to him in a hushed tone. "Your wife is in good hands and would probably benefit from a calm atmosphere. Why don't you grab a cup of coffee and head into the waiting room while we find out how to best help her? I promise I'll stay by her side the entire time."

Tony looked at Alma as if she had just told him that she was going to make everything better. The flush in his face drained almost instantly and a weary look replaced the anxious one. "You're right. I'm just in everybody's way here." Turning toward Anne's conversation with the doctor, he interrupted, "I should probably go sit in the waiting room. I'll be right out here if you need me. I'm not going anywhere. Okay?" A look of worry crossed Anne's forehead when she saw Tony reaching for the door handle, but was replaced by a wave of relief when she realized the OB/GYN nurse was Alma.

Alma approached Anne's side and touched her hand. "I'm going to stay with you until you're ready to head back home with your husband. Would that be all right with you?"

Anne gratefully nodded and visibly relaxed. "Oh. Alma. Yes. I'm so glad you are here." Together the doctor and Alma worked in synchronized motions, attaching monitors to Anne, taking her blood pressure, conducting an exam, and answering her questions. Several minutes after the doctor completed the exam, she left the two friends alone. Alma stood next to the exam table, monitoring paper charts that rolled out of the machine, nodding reassuringly, and smiling. "Anne, everything is looking good. You're doing fine."

"Thanks, Alma. I don't know what I would have done if you weren't here." She reached out and rested her hand on Alma's arm. "Did you meet my husband, Tony? He was freaking out, wasn't he?" Anne wrinkled her nose in a distasteful expression, indicating her embarrassment over her husband's behavior.

Alma nodded, "Yes, I did. He was worried about you and the baby. It's nice when a father is as concerned as he is. We get some fathers around here who don't even seem to be interested—and even more fathers whom we never see. I'll take anxiety over indifference every time." Alma patted Anne's hand and winked at her friend, "You've got yourself a keeper there, Anne."

Anne smiled, and Alma continued, "God has blessed you richly—both you and Tony. Sometimes we wives get so caught up in day-to-day demands that we forget to thank God for all the many ways He provides for us through marriage. I'm glad that we're working on honoring those blessings with our small group. I feel like big things are happening and we're becoming more of the women God intended for us to be."

"Thanks, Alma. You're right." Anne smiled and as she did, the door slowly opened and a composed Tony poked his head into the exam room cautiously, but with a smile, "How's my beautiful wife doing?" Alma took one more look at the monitors and, feeling confident that both Anne and her baby were perfectly healthy, excused herself. She exited the room just as Tony lovingly cupped his hands around Anne's face and began to speak tender words into her heart.

Chapter 31 — Dare #21: Alma, Mona

And the wife must respect her husband.

Ephesians 5:33 NIV

After working the entire day on Saturday and sitting through a late hockey game, Alma longed for rest. Thankfully, the Agitators had done poorly in the Thanksgiving hockey tournament and didn't qualify for a spot in the playoffs on Sunday. Rather than trekking out into the rainy November weather, she was grateful for the large block of Sunday free time she unexpectedly had before her. Although no parent ever confessed it, Alma suspected she wasn't the only one who rooted for the opposing team during holiday tournaments.

Marco continued to be disconnected from the rhythm of the family and had spent the last three days in near-isolation, warming up leftovers and eating in front of the television. Alma had invited him to join her at church, but he declined. She had been so busy shuttling to hockey rinks and cooking that it had been easy to push away her thoughts of sadness. Now that the tournament was over, Alma felt the weight of loneliness settle over her like a heavy burden. The toll of Marco's emotional absence during this holiday had pained her so deeply that she wasn't looking forward to Christmas.

Alma went to church with Alicia, Mateo, and Max, brushing off questions from other parishioners about her husband's absence. Forcing a smile, she led her children into a pew near the front and tried to quell the tears that threatened to fracture her composure. The rhythm of the familiar worship rituals calmed and steadied her nerves, but then the morning message hit her squarely in the chest. The priest had been reading from the Bible in the book of Luke where the Virgin Mary learns she is to be the mother of the promised Messiah. Rather than fretting over the cultural ramifications of being an unmarried mother, Mary rejoiced. Alma was reminded that in the midst of our darkness of sin, God blesses us. The priest urged those present to shine because God kept His promise of truth and light by sending His Son, our Savior. No matter her circumstance, Alma could also rejoice in the confidence that God will fulfill His promises of salvation and eternal life.

Hidden partially by reading glasses, hot tears rolled down Alma's cheeks. She knew that God wanted her to receive His daily gifts with open hands, and that she wouldn't be able to grasp hold of them with fists clenched in anger and worry. Slowly, she relaxed her hands and turned her palms upward, releasing the grip of pain and sadness on her heart. No matter her situation, she would trust God.

Alma knew that God loved Marco and had plans for her husband that were part of a bigger picture—one that perhaps neither of them would ever realize—but it was her responsibility to trust God and let Marco be led through the dark storm in which he resided. It wasn't Alma's job to fix whatever was plaguing her husband; rather she would be obedient to God by showing love and respect to Marco. She wanted the love of Jesus to shine into all the dark places of their home.

Later in the day, Alma had Mateo and Max bring down the Christmas boxes from the attic. Looking at the familiar decorations brought wistful memories of happier Christmases when Marco wasn't distant. Along with Alicia, the four put up the tree, hung the lights, and displayed the nativity scene. Looking at the baby Jesus in the manger, Alma was reminded that God sent His only Son to pay for our sins, and that she could rejoice in that knowledge, no matter what. With a considerably lighter heart she went to the kitchen and cooked a traditional Mexican meal of enchiladas, rice, and beans. It was a family favorite, but Alma didn't make it to draw Marco out of himself, nor did she have any expectations for gratitude from her husband. Instead, she cooked with a joyful heart of thanksgiving for God's abundant blessings.

Muslims were forbidden to cook and serve a turkey on Thanksgiving Day, so Aahil's eyebrows rose high Sunday afternoon when he saw the large bird baking in the oven. Mona had never deliberately defied Muslim tenets, but hearing Stephen's descriptions of the food traditionally consumed by non-Muslims during the holiday made her curious enough to experiment with some of the easier recipes she found online. She had even considered saving some of the leftovers in order to give them to Stephen, who had moved into a small apartment and would be spending Thanksgiving alone for the first time in his life. In the end, she decided there wouldn't be time in the busy hockey tournament schedule to squeeze in a road trip getaway to meet him face-to-face. Mona had no intention of getting involved with Stephen—they were just friends who were bound by a similar, painful experience and found comfort and acceptance in each other.

Mona's phone blipped and she reached for it, feeling a slight acceleration of her heart in anticipation of the message. It was her sister grilling her about the decision to make a non-Thanksgiving turkey. The two texted back and forth for several minutes, and Mona nearly missed a message from Stephen.

"How was your Thanksgiving dinner?" he texted.

"It was good. How do you eat all that turkey in one meal?" she asked.

"LOL. You aren't supposed to eat it all at once. Leftovers are part of the tradition."

"Oh."

"Want to know what I did for Thanksgiving?" he asked.

"Sure."

"I went to a family restaurant for a traditional meal for one," He texted

"You ate alone?"

"Yes. All my friends had plans with their friends and loved ones."

Mona felt sorry for Stephen and didn't know how to respond to his last text. While she was considering, another text came, "Don't worry. Being alone was better than eating a meal with a cheating spouse who lied to my face. Can you relate?"

She inhaled sharply as Stephen's words reawakened her angry feelings toward Aahil for his supreme betrayal. She thought of the times he had introduced her to female coworkers at company picnics or holiday parties, and wondered which woman had dethroned her from the pedestal of her husband's attention and affection. Was she smarter? Younger? Thinner? What role wasn't Mona capable of filling that caused her husband to turn to another woman? Where had she failed?

For lack of better words, Mona sent Stephen an emoji of a smiling character who was raising his hand. Within seconds, Stephen returned her emoji with one of his own—a winking smiley face with the words "We're in this together, Mona."

She replied simply, "Yes we are."

Chapter 32 — Small Group Meeting Dares #19–21

It was the first week of December and the rink's smiling turkey cutouts had been replaced by grinning snowmen and penguins. A large cardboard box marked "coat donations" crowded a small Christmas tree that sparkled with tinsel. One by one, the hockey moms took their places around the meeting table, until all six women were seated. Anne looked at the women's faces and wondered if she should continue to act as group facilitator or let Maxine resume her role as leader. Anne respectfully waited for a couple of minutes past their regular start time and noticed that Maxine avoided eye contact, and fiddled with the bookmark in her thick, leather-bound notebook.

Anne took the hint and began the meeting by officially welcoming Maxine back into their group and reading the group guidelines aloud. After dispensing with the business, Anne surprised everyone with a suggestion, "Ladies, if it's okay with all of you, I just want to start our meeting tonight with a prayer of thanksgiving. Over the weekend, I experienced a pretty big scare with the pregnancy." At the mention of pregnancy, Maxine looked in surprise at Anne, who bowed her head and folded her hands. "Dear Lord, thank You for keeping me and the baby safe. Thank

You for sending an angel named Alma to comfort me in my distress." With that, Anne peeked her eyes open and looked at Alma, and continued, "Thank You, Father for her wisdom and her skill and her great faith in You. Amen." A murmur of "Amens" echoed around the table and all but Mona, who refrained from praying, reopened their eyes and unfolded their hands.

Having opened the meeting with a prayer, Anne grew quiet and let the other women take turns sharing their experiences with Dares #19, 20, and 21. Joyce eagerly spoke first. "These Dares had a profound effect on me. If you can believe it, I started organizing and de-cluttering the enormous Christmas collection that I'd amassed over all the years I've been married." Joyce's arms reached wide as if she were showing a vast bulk. "Jim didn't know what hit him, but he certainly didn't complain when I asked him to take a total of 22 boxes of donations to the thrift store." A collective gasp of approval affirmed Joyce in her work and she revealed more. "Once I got started, I didn't want to stop. Normally I'd have spent the entire holiday weekend pigging out on leftovers and binge-watching reality television. This year was a complete turnaround. I was so revived by reducing the Christmas items that I moved on to my bedroom dressers and donated things I'd been saving from my early years of marriage—things that would never fit, even if I tried." All but Jessica, who was still in her 20s, smiled and nodded in recognition of the truth Joyce had uttered.

She stopped speaking and looked pensive for a moment before revealing, "I think I just realized something important. All the clothes from my younger years were cute and attractive, a couple of items were, dare I say, racy!" Joyce wagged her eyebrows up and down in a suggestive manner. "But, you know, the only clothes I wear now are my work smocks, clothes for cleaning around the house, and the same Sunday outfits I've been wearing since the early 1980s!"

Jessica's eyes widened and she interrupted, "Wow, Joyce, you have clothes older than me!" Realizing that she had spoken out of turn by the hurt expression on Joyce's face, Jessica tried to make amends, "I'm sorry, Joyce, I shouldn't have engaged in cross talk, but I know a lot about fashion and if you'd like, I'd be more than happy to help you find some new things."

Joyce quickly covered her feelings from Jessica's offensive

remark about her antique wardrobe. "That's okay, Jessica, I was finished talking anyway and with a new granddaughter, one kid in college, and the youngest in hockey, my budget can't afford a shopping spree right now."

Not to be rebuffed, Jessica tried another advance. "Joyce, let me help you. The three Dares this week got me to reevaluate my closets too. I had way too many outfits—some of them were recent purchases that still had their sale tickets. I returned an entire stack of items to the boutiques they came from, resulting in a hefty credit at several of my favorite shops." Her smile reflected her frugal instincts. "I've forbidden myself from buying any new outfits for at least a year, and unfortunately, merchandise credit expires after six months. Joyce, if you let me take you shopping, you'd keep me from wasting a pile of money." Jessica eagerly looked at Joyce with pleading eyes. "What do you say? Will you join me?"

Before Joyce could answer, Mona looked up from the cell phone she was trying to hide under the table and playfully taunted, "If you don't, Joyce, I will!" The women laughed and Joyce looked at Jessica. "Okay. Why not? Let's go shopping." As the meeting continued, Mona's attention returned to covert texting and Joyce thought about what she had agreed to do—she, the eldest woman in the group was about to go shopping with the youngest of the hockey moms. She wondered what the perky 29-year-old could possibly know about arranging clothing to camouflage sagging skin and lumpy flesh. Joyce suspected their outing would be futile, but she thought it was nice of Jessica to offer.

When it was Maxine's turn to share, she squared her shoulders and looked directly into the faces of the women seated around her. "I've been working hard on the Dares all this week. To be honest, right from the start, I didn't put enough time and attention into this group work." She lifted her hands in admission. "I attempted to squeeze our homework in between phone calls or meetings, and only wrote answers that I thought sounded good. Honestly, I didn't think that I really needed to learn how to treat Samuwel, because I thought our arrangement worked. Sure we bickered and teased each other, but that's what every married couple does. Don't they? I mean, no marriage is perfect."

Maxine paused and stared at the ceiling for a few moments.

"I thought my life was on track. The job is great. The kids are good. I thought everything was fine in my marriage. So fine that I only offered to lead this group to help the five of you sort out the problems in your marriages." Her eyes dropped to the table for a few moments before taking a peek at the women who were all listening attentively to her confession. "But the cold hard truth is that my marriage is in trouble and something needs to change. Everything I've been told about relationships—especially marriage—isn't working." At the last admission, Maxine's strong voice cracked and tears filled her eyes and threatened to spill down her cheeks. "As women, we're told to work hard and demand equality. They tell us to challenge the men in our relationships and take the lead role in making decisions, negotiating conflicts, and even in bed." She balled up her fists in frustration. "The world celebrates female promiscuity and antagonism but doesn't give any clues about creating and maintaining unity in marriage." She raised her fist and banged the table in front of her. "It's not fair! We're taught the world's rules of the road and practice them faithfully, only to find those are the very ways of living that weaken marriages and destroy families."

Maxine abruptly stopped talking. Squeezing her eyes shut, she covered her face with her hands. Her shoulders convulsed forward and from behind her fingers tears broke their barriers and silently tumbled onto the cold table in front of her.

Chapter 33 – Dare #22: Maxine, Alma, Anne

Whatever you do, work at it with all your heart, as working for the Lord, not for human masters, since you know that you will receive an inheritance from the Lord as a reward. It is the Lord Christ you are serving.

Colossians 3:23–24 NIV

Maxine finished reading the next chapter of *The Respect Dare* and sighed. She had been wrestling with the vast difference between modern culture's concept of marriage relationships and the biblical view, which she had been intensely studying the past two weeks. Some of the ideas in *The Respect Dare* were old-fashioned and challenged wives to act as if the feminist movement hadn't taken place. Since the very first Dare, Maxine's response to each reading was to grit her teeth and roll her eyes upward in contempt. Discovering Samuwel's social media relationship with the preschool mother, however, had caused her to reexamine whether society's way of doing marriage was suitable.

Could it be that while industry, technology, and fashion trends advanced, the basic needs of men and women hadn't changed since the beginning of time? In relationships, a woman's strongest desire is to be loved by her husband. Pondering this, Maxine acknowledged that more than anything, she wanted to captivate Samuwel's heart and feel the warm embrace of his love. She certainly had felt his adoration when they were dating in college. Maxine smiled when she recalled how infamous Samuwel had become on campus for ambushing her with expressions of undying love. Once, in their junior year, he burst into the middle of a lecture hall with a large bouquet of wildflowers in hand, reciting a love poem to Maxine that he'd written himself. The philosophy professor seemed irritated by the interruption, but then recovered by launching into a new direction—the precarious balance of love and respect in relationships between men and women.

Maxine had been so dazzled by Samuwel's bold display of affection that she had little opportunity to absorb the life lesson her professor was sharing. Working with the other five women on *The Respect Dare* had awakened her memory. The predominant driving force behind relationships was different for males and females—women needed to be loved, and men needed respect. Maxine smiled as she remembered the collective groan that erupted at the mention of respect for men. Tonight though, she considered the possibility that the philosophy professor's premise may have been right all along.

Was it possible that two critical ingredients of a healthy marriage were love and respect? It was ironic that these exact components were ignored, if not rejected entirely by modern society. Maxine thought of the ways women were discouraged from displaying any sort of weakness or submission to their mates. At the office, male employees were cautioned away from deferential gestures such as holding open the door for a woman or offering to push her car out of a snow pile in the parking lot.

It seemed the very lessons the world had been throwing at Maxine were in direct conflict with the respectful ways she needed to interact with Samuwel. When she really thought about it, she secretly wanted to try some of the suggested Dares in her book—to demonstrate respect for Samuwel—but it felt like a nullification of her strengths, her skills, and the progress of all womankind. She tapped her fingers on the book before her and uncertainty invaded her thoughts. What if the persistent messages to overpower and disregard men were the actual undermining treachery?

The washing machine in Alma's basement had been running steadily all day. With the exception of a quick run to practice and grocery shopping, her Saturday had been filled with dirty laundry. Because she worked full time, the responsibility for clean clothes lay squarely on the shoulders of their owners. None of the kids were great at keeping up with the task, and frequently large, smelly mountains rose from the floor of their bedrooms. Marco, on the other hand, usually took great care with his clothes. Early on in their marriage, Alma had washed a load of their laundry together and a single rogue red sock, which had been lodged in the leg of Alma's work scrubs, tinged three of Marco's white dress shirts a soft, pastel pink. From that day on, Marco kept his dirty clothes away from Alma.

Lately, however, the clothing that Marco had worn to work lay in tall stacks in their laundry room. In addition to brooding, he was beginning to neglect his appearance. Alma knew he was dealing with mounting pressures at the plant where he managed a large team. Operations had been changing over the past few quarters and there were rumors that the company might move production to Mexico, where costs were only a fraction of what they were in the United States. Alma attributed his recent change in behavior to his worries about providing for their family. Fortunately, Alicia had received an academic scholarship for college, but Mateo and Max would soon be exploring the costly world of higher education, and their prospects for academic scholarships were less likely.

Nearing the end of her chores in the early evening, Alma's eyes locked on her husband's dirty clothes lying in a pile. She was tired from a hard week at work, coupled with late hockey practices, and several phone calls from Anne who had all the usual questions about pregnancy. Wanting nothing more than to bring the last basket of folded laundry into her bedroom and take a nap, Alma thought about the latest Dare—to serve the Lord by working heartily. Marco had left the house before sunup to work a double shift and was wearing the last clean dress shirt he owned. He wouldn't be home for hours, and in order to wear a clean shirt on Monday, he would need to spend his Sunday night washing clothes. Alma suddenly felt compassion for the man who worked so hard, yet whose future was unsteady. She knew instinctively that he wouldn't acknowledge any of her efforts, but putting down her basket of fresh smelling clothes, Alma began to carefully separate his darks and lights.

Washing one load after another, Alma found a rhythm in folding socks, ironing shirts, and hanging pants. As she worked, she reflected on the sacrifice that Jesus made for her, how He took on the humble form of a sinless man, interacted with the most rejected people of Jewish society, and was crucified—the lowest form of punishment at the time—in order to pay for the sins of all mankind. Jesus Christ offered redemption to all who believed in Him, and yet was rejected by the Jews, who were indifferent to His sacrifice for them. A wave of gratitude swept over her and she noted how the sacrifice of washing her husband's clothes was so small in comparison to Jesus' sacrifice. She thanked God for sending His Son for her salvation and dedicated the efforts of cleaning Marco's laundry to the Lord.

Anne hung up the phone and breathed a deep sigh of relief. Her obstetrician had patiently answered the pregnant teacher's long list of questions that couldn't wait until the office visit next week. Pregnancy completely baffled Anne, who was used to researching answers and solving problems without consulting anybody. Now that she was expecting, however, she needed the reassurance of an experienced professional to accompany her research. In her quest for a deeper understanding of all the changes that occurred during gestation, she had turned to Alma for help. After Alma had been such a godsend during the scare a couple of weeks ago, Anne began to see her as someone more than a fellow hockey mom.

Alma had not only stayed by Anne's side while she feared

for the life of her unborn child, but she also helped her recognize several of Tony's positive qualities. Anne spent so much time scheduling projects and ticking them off her mental checklist that she had only been able to see his shortcomings. Focused on his excessive weekend drinking, she harbored resentments and manipulated attempts to fix his character flaws. Over the past several days, Anne realized that she had been comparing Tony to descriptions of colleagues' husbands—thoughtful, neat, and expressive men who surpassed the realities of her own husband. She was grateful now to have a friend in Alma, whose marriage would certainly become harmonious again, given Alma's positive outlook, faith, and trust.

Chapter 34 – Dare #23: Jessica, Joyce

Rather, it should be that of your inner self, the unfading beauty of a gentle and quiet spirit, which is of great worth in God's sight.
1 Peter 3:4 NIV

Jessica pulled her luxury SUV into Joyce's crumbling concrete driveway. She turned off the engine and was about to slide off the grey leather seats when Joyce darted out of her house and jogged toward the car. Jessica suspected Joyce was embarrassed by the size of her small bungalow, but compared to the trailer home Jessica once lived in, the single family home seemed like a mansion. "Hey, Joyce, you're fast! You didn't even give me a chance to get out of the car!" Jessica motioned to the passenger door. "Come on in."

Joyce opened the door and paused for a moment, inhaling the new-car smell and taking note of the clean interior of the SUV. If it weren't for the two car seats in the back, she would never have thought that Jessica had children. Remembering the days when her kids were small, Joyce recalled the myriad of stickers that obscured most of the view in the back windows, and the cookie

---

DARE TO RESPECT

crumbs, broken crayons, and wet scraps of paper that littered the floor of her old minivan.

"Hi, Jessica, thanks for inviting me." Joyce didn't know how to include all the things for which she could be thanking Jessica.

Jessica graciously responded, "Don't mention it, Joyce. Believe me, you're doing me a favor by giving me the chance to do my favorite activity without bringing more stuff into my closets. I'm only allowing myself to purchase one thing today, and that's a gift for Bob."

Joyce relaxed, "I've been looking forward to our outing all day. Mondays are my only day off from work, and how fortunate that it's your daughters' cultural day at the . . . learning studio?"

Jessica backed out of the driveway. "Yes, the girls spend Mondays at a private center that specializes in educational experiences for toddlers and preschoolers. The girls will play with musical instruments, listen to stories in Mandarin, dance to World beats, and do just about every type of activity that might possibly stimulate their little brains." Joyce's eyes widened and Jessica realized that she probably sounded snobbish and changed tactics in order to try to put Joyce at ease. "Things are certainly different for my daughters than they were for me when I was growing up in a trailer park."

Joyce's face registered surprise at the revelation of Jessica's humble beginnings. "I had no idea you didn't grow up in the lap of luxury, Jessica."

"Well, I had a lot to learn when I first married Bob. I spent a lot of time studying fashion magazines, etiquette guides, and eavesdropping on conversations at fancy dinner parties. The fact that none of the other wives would speak to me during those first few months was actually a blessing in disguise—it gave me time to construct a back story for myself that was truthful but covered up the fact that I was poor as dirt when Bob met me."

Joyce immediately felt both compassion for this young woman and guilt for having similarly rejected her. "Well, you certainly fit in with all of the other . . . um . . . high-society folks that I see around the hockey rinks."

Jessica dismissed Joyce's compliment with the wave of a hand. "I may look all polished on the outside, but on the inside I'm

155

still a country bumpkin who prefers frozen pizza over lobster and caviar."

Joyce snorted, "Well then Jessica, I think you and I will get along like two peas in a pod." Together the women went from one boutique to another, stopping once for an early lunch and again at a beauty salon where Jessica surprised Joyce with a manicure, facial, haircut, and style. "An early Christmas present," Jessica explained when Joyce tried to protest. By day's end, both women were exhausted and thoughtful as Jessica drove Joyce home.

"I've enjoyed our day together, Joyce." Jessica was quiet for a moment then continued, "I haven't had a girlfriend to shop around with since I moved to Chicago." Her voice grew quiet as she continued, "It's been hard for me to make friends here. I don't understand it completely, but other women seem to keep their distance from me. Last year, the other hockey moms rarely even said hello to me, even though I went out of my way to be friendly." Jessica stared straight ahead into traffic and her voice became so shaky that Joyce had to strain to hear. "At the girls' dance class and learning studio, the other moms were nice to me at first, but after a few weeks, they seemed guarded. Bob told me it was my imagination and I was being too sensitive. He would know, because he's met them all several times when he offered to pick up the girls." Jessica stopped talking and Joyce, with her new stylish hairdo and painted nails, was unsure how or even if she should respond.

Before Joyce could formulate a proper sentence, Jessica changed tacks and her voice resumed its normal strength and volume. "I'm sure he's right. I just need to keep putting myself out there and sooner or later things will get better."

As the SUV pulled into Joyce's driveway for the second time that day, Joyce's troubled thoughts jumbled her words. All she could do was look up at Jessica, whose eyes were bright with tears, and spit out "I'm glad we're friends, Jessica. Thanks for everything."

A large knot formed in Jessica's throat at Joyce's sincere tone, and she shook her head in a quick and barely perceptible motion. As if erasing the previous moments of deep truth, the perfect smile with pearly white teeth reemerged on Jessica's face. Her pert voice bounced around words that were as artificial as the color in Joyce's hair. "I had a great time today, Joyce. Let's do it again some time." With that simple statement, the open heart that had revealed the authentic Jessica from the trailer park was shut.

It was too late to go back, however. Joyce had seen into Jessica's reality, and it wasn't nearly as perfectly shaped and polished as her fingernails.

Mona was shopping online for a token of her love and respect for Aahil. Searching through a wide variety of online stores had provided no inspiration for the gift she was to purchase for the current Dare. The gift was supposed to represent the positive qualities of her husband's character and demonstrate her recognition of those aspects. From one website to another, she couldn't find anything that reminded her of Aahil.

Taking another approach, she thought about the admirable qualities of her husband. She thought about the man she married in the late 1990s—kind, gentle, honest, and dedicated to providing for his family. Remembering their early days of marriage, she could easily picture Aahil leaving home before the break of day to put in long hours of work at the burgeoning software company. Her imagination followed him to work, right up to the moment when he sat at his desk to untangle a mass of digital commands. She felt her stomach jump and a shiver of ice ran down her arms when her mind brought to view a woman approach his desk. Pushing aside the framed photo of their family, Aahil gazed up at the salacious temptress whose large teeth snapped at the opportunity to lure him away from an honest life.

While Mona had been at home accomplishing the business of caring for their family, Aahil talked and laughed at work with the other woman, who brought him food and gossiped with him about office affairs. The Jezebel confided in him about her problems with an ailing parent, and he came to her aid whenever there was a programming problem too difficult for her to solve. Aahil was careful to keep his thoughts about Mona separate from the growing relationship with his female co-worker, but over time the two grew more comfortable and connected to each other. While the illicit intimacy grew, Mona's husband continued the ritual of praying daily at the mosque and expressing love to his wife. Unaware of the threat poised to destroy her family, Mona sacrificed sleep for late night hockey practices and rose early each morning to make a lunch for Aahil to take to work.

As the horrible fantasy rolled in Mona's mind, the icy chill in her arms traveled down her shaking legs. Her heart pounded and her chest constricted with every breath. Wishing to erase these thoughts, she pushed herself abruptly away from the computer, but not before envisioning the door to Aahil's office swing shut and hearing in her mind, the frozen click of its steel lock sliding into place.

Chapter 35 – Dare #24: Alma, Jessica

Be still and know that I am God.

Psalm 46:10 NIV

Rest. The title of Dare #24 was "Rest." It was two weeks before Christmas and each of the hockey moms in the Respect Dare small group yearned for rest from their demanding schedules. Added to the pressure of work, practice, games, meals, and homework were Christmas parties to attend, presents to wrap, and trees to decorate. Five of the six women laughed out loud when they read instructions to rest and listen to God's voice. Only one woman stopped and listened—Alma.

After wrestling with her marriage discontent for months, Alma had finally surrendered. Marco continued to be moody and evasive. He rarely spoke to his wife, and when he did, it was with sarcastic or angry tones. Despite his behavior, she entered a state of peaceful acceptance fueled by frequent periods of quiet with God. She was grateful to recognize that she didn't have control over her husband's attitude or relationship with their children. She couldn't change him, nor could she fix the problems he was facing.

While the frenzied pace of preparing for Christmas celebrations and traditions increased around her, Alma became still. She looked for God's handiwork dispersed throughout her day and found pleasure in unexpected places—an open parking spot near the office, a feathery snowflake floating to earth, a perfectly sharpened pencil, the healthy cry of a newborn, and sweet smelling hockey equipment fresh from the washing machine. Inexplicably, the time and attention she spent noticing God's blessings around her didn't impact the limited time she had to accomplish daily tasks. She no longer felt rushed or squeezed for time. Instead, she felt as if each new discovery added minutes to her day.

The idea of accepting her new reality in marriage had been foreign, but once Alma found herself at the end of her wits, she realized there was nothing left to do but let go. The future was still unclear, but she had left the business of planning to God and held fast to her faith in His promises. God would not let her go and would always be with her. His plans for her were perfect, and she could choose to pave her own perilous way, or walk on the smooth path that her mighty Father was constructing.

Alma knew there was also a separate and perfect path for Marco. She didn't know exactly what demons he was facing, or what lay ahead on his journey, but she knew that God's love for her husband was richly abundant and that His lessons would be learned in time. It was up to Marco whether he would submit to God's leading or not.

Jessica had been careful when wrapping the single item she had purchased on her shopping trip with Joyce earlier in the week. The exquisite, single-edged Katana sword was crafted of the finest metal, and to Jessica, it represented Bob's refined character and the power he exuded in every situation. Joyce had admired the beautiful dragon engraved on the curved steel blade and assured Jessica that her husband would treasure such a meaningful gift.

Bob had been tied up in court and didn't have time to come home before dinner, so she agreed to meet him at the restaurant.

Jessica arrived first and waited expectantly with his gift at the best table in the room. Arriving 45 minutes late, Bob seemed rushed and distracted when he ordered a drink and looked sharply at the box in front of his wife.

"What's in the box?" he demanded.

Jessica shyly responded, "It's a gift for my husband," and pushed the box across the table.

Bob reached for the gift, hastily unwrapped it, and politely thanked Jessica for the sentiment. She didn't even have a chance to explain the meaning behind her gift before he launched into a long rendition of the demands placed on his shoulders. Jessica listened patiently, despite complete ignorance of the specific complexities of corporate law. When Bob's scotch arrived he emptied the glass in one large gulp before rising from the table.

"Sorry to do this to you, Babe, but I've got to get back to the office. There's a very demanding client that needs my full attention. I'll be home late, so don't wait up." Without saying another word or waiting for a response, Bob maneuvered his way around the smartly dressed waiters serving plates of food to other diners. Jessica saw the back of his head as the maître d' held the door for Bob's hasty getaway.

Deflated, Jessica sighed and looked helplessly across the table where her husband had been for less than five minutes. Lying across the empty plate was the forgotten Katana that held so much meaning for her. Next to the sword, the ice cubes shifted audibly in Bob's empty glass tumbler, and mirrored the melting of Jessica's hopes.

Chapter 36 – Small Group Meeting Dares #22–24

For there is nothing hidden that will not be disclosed, and nothing concealed that will not be known or brought out into the open.
Luke 8:17 NIV

A low wolf whistle reverberated in Anne's cheeks when Joyce entered the meeting room at the ice arena. "Wow, look at the hot mama that just walked in!" The rest of the women halted their conversations to stare at the most mature member of their small group. Joyce was wearing a pair of flared silk trousers with a long sleeve cashmere sweater. Silver earrings dangled from her ears, accentuating short, wavy hair with warm auburn tones. Softly blended colors brightened her face, creating a smooth, dewy effect that drew attention to her dazzling hazel eyes.

Joyce did a dramatic turn before sitting down at the table. Anne asked, "How did Jim react to your makeover?"

A large smile crept across Joyce's face. "I think it took him by surprise. When I walked in the door his eyes grew wide and he had the goofiest look on his face. He didn't carry me off to the bedroom, but I think we're moving in the right direction." By the contented grin, it was evident that she was pleased with the changes in her appearance.

Alma chirped happily, "Joyce, you look *muy hermosa*, very beautiful!"

Not wishing to take all the credit, Joyce explained, "This was all Jessica's doing. She's a wiz kid with fashion and knows how to hide certain body flaws that I'm not going to mention. But let me just say that the right bra can do wonders for a woman's confidence!" The women laughed in response.

Anne, who was barely into the second trimester of her pregnancy, had been struggling to make any of her old clothes fit before transitioning into maternity wear. She looked down at her chest and suggested, "Well, maybe Jessica could help me figure out how to stuff these growing girls into something more suitable than my lacy bras. They're being stretched like a slingshot ready to recoil!"

Just then, the door opened and Jessica entered the room, looking worried, "Did someone mention my name?" She applied her best grin, but Joyce, who knew the insecurities that lurked under the surface, replied, "Yes, Jessica, we were just talking about your amazing ability to match the right clothes to a woman's body. I think Anne might be jealous of my makeover." Joyce winked at Jessica, who relaxed and let a smile radiate from her heart.

"Let the record show that I'm jealous, and it's because my pants are being held together with two paperclips and a rubber band!" Mona's eyes grew wide in surprise at Anne's confession.

"I guess there's at least one benefit to dressing in traditional Muslim attire." Mona wore mostly American clothing and only the occasional *hijab*, or head covering, to demonstrate her religious affiliation.

"Well, Mona, I may have to raid your closet soon. I don't think I'm quite ready to announce to the world that I am going to have a baby in five months." Anne pulled out the group guidelines and read the list to the assembled group. Together the women shared their experiences with the week's Dares and reactions (or lack of response) from their husbands.

When the topic turned toward the gift purchased for their husbands as a token of their love and admiration, Jessica was the first to share. "Before my shopping adventure with Joyce this week, I spent a lot of time thinking about what to purchase for Bob. It seems he already has everything a man could need or want, but still I wanted to get something that would be special to him. In the end, I settled for a vintage Katana—a traditional Japanese sword wielded by the most elite of warriors. It is such a beautiful piece."

Joyce, not able to restrain her support for Jessica, chimed in, "You bet that thing was beautiful. I couldn't believe my eyes when the owner of the specialty shop unsheathed it. It was simply breathtaking." Joyce stopped and saw all of the women staring at her, "Oops, sorry, I've done it again—'no cross talk during meetings,' sorry—but Jessica's gift was extraordinary, you should have seen it."

"Thanks, Joyce, but I wish Bob had shared your sentiments. I made reservations at our favorite steakhouse, and frantically shuttled the girls to the babysitter in order to make it to the restaurant on time." Jessica paused when she noticed the expressions of encouragement on the women's faces. "Only to find myself alone waiting for my husband for nearly an hour. By the time Bob finally arrived, it was almost 8 o'clock. He opened the gift and dashed out of the restaurant before I could even say more than a few words." Recognizing both sympathy and suspicion from several of the women, she started to backtrack in order to protect her husband's reputation. "It's just that he's been so busy lately with a major takeover and negotiating multiple owners' holdings— I probably should have waited a few more days until things were calmer to complete the Dare."

"But what about the sword? What did he say?" Joyce interrupted, but then caught herself. "Oops. Sorry. Again." She rolled her eyes and slapped an open palm on her forehead.

"He said nothing about the gift. I don't even know if he remembers getting it. He just opened it and then left it lying on the table when he rushed back to work." This time Jessica's voice was lower and less animated than her usual cheerful tone. "I don't feel like my sentimental gift held any meaning for him. So, that's all I've got for tonight." She held open her hands to the group and waited for their judgments.

The women remained quiet for several long moments until Alma spoke up. "It's like the book says, 'do everything for God's glory' without harboring expectations of our husbands' responses. I think after so many months of waiting for Marco to change, I've finally accepted the things I cannot change. No matter how hard I tried, I couldn't get Marco to reciprocate with even one kind word. Every positive attempt I made ended in disappointment and drained me of a little bit more hope. I finally hit a point where I'd tried everything and ran out of plans to fix things. So I've left Marco in God's hands now. And you know what? I've been able to notice many other blessings all around me that I couldn't see when I was so focused on the difficult situation with my marriage." She finished speaking and looked into the faces of her friends and peace washed across the deep crevices around her eyes. "Jesus is at the center of my life, and it's from Him I receive my strength and hope and courage and peace. And I guess that about sums it up for me."

When Alma concluded her share, Anne stood up, walked around the table, and embraced the woman whom she admired so deeply. Whispering so only Alma could hear, "Thank you for sharing that with us, Alma. You have become such an important person in my life. Thank you." Alma patted the back of her friend, who enveloped her in the fiercest hug she'd ever experienced.

While Anne made her way back to her seat, Maxine cleared her throat and began, "I have something to share." The women shifted their attention to the other side of the table, "As you know, I'm making up for lost time in my Respect Dare work. I've been doing lots of thinking about the ways I interact with Samuwel. Every mainstream attitude toward marriage that I've enacted has had a destructive impact on my relationship. I admit my culpability, but I'm also hurt by his platonic interactions with other women. Despite the fact he didn't cross any physical lines with the blonde divorcee at the kids' preschool or the woman at my work event, I feel betrayed. Instead of pouring his energy into our relationship, he was stoking other fires on the backburner. It sickens me when I think of how much time my husband spent having intellectual access to other women—sharing things he probably wouldn't share if the relationship was limited to face-to-face interactions."

Maxine's words had captured every bit of Mona's attention. Her conscience pricked at the similarities between

Samuwel's platonic, yet frequent, interactions with other women, and her own relationship with Stephen. The pain in Maxine's voice was significant, and she was a strong, fierce, independent woman. If she could be hurt so deeply by recurrent exchanges between her husband and another woman, Aahil would be similarly wounded. As if on cue, Mona's cell phone started vibrating. Without looking at the caller's name, she knew it was Stephen and quickly sent the call to voicemail.

As the meeting neared its close, the women discussed the upcoming Christmas tournament schedule and holiday plans. Anne suggested, "Ladies, with our busy Christmas schedules, plus hockey and shopping, how do you feel about taking a few weeks off during Christmas break? I'm so tired these days, I can barely keep awake after dinner."

Maxine agreed, "I think it's a good idea, but we should still keep working on Dares. It might be a good time to practice some of the new skills we've been learning these past weeks." The women agreed to complete two weeks' worth of Dares over Christmas break and regroup when the kids returned to school. As they were gathering their books and reaching for winter coats, Joyce shared a caution, "Remember that while we're in the season of celebrating the birth of our Lord Jesus Christ, we may face situations that challenge our resolve to respect our husbands—things like family gatherings, gift exchanges, overindulgence of alcohol. Just be on guard against the evil one's traps."

Anne nudged Joyce in the ribs, "And on that note, a very merry Christmas to you, too!" The women exchanged hugs and wishes for a Merry Christmas. Mona refrained from the exchanges, making a hasty exit for the parking lot with a worried frown and a blinking cell phone.

Chapter 37 – New Year's Eve Party

Finally, all of you, be like-minded, be sympathetic, love one another, be compassionate and humble. Do not repay evil with evil or insult with insult. On the contrary, repay evil with blessing, because to this you were called so that you may inherit a blessing.
1 Peter 3:8-9 NIV

"5...4...3...2...1... Happy New Year!" Party horns blew and fireworks exploded outside the large wall of windows overlooking a manmade lake. Anne and Tony's guests kissed and toasted the New Year with crystal flutes of champagne. A small jazz trio played celebratory music in the corner of their grand foyer near the 9-foot Christmas tree. In addition to business contractors and clients, Anne had invited her friends from the Respect Dare Small Group to attend their annual New Year's Eve party.

With the exception of Alma, all the women were in attendance with their husbands. Jessica and Bob dazzled guests on the dance floor with their glowing tans and perfectly choreographed dance steps. When Bob twirled Jessica, her shimmering silver dress floated, then delicately curved around her legs like the spiral staircase on a wedding cake. Together their movements were smooth and the performance flawless. Jessica's dazzling white smile and heavy dose of expertly blended concealer completely masked the fact that her feet were in searing pain and she was exhausted from caring for two sick babies.

Across the dance floor, Joyce and Jim were the polar opposite of Jessica and Bob. The older couple danced to their own rhythms on the margins of the partygoers. Jim's movements were abrupt and exaggerated and he looked as uncomfortable in his new suit as Joyce did in her 2-inch heels. All the while, Jim's facial expressions volleyed between concentration and self-deprecation. The two weren't much to look at, but together they laughed and clung to each other like two mountain climbers scaling sheer cliffs in tandem.

Anne scanned the dancing partygoers trying to locate Mona and Aahil. Finally she spotted them in the grand foyer, deep in conversation. By the looks of things, Mona wanted to dance badly, but her husband resisted. Perhaps it was a religious issue, Anne thought, and before she could intercede with an offer of champagne, Maxine and Samuwel interrupted her thoughts. They were nearly out of breath as they approached their hostess to beg forgiveness for leaving early. "Anne, thanks for inviting us to your party. We had a wonderful evening, but have to get back home to relieve Cynthia who's probably trying to wrangle her brothers into bed with little success."

By the way Samuwel was looking at Maxine, Anne suspected there was another urgent need that was calling them home. "No worries, Maxine. Samuwel, it was wonderful to meet you finally. I hope to see you again soon. Perhaps at the hockey tournament later this month?"

Samuwel put his arm around Maxine's waist, "Yes, that sounds like something the whole family might have a fun time doing this year. Perhaps I'll see you at the tournament." Samuwel took the coats from one of the wait staff and helped Maxine slide into her floor-length fur before donning his own leather coat. He held the door open for Maxine, but before exiting she leaned to the side and whispered into her friend's ear, "Anne, *The Respect Dare* is working! I can't believe how different things are in our home." She hugged Anne's shoulders and dashed out the door with

Samuwel at her side. Together the two held hands in the falling snow while they made their way to their car that the valet had warmed and brought to the front of Anne's home.

Anne watched Samuwel open the car door for Maxine and was startled when Tony came up behind her. "Hon, we're almost out of beer." It took a moment for Anne to make sense of what Tony had just said, but once it registered, she became completely incensed. Anne ordered three cases of champagne and four crates of his favorite German beer, plus enough top- shelf liquor to open their own martini bar. Looking at Tony's reddened face, Anne knew that he had already enjoyed more than a few beers this evening. She clenched her fists. She and Tony had had lengthy discussions about his drinking over the past couple weeks and he had promised to cut back, but apparently had already drunk his way through the evening supply and needed more.

Anne's eyes narrowed and she thought about how to chastise her husband subtly enough so they weren't the main topic of tomorrow's gossip column. She would have to keep her voice as low as possible and make sure a smile plastered her face when she blasted him for breaking his promise. As she formulated a sentence from her handy arsenal of belittling vocabulary and expressions, she caught herself. For months she had been taking new steps toward more respectful interactions with her husband. Some of the tasks, such as purchasing a token gift or leaving love notes for Tony to find, had been lighthearted and engaging. Other Dares had been humbling, particularly the one where she asked if he ever felt she said things that made him feel less than a man. In both cases, the tasks were assigned based on the designated schedule and small group meetings—and were implemented only after she had the luxury of carefully planning each scenario.

Suddenly Anne found herself in the midst of an authentic opportunity to practice some of her new respect skills. Yet here she was, ready to go from zero-to-sixty in three seconds. She needed to ease off the accelerator and let the engine idle for a few moments. She took a few breaths—the first was painful, as her chest had constricted with the sudden flood of adrenaline brought on by anger. After she was able to catch her breath and had unclenched her fists, she looked Tony in the eye and as calmly as if she was folding laundry, asked, "Did I hear you say that you've gone through all the beer I ordered for the party?"

Tony's face was anxious as the question was delivered. He had been growing tense watching Anne's face change expression several times between the time it took him to ask and her to answer the question. Her calm and even words tamped down the argument he feared would erupt in fiery flames. He relaxed and smiled, "No. What I said was that we just finished the first crate of beer, and I need to go into the garage to get another." He put his calloused hands gently on his wife's shoulders and leaned in to kiss her forehead and then her lips. "Have I told you how much I love you lately?" He squeezed her shoulders and stepped around her to open the door leading to the garage.

Anne stood still in the foyer, struggling to comprehend what had just happened. Twenty seconds ago, she was ready to tear down her husband, possibly in front of all their guests—over a complete misunderstanding. Because she had been inspired by grace to pause a moment and ask for clarification, their marriage received a boost instead of bullet holes. In amazement she closed her eyes and thanked God for this teaching moment—the first miracle of a new year.

Chapter 38 – Small Group Meeting Dares #25–30

As the women entered the room and greeted each other, the mood was unusually somber. It had been several weeks since they'd had a small group meeting and each had much to share about their progress over the holidays. When all were assembled and Anne had finished reading the group guidelines, looking directly at Joyce when she read the rule about 'no cross talking,' she asked if anyone would like to begin sharing about their work in dares #25 through 30.

Maxine raised her index finger, indicating she wished to speak and began, "Over the past couple of weeks I have noticed big transformational shifts in my marriage." She explained, "I've been doing the Dares, just as the author has suggested, even when it made me uncomfortable or if I thought the Dare was naïve. I resisted developing expectations of Samuwel's response to my changes, but was delighted when he began to act differently around me. Even if he didn't outwardly acknowledge a specific action I'd done, like a favor or small task, he began to treat me with more care." Maxine, not frequently challenged when looking for solutions to problems, seemed perplexed at the balance shift that had taken place in the relationship with her husband. "How quickly he responded to my new approaches! I can't believe these simple changes in my behaviors have changed the whole dynamic in our home. For the first time in a long time, I'm feeling a protective kind of love around and above me coming from my husband." She searched the faces of the women sitting around her for answers. Receiving none, she continued, "If I'd known all it would take to improve my marriage was a bunch of simple Dares, I would have done them long ago!"

The women remained quiet, because each of them knew that completing the Dares hadn't been the same magic bullet for them that it had been for Maxine. Looking thoughtful, Anne began to speak, "The Dares have been changing my marriage also, but over Christmas break I learned that practicing them in real-life situations is tough, but worth it. At our New Year's Eve party, instead of blowing up at Tony over a situation I perceived was happening, I was able to ask for clarification. That was a great success for me, and a good moment for us as a couple." She paused and then added, "Several hours later I got the opportunity to practice the fine art of setting boundaries. I awoke to an empty bed and discovered that my husband had continued drinking with several of his buddies long after our guests, the servers, and the cleaning staff had all gone home." Her lips tightened and she clasped her hands together, "I entered his den where I found him, completely inebriated, smoking cigars, and talking very loudly. Instead of launching into a demeaning and hurtful verbal attack I calmly approached my husband and told him that he woke me from a sound sleep. Of course, he apologized quickly, kissed me, and then promptly asked me to bring more beer from the garage." She paused and then sat a little straighter in her plastic chair and folded her arms across her chest in defiance. "I refused and went back upstairs to our bedroom. The next morning instead of cleaning up the beer bottles, cigar stubs, and garbage, I tried something different. I handed Tony an empty garbage bag and a can of deodorizer, pointed out the vacuum cleaner, and went shopping for maternity clothes." A look of accomplishment spread across her face as she unfolded her arms. "When I returned several hours and one glorious massage later, I discovered that he had not only cleaned and aired out the den, but he also got the boys to clean their disgusting rooms." Anne folded her arms over her growing belly and smiled with satisfaction. "I was so proud of myself for setting boundaries that I treated myself to a luxurious bubble bath in my new master bathroom."

As soon as Anne finished speaking Joyce leaned forward and opened her mouth as if to speak. Catching Anne's narrowed eyes looking directly back at her—almost daring her to engage in cross talk—Joyce leaned back and closed her mouth. Instead, she let her approving nod convey the fondness she was feeling for Anne.

With so much attention shifting in her direction, Joyce took the opportunity to reveal her plans for a romantic interlude with Jim. "As you know, Jim and I have been very lax in the intimacy department. I figured the author of *The Respect Dare* would have to include at least one chapter about sex, and boy, if chapter 28 didn't lay it out there for us." Joyce's sheepish grin conveyed her uncertainty. "I've got reservations at a romantic hotel this weekend, and am ready to . . . um . . ." She struggled to formulate the word and finally blurted it out. "SEDUCE him with wine, massage oil, and even an intimate nightgown with barely enough lace to cover my . . . um . . . parts." Her face blushed bright red. "I tried it on and nearly broke a rib from laughing so hard when I looked at myself in the mirror. Nevertheless, I'm going boldly forward into new and uncomfortable horizons." She looked up at the ceiling and brushed a thick strand of recently highlighted hair from a neatly arched eyebrow. "So that's the plan, and no matter what happens I'm going to fulfill this Dare. Wish me luck, girls!" With that invitation, all of the women expressed their approval. Maxine cheered and even Anne broke her own rule of no cross talk, "Go, Girl!" At Anne's transgression of the rules, the women released joyful giggles and gentle encouragements to the group member who notoriously defied the rules in search of affirmation.

After a while, the women grew quiet and Jessica spoke in an unusually flat tone, "Well since we're talking about Dare #28, I guess I'll share my experience." Even though Mona was seated directly across from Jessica, she had to lean forward to catch the entire contents of Jessica's timid share. "My sister, Marilee, surprised me by coming up from South Carolina to watch the girls for New Year's. Bob and I had a wonderful evening at Anne's New Year's Eve party, and I was excited about revealing my new negligee when we got home. It was so pretty—it was sheer and had lace with pearls—absolutely stunning." Jessica paused a few moments and ran her hand over imagined silk before continuing with her story. "I thought it would catch Bob's eye and give me the confidence to make the first move—something I've never done before." Jessica looked at Alma's peaceful face that offered unconditional acceptance and took a deep breath. "When we got home, I went into our bedroom to put on the new gown and Bob checked his messages before coming up. I was nervous and rushed through my clothing change so he wouldn't see me before I was ready." Jessica's hands were in motion, imitating her hurried state of movement. "Well, I shouldn't have rushed, because he didn't come for a long time—so long that I had time to change, brush my hair, adjust my makeup, and pick up the clothes lying around the room. I was getting impatient, and just about to go downstairs when our bedroom door opened, and I noticed that Bob's face was red and his eyes looked . . . I don't know . . . strange."

Jessica stopped talking and searched through her purse for a half-empty water bottle, opened the cap with shaking hands and took several loud gulps before clearing her voice. "I took a deep breath and walked across the room toward him. I put my arms around his shoulder and whispered something suggestive in his ear, before kissing his earlobe." Her even, peach-tone face turned scarlet and blotchy. "And then he laughed. He looked down at me with a disgusted look and laughed at my pathetic attempt to set the mood. He told me I was too simple and if I really wanted to do my part in the bedroom and make him happy, I should . . . ." Silence stopped all movements in the room. "That I should get my sister to join us."

Jessica searched the faces of each of the women for traces of shock or judgment. She found none, but felt suddenly too exposed and quickly backtracked. "I'm sure he was just joking. Right? My husband didn't really mean what he said." She looked up at the ceiling tiles and then back at the group. "No, definitely not . . . or if he did, it was only because he drank too much champagne." Jessica, apparently done talking, fell silent and became intently focused on her cuticles, stroking the perfect pink streak of gel polish on her round-shaped nails.

Joyce remained seated and mute, suddenly grateful for the

no cross talk rule. After it was clear that Jessica was finished, Mona, who had been unusually quiet all evening, broke the awkward silence. "I have something to share." In unison, five heads quickly turned to face Mona. She waited for several moments before beginning, took a deep breath, and plunged in. "For the past few months, I've been texting and talking with Stephen, a man I met on a cheating spouse support website. At first we only messaged each other on the public blog site, but then he started sending me private messages. He left his cheating wife, and was hurting a lot, so we exchanged phone numbers and began talking and texting on a regular basis." She paused, but didn't raise her eyes to face the women. "He got an apartment and started calling me late at night, sometimes catching me while Samir was in hockey practice, and other times he left a voice message. He was lonely and broken. I was just being supportive by responding to his messages. I had no romantic interests in him whatsoever. After a while, his texts started to take on a different tone—like they could be taken in a suggestive way."

Mona took a deep breath and intently studied the floor tiles. "Over the winter break, Stephen told me that he was travelling to Chicago on business and invited me to meet him for dinner. The restaurant was downtown, so I told Aahil I was meeting my sister in the city for shopping. He drove me to the train and cautioned me to be careful, but to have a good time."

Mona gulped and began to twist the gold band on her ring finger. "When I got to the restaurant, I was shocked. It was small, dark, and almost entirely lit by candles. I recognized him because of pictures he'd sent to me, but also because he was the only person sitting alone at the tiny tables. I was nervous at first, but by the time dessert came, we were both laughing and enjoying each other's company. After he passed the waiter his credit card, Stephen took my hand and looked right into my eyes. I started to pull away, but the pain in his face over losing his marriage just overwhelmed me. I left my hand in his and listened to him describe the sad details of his new life."

A look of distress passed over her face and she bit her lower lip. "He asked me to join him in his hotel room for a drink, assuring me it was only a drink between friends and nothing more. But when we got up to his room, he kissed me." Mona stopped abruptly and sucked in a large gulp of air. Her dark eyes glistened with wetness and she shut them tightly. "And I kissed him back."

Raising her face to the group, her voice became anguished. "All this time I've been punishing Aahil for being tempted into the arms of another woman, and suddenly I find myself in the arms of another man! I left as soon as the kiss ended, and haven't returned any of his calls or texts since. But I'm all mixed up now. I'm confused about how I strayed so far out of bounds. I hate myself for being no better than all the other cheating spouses!" She balled up her hand and began to knock it on the side of her head. "You talk about your God that is full of love and forgiveness, but Aahil did something that isn't forgivable. Now I did something that isn't forgivable."

Before Mona could deliver another series of blows to her temple, Maxine grabbed her wrist. She wrapped her hands lovingly around Mona's fist and whispered in her face, "Nothing is too big for God to restore. No sin is too large for him to forgive."

Mona looked up at Maxine's face so close to her own. There were dark streaks of eyeliner marking lines of pain down Mona's cheeks, but her forehead smoothed and her eyes opened wide as she whispered only two words—"Show me." Maxine nodded her head and wrapped her arm around Mona's shoulders and gave them a gentle squeeze.

The room filled with a quiet reverence as the women reflected on all that had been shared. Alma, who had listened quietly as each woman shared her story, finally spoke in a tired, monotone voice, "Between Christmas and New Year's, Marco had a stroke." A stunned stillness filled the room and deep lines of concern cut across Joyce's face, while audible gasps could be heard from around the table.

Alma adjusted her position, sitting a little straighter in her seat. "Two nights after Christmas was our 20th wedding anniversary, and despite all the silence and difficult moments over the past few months, Marco offered to take me out to celebrate." Alma looked down and laid one hand neatly over the other, lining up her fingers until each was perfectly paired with its mate. "We were all dressed up and about to leave, when Marco started having difficulty speaking and couldn't stand up without leaning to the side. I suspected that it was a stroke and knew it was critical that he be taken to a hospital within two hours of the incident. I called 911 and we were rushed to the emergency room. They confirmed my suspicion and administered the medicine in time to halt the progression of damage. The effects of the stroke were bad, but would have been much worse if he hadn't been treated so quickly." Alma's calm, professional voice began to waver. "He's still in the hospital, and they don't know if he will ever speak or walk again." Her lips pressed together and her chin began to tremble, "I . . . just . . . don't . . . ." The words were choked in her throat and hot tears splashed down onto her unmoving hands. Her face turned downward, and her shoulders heaved forward. A single moan rose as if from the depths of her soul.

Joyce was the first to jump to her feet and rush to Alma's side. She squatted so low that Alma looked directly at Joyce's face, "You aren't alone, Alma. I'll stay by your side for as long as you want." Joyce's unflinching words emboldened the other women to break from small group norms. One by one, the women rose and surrounded Alma, and offered words of encouragement, support, and friendship.

Anne's clear voice rose above the rest, "Alma, we've got your back. Whatever you need, we'll do it. We'll be there. You'll never be alone with us around."

Alma looked up and her eyes grew wide with the circle of women who had knitted themselves like a protective blanket around her. As she absorbed Anne's promise, a weak smile returned to her lips. "What more could I ask for? God has blessed me so richly with your friendship."

Joyce straightened and looked across the room, squinting her eyes as she considered and then amended Alma's words. "We're more than friends, Alma. We are sisters now."

Chapter 39 – Dare #31: Anne, Alma

Better to live on a corner of the roof than share a house with a quarrelsome wife.

Proverbs 21:9 NIV

It was Saturday afternoon. Anne had had a tough first week back to school after Christmas break. The growing baby inside her was taking up more energy than she thought possible, and she wondered how she would be able to continue teaching after entering her final trimester. There were a dozen tasks to accomplish before the end of the day, but she reclined on the couch in the family recreation room. She had wrapped a soft chenille blanket around her shoulders and sipped tea from a large round mug she had thrown on a pottery wheel several years ago.

Transfixed by the fat snowflakes that floated lazily onto the outdoor deck railing, Anne contemplated her interaction with the drunken Tony after their New Year's Eve party. She had denied his request for more beer without being disrespectful or compromising her needs. She was proud of the way she'd handled the situation and realized that while some of the Dare challenges may have felt forced, the practice of engaging her husband in respectful ways was starting to take root. Determined to expand her respect toolbox in a lasting way, Anne committed herself to doubling her efforts in completing the final ten challenges in *The Respect Dare.*

Just as she finished her tea, Tony entered the recreation room, halting abruptly when he saw her on the couch. "Is everything alright? Do you feel okay?" His worried expression conveyed the deep concern he had for his wife, particularly after their scare several weeks ago.

"I'm fine, Honey, just enjoying the winter wonderland scene outside the window while the house is quiet. The boys are out trying to earn some money shoveling neighbor's driveways, but I don't think they'll be successful since most of the block uses a private snow removal service."

Tony smiled. "And you decided not to tell them, so they would get away from their video games and spend some time outdoors for a change, right?"

Anne smiled back. "You got it!" They laughed together and Anne noticed the tools in Tony's hands, "Are you starting another major remodeling project?" A worried look wrinkled Anne's forehead.

"Nothing even close to that," Tony assured his anxious wife. "There are some racks in the garage that I'd like to install so Pete can hang his wet hockey equipment out there instead of stinking up the house after every practice." It was a project that was long overdue, considering Pete's sour-smelling gear had been making Anne sick since the season began several months ago. "Want to keep me company?"

Anne looked down at the overflowing basket of laundry that needed folding and the messy stack of ungraded papers on the end table. Running her hand over the warm blanket tucked around and under her thighs, she was unsure if she should waste any more time neglecting her looming responsibilities only to sit and watch Tony work. Noticing the eager look in his eyes, she changed her mind and followed her husband, who began whistling the moment the garage door opened.

Anne watched Tony's focused movements as he measured and marked places where he would drill and attach extra-long hooks for hanging large hockey equipment. Sitting on the space he had cleared for her, she spied several tasks she could accomplish while Tony worked—organize his tools, sweep the floor, or throw away scattered pieces of wood. She also considered several topics of conversation they could explore. Before launching into action though, Anne remembered the present Respect Dare of being fully present with her husband, and remained still. She allowed herself to relax and appreciate the simple pleasure of watching her husband work. He glanced up several times to see if she was still looking, and smiled each time their eyes met. No words passed between them, but she could sense her husband's contentment.

After 40 minutes, Tony stopped whistling and spoke as fluidly as if they'd been conversing the entire time, "I've been thinking about checking out that Monday night group at church."

The sound of Tony's voice startled Anne from her own thoughts and she cocked her head, not understanding his meaning, and reiterated his words for clarification, "What Monday night group at church?"

Tony's voice was casual while he continued working on the project, "I think it's called Celebrate Recovery." With that, he squeezed the trigger on the drill and began a succession of tightening the evenly spaced screws that spread along the wall.

Anne's eyes opened wide and she stared blankly at Tony's back as he continued to work. Celebrate Recovery was the Christian equivalent of a 12-step program to support believers' recovery from hurts, hang-ups, and habits, including alcoholism, co-dependency, and other addictions. Her mind started racing as she thought about what people at church would say if he went to that meeting, and then counted how many months of sobriety he could amass before their baby was born.

Before she could share her thoughts and plans for his recovery, he continued, still facing the wall, "Yeah. A couple of days after our party, Joe from church told me how much his life changed for the better when he turned to God instead of the bottle." Her mouth opened to speak several times, but she shut it each time, remembering one of the Dare's challenges was to allow her husband time to process things in his own way. After several long minutes of silence, he spoke again. "Let's go check it out. They serve dinner at 7:00 and the meeting begins at 7:30." Anne's mouth began opening and closing again before clamping her teeth down on her lips to prevent herself from breaking his momentum. By the time he turned to face her, her expression had changed from baffled to placid. "So, what do you think, Anne? Are you in?"

Anne gently smiled and said, "I'm all in, Tony."

Alma finished her shift at the OB/GYN office and crossed the long bridge that connected the professional building with the main hospital. Marco had been transferred to the rehabilitation floor in order to begin a routine of occupational, speech, and physical therapy. Despite the high quality of care he had received, there had been little improvement in his condition over the two weeks since his stroke. The doctors were still unsure to what degree he would regain his ability to walk or speak.

Entering his room, Alma saw Marco propped up in bed with his eyes closed. The television was turned to a soccer game between rival teams from Barcelona. The announcer was giving a smooth, running commentary of the players' actions in Spanish, and after the referee issued two yellow cards and one red card for unsportsmanlike conduct, a goal was scored. "GOOOOAAALLL!" The commentator's deep voice bellowed out the cry for such a long time, Alma was convinced he did inhalation exercises to maintain his breath for such occasions.

The exclamation roused Marco from slumber and he opened his eyes, dazed and excited at first, then clouded as he took in his surroundings. Alma dragged her chair closer to the bed, and without a word reached under the blanket and took his slack hand in her own. Together they sat, fingers intertwined, and watched the soccer game to its completion. Lowering the volume as the players were interviewed, Alma turned to face Marco. The right side of his face sagged; distorting the face of the handsome man she had loved for such a long time.

In recent months, Marco had become distant, even harsh at times. If Alma was truthful, it was duty and obedience to her marriage vows, not admiration, which had kept her with him. One morning, in the middle of one of the most painful and difficult times with her husband, Alma realized with surprise that she no longer loved him. As despair had filled her heart, she remembered the wise words of her mother, "It isn't love that keeps a marriage together. Rather, it is marriage that keeps love together." Holding fast to the belief that love isn't an emotion, but a daily decision, Alma had trudged through her days, hopeful for change.

Looking at Marco now, Alma realized that while his physical form had changed, she was unable to detect any positive changes in her husband's heart. He no longer was able to communicate through words and his body was incapable of avoiding physical contact with his wife. Alma continued to hold his hand as she gave him updates on their children. Alicia had begun reviewing potential roommate matches for the fall semester. Max attended his first boy/girl party, and Mateo's hockey tournament over the long Martin Luther King Jr. weekend would be in Madison again. Marco's eyes were the only window into his thoughts, but it had been such a long time since Alma had looked deeply into the caramel-colored portholes, she was uncertain of what he was thinking.

With no other news from home, Alma grew silent. Thoughtful. Perhaps she could use this time of imposed quiet time to pray with her husband. "Marco, I'd like to pray together like we used to when we were first married." She searched his face for any indication of rejection, and seeing none began, "Dear Father in Heaven, thank You for providing wonderful doctors and nurses to care for Marco as he recovers. Please give him strength to do the work being asked of him during therapy. Protect him from any evil and reassure him of Your great love for him and mighty power to heal all things. Amen." Alma stood up from her chair and kissed her husband's forehead. Stepping back there was no perceptible change in Marco's expression giving any indication if the prayer had reached his heart.

Alma promised to return the following day after church and hastily turned and exited his room. She walked rapidly down the hall, past the nurses' station, and into the elevator. She waited until the doors closed, enveloping her in solitude, before she allowed the sobs to escape the tight space in her chest.

Chapter 40 – Dare #32: Mona & Maxine

And let us consider how we may spur one another on toward love and good deeds.

Hebrews 10:24 NIV

Mona logged into her husband's cell phone account. He was the primary owner of the family's cell phones, but she had online access to pay bills and monitor usage. In the past, she visited the website numerous times each day, searching her husband's phone usage for an unfamiliar number that might belong to the other woman. Today, however, Mona selected her own phone number from the menu of options. Scanning the first page of text message records, she recognized Stephen's number instantly. She scrolled down and saw that his number was the most frequently texted number. In some cases there were 30 exchanges in a single day. Many of those were during late night hockey practices, and there was a pattern of daytime texts that were exchanged while Aahil was away at work. Page after page of records. Mona realized that over the course of the last month, hundreds, if not thousands, of texts had been exchanged with

Stephen.

Mona couldn't remember the specific content of any of the
texts, but was certain they weren't flirty or suggestive. The texts
were friendly and familiar—definitely not sexting—but a heavy
feeling began to form at the pit of her stomach. There were no
saved texts between the two, because she deleted the threads each
time the phone left her hands. She didn't have anything to hide, but
knew Aahil wouldn't understand the friendly relationship, and
didn't want him to think she was being unfaithful.

Selecting talk minutes from the online menu, Mona pulled
up phone call records and the heavy feeling in her stomach rose up
to her throat and made her shoulders shiver. Nearly all of her 495
minutes had been spent with Stephen. Mona wondered how it was
possible that so many minutes and texts had amassed. She berated
herself for betraying her principles of fidelity.

Guilt hung heavy and pressed hotly on her back and
shoulders. How could she have gotten so involved with Stephen?
Despite her wholesome intentions, she had been drawn into an
emotionally intimate relationship with a man that was not her
husband. At the beginning, they shared only stories and
encouragement in the wake of their respective spouses'
indiscretion. Her pain had been constant and his messages
provided brief respite from her anguish. Over time, though, she
experienced a little thrill each time the cell phone notified her of an
incoming call or text, no matter how innocuous the content. It
meant that someone was thinking about her and taking time to
share a short greeting. In hindsight, she realized that over time
their relationship had evolved into a gateway to the physical realm.
She had felt a strong physical pull when he had kissed her, and
wanted nothing more than to escape reality and drown in his
embrace.

Remorse swept over her as she sat staring at the computer
screen. Damning evidence of her transgressions overwhelmed her
and the sick feeling in the pit of her stomach rose quickly. She
leaned forward and retched on the floor. After catching her breath,
she looked up from her bent position and spied the cord that
powered the family's computer. The Internet had provided the easy
pathway into a clandestine relationship with Stephen. Reaching
forward, Mona violently yanked the thick power source from the

wall. She heard a pop and a snap as the electronics gasped for electricity, effectively disabling the computer as abruptly as she had ended things with Stephen.

Holding the thick cable in her hands, Mona looked at the mess between her feet and thought with despair about the level to which she had sunk. She felt shame over the disgrace this would bring to her family. Was the betrayal in an emotional affair somehow more acceptable than in a physical one? She had shared her heart and mind with another; Aahil had shared his body. She had spent countless hours emotionally entwined with Stephen, when Aahil had spent mere minutes. She concluded that her infidelity was just as disloyal as her husband's had been. She knew without a doubt that the condemnation she deserved would be delivered in this world and in the next for eternity.

Before Mona could get up to retrieve cleaning supplies, her phone rang. Instinctively reaching for it and anticipating Stephen's familiar number, Mona saw a number she didn't recognize. A frown of worry distorted her face and she answered brusquely. "Hello? Who is this?"

The line was quiet for a second. A hesitant female voice filled Mona's ears. "Hi Mona. It's Maxine . . . from our small group."

Relief flooded Mona's heart and words spilled from her mouth, "Oh, Maxine! I'm so happy you called." Not sure how to continue, she abruptly stopped talking.

Maxine explained, "I just wanted to call and see how you were doing. After our meeting last week, you left the rink so quickly I didn't have a chance to talk with you."

Mona tried to cover her inner turmoil by speaking more loudly than normal, "Oh, I'm fine." Her lack of explanation indicated that she was anything but fine.

Maxine pressed on, "I was wondering if you wanted to talk more about . . . ."

Before Maxine could complete her sentence, Mona completed the thought, "Uh, the thing I shared at our meeting a few nights ago, about . . . ?" In frustration, Mona balled her free hand into a fist and clenched her eyes shut. Of course she couldn't pretend like nothing had happened after confessing her clandestine emotional affair with Stephen. "I'm feeling terrible about . . ." She struggled to describe him without saying his name, "my friend from the support group . . .?" Any further words were stuck in the back of her throat, strangled with the bile that was rising there.

Maxine sensed the futility of having this conversation with Mona over the telephone and suggested they meet at the coffee shop that was several blocks from the hockey rink. Half an hour later, Mona tentatively opened the heavy glass door and spotted Maxine waving and sitting on a large sofa near the back. She ordered an herbal tea and joined her friend who was feasting on a large chocolate croissant.

Maxine laughed at Mona's shocked expression over the unhealthy snack. "There's a gym at work and I'm going to have to spend a lot of time on the elliptical tomorrow at lunch. But today we indulge." Taking a large bite of her croissant, she motioned her hand toward an almond biscotti, indicating Mona could have it.

"Thanks but no. My stomach's a little upset today, and I don't want to push it."

Maxine's experience with coaxing information from employees helped her address Mona in her anxious state. "Oh?" This single syllable was powerful enough to elicit unsolicited gossip, true confessions, and long stories about dysfunctional office dynamics. It was equally effective with Mona.

"Oh, Maxine, when you called I was so upset. I had been looking at my cell phone usage over the past month and realized just how much time and attention I've been pouring into my relationship with Stephen." Mona wrung her hands so tightly that Maxine noticed they were turning a raw shade of red. "It seems there have been hundreds—no, thousands—of texts that passed between us, and probably as many minutes spent together in phone conversations." She squeezed her eyes shut and pressed her fists against her forehead. "I did this. No one tricked me or forced me into a secret relationship. I've been a complete hypocrite—condemning Aahil for his infidelity, all while I've been involved with another man. My marriage is ruined and our family will be torn apart." She opened her fists and pushed her fingers into her hair.

Maxine could see that Mona's hands were shaking. Grateful that she had listened to the Holy Spirit's prompting to reach out to Mona after church, Maxine reached forward and gently pulled Mona's hands into her own. She held them tenderly, yet firmly. "Mona, you made a terrible mistake, but it can be forgiven."

Mona left her hands in Maxine's grasp, but shook her head back and forth. "No, no, no. In my religion, adultery is unforgiveable. Just because Aahil had an affair, that didn't give me the right to ignore my vows of faithfulness and loyalty. In my country, we could both be put to death for our dishonorable actions."

Maxine patted the shaking hands of her friend, "In my religion, we believe that there was One that bore the punishment for all sins, redeeming us from an eternity of painful consequences. Jesus Christ was without sin, yet He died the most shameful sentence of death any criminal could receive—crucifixion on a cross. His blood paid the price of my freedom."

Mona pulled her hands away from Maxine. "I've listened to you and the rest of the women in our group talk about Jesus' forgiveness and your relationship with Him. Week after week, the story of His salvation never changes, and it sounds nice, but your Jesus did not die for my people."

Maxine looked straight into Mona's eyes, "Jesus loves everybody, and wants to spend eternity with us in heaven. The only way is through faith. We have a Bible verse that sums up the Gospel equation simply and beautifully—'For God so loved the world, that He gave His one and only Son, that whoever believes in Him shall never perish, but have eternal life. For God did not send His Son into the world to condemn the world, but to save the world through Him. Whoever believes in Him is not condemned, but whoever does not believe stands condemned already because they have not believed in the name of God's one and only Son.'" When Maxine finished speaking, her eyes were bright with joy and her smile was wide and dazzling.

Mona looked up at the ceiling. She took a deep breath and began, "I think I'd like to know more about your Jesus."

Maxine reached for Mona's hand a second time, "I would like to tell you all about Him. It's the greatest love story ever told."

Chapter 41 – Dare #33: Joyce, Jessica

Make every effort to live in peace with all men and to be holy; without holiness no one will see the Lord.

Hebrews 12:14 NIV

It was Tuesday morning and lingered at the kitchen table after dropping Justin off at school. A strawberry-cream cheese coffee cake taunted her. Since her shopping and beauty excursion with Jessica several weeks earlier, Joyce had been careful to avoid sugary foods that set up cravings for excess. As a result of her efforts, there were seven fewer pounds of flesh around her middle, and she thought her double chin was a little smaller when she studied her face in the mirror.

Joyce was delighted by the changes in her body and outlook, but the sweet temptation in front of her captured her attention numerous times as she tried to read Dare #33. After rereading the same paragraph three times, she finally stood gruffly and grabbed the coffee cake and serving knife. Carrying both to the kitchen counter where dessert plates were stacked neatly in the dishwasher, she cut a thick slice. Right as she was about to lift the cake onto a plate, she shouted, "No! I don't want to undo all my hard work. Jesus, give me strength!" She grabbed one end of the cardboard platter and folded the coffee cake onto itself. Mashing the two halves into each other with the push of her fist, she cried, "HA! Take THAT!" With a triumphant sweep of her arm, she lifted the object of her morning obsession and dramatically dropped it into the opened garbage receptacle.

Returning to the kitchen table, Joyce clasped her hands and bent her head low. "Thank You, Lord, for giving me the strength to avoid temptation today. Please make me crave You more than I crave sugar."

She returned to the table where she had left her book and journal and carried both into the living room. Settling into her favorite recliner, she took the challenge of Dare #33 and pondered the myriad of ways she had tried to manipulate her surrounds over the years. "Humph," she grunted aloud, "that stupid Eve, she eats the forbidden fruit, and I bear the consequence of her sin—a lifelong desire to control my husband!" Seriously wondering if there was enough ink in her pen to record all the instances, she decided to write overarching categories of the ways she attempted to control Jim:

1) *Try to get him to _do_ the right thing,*

2) *Try to get him to _say_ the right thing,*

3) *Try to get him to _think_ the right thing.*

"Yes," she thought, "that ought to cover pretty much everything." After a few moments she imagined the detailed answers that Jessica and Anne always produced at their meetings, and knew there was more work to be done in this area. So she started with today's manipulation, "I told Jim to wear his hat and gloves when he went into the garage to work on the clunky snow blower. That was *helpful*, wasn't it?" Remembering the heated discussion that ensued after he refused to don the garments, Joyce could see how she, in retrospect, had bullied him into doing what she thought was best. She added it to category one.

The evening before, Joyce had cajoled Jim until he called his sister and wished her a happy birthday. She added this to category two. Yesterday at breakfast, Joyce badgered Jim about the health benefits of eating chia, kale, and quinoa until he acquiesced and agreed that he would enjoy eating those ingredients on a regular basis. Category three.

Joyce continued writing transgressions. After only 10 minutes, she had covered three pages in her notebook, evenly representing each of the three categories. Her eyes opened wide when she realized how many times she meddled in her husband's behaviors—and she had only gone back four days! It almost seemed if each day was a constant struggle of convincing and manipulating her husband into one thing or another.

A thought occurred to Joyce and she began flipping back in her journal until she came to an entry from Dare #7—the day she had asked Jim if there was ever a time she made him feel like a child. She recalled his uneasiness at being confronted with that question. Jim had looked down at the floor, shoved his hands in his pockets, rocked back and forth on his heels and toes, and after several attempts at answering, had simply replied, "Nope" and exited the room as fast as his dangerously-worn slippers would allow.

Joyce's lips pressed tightly into a straight line and the skin around her eyes wrinkled deeply. It had become painfully obvious that she'd spent the better part of 40 years attempting to control Jim's thoughts, words, and deeds. She, like Eve did with Adam, tried to take the lead on nearly every situation. The result was . . . disastrous. The intimacy in their marriage had completely eroded away with every demanding order she issued. Instead of feeling like a virile man, Jim probably felt like a castrated eunuch. Joyce grimaced. It was going to take a lot more than a costly makeover and some lacy undergarments to put things right in their bedroom. After thinking a few moments, she knew exactly where to begin.

Jessica was rushing to pick up the girls' toys, shoes, and play-date backpacks before Bob came home from work. He had been working tirelessly over the past two weeks on a conglomerate takeover and his temper seemed hotter and his fuse shorter with Jessica for as long. She was searching for 3-year-old Ashley's coat, but was having no luck in the foyer, dining room, or living space. On a hunch, Jessica walked toward Bob's office. She remembered the girls playing Hide-the-Coat after lunch, and she suspected Ashley's daring personality had brought her into the room where she was warned never to enter.

Jessica rolled her eyes and very carefully pushed open the office door. Her eyes scanned the room, and she caught a glimpse of a pink hood, peeking around the side of Bob's desk. She grimaced and strode slowly across the wide room to retrieve the forgotten item. Bending over, she noticed several messy stacks of paperwork, spread across the desk. Standing up with the jacket in hand, she recognized the papers in one stack were from her credit card. Bob never shared financial information with Jessica. She didn't know how much they had in savings or even how much they paid each month for the electric bill. Bob had dismissed her early inquiries by informing her that he would always provide her with whatever she needed, and she didn't have to concern herself with his net worth. Coming from nothing, Jessica was satisfied with his answer, but now, seeing the charge card records out in the open, she grew curious.

Jessica tilted her ear toward the entry door, and hearing neither the girls on the baby monitor, nor Bob's car in the garage, she picked up the statement. At first the numbers with all the zeros swam in front of her eyes. It was unfathomable that her monthly spending for December ran into the tens of thousands. Scanning the charges, she felt her face grow hot with shame at the knowledge of how much money she had spent purchasing Christmas presents for Bob, Bobby Jr., and the girls.

As she lowered the statement back to its place on Bob's desk, Jessica noticed another statement—this one from Bob's credit card. A new wave of inquisitiveness inflamed her fingers, and she carefully lifted the eight-page record. The first charges were from Bob's suit maker, hair salon, and a string of coffee shops. Many of the other vendor names were vague and unfamiliar —exotic names of orchids were followed by "Enterprises," "Inc." or "LLC." Confused, she counted 23 charges from such businesses, some as large as $7,350. Rationalizing that those payees must be related to the corporate takeover he had been expediting recently, she stepped sideways and pushed the button on the large, flat-screen computer monitor.

The image that flashed before her eyes brought immediate reassurance to Jessica's rapidly beating heart. As beautiful as any family could ever hope to be, their family's Christmas portrait was Bob's wallpaper on his computer. Still inquisitive about the unknown merchants, she did a quick online search of the first company name. The links provided by the search engine provided vague references to commerce and services, but an uneasy feeling rose up and would not go away. One search after another seemed fruitless until a small "ping" sound escaped the high-end surround-sound computer speakers Bob had installed in the office. A red, flashing tab at the top of the online session screen caught her eye and she automatically clicked it with the wireless mouse.

The image that filled the screen and Jessica's mind was vastly different than the earlier family photo that conjured warm, safe feelings. Her stomach turning and legs shaking, she could hardly process the hard-core pornographic scene that invaded her mind. Repulsed, but incapable of tearing her eyes from the raw images before her, her knees buckled and she fell into the soft leather executive chair. Indecent sound waves pulsed in her ears from cleverly hidden speakers in the headrest. The screen started to shrink. As the larger than life images were pulled back into the screen, elegantly scripted letters floated to the surface, closely followed by the company's logo—an exotic, purple orchid that flashed with directions to "Click Here for More."

Dazed, Jessica fumbled with the mouse. Before she could click the blinking flower, a heavy hand roughly grabbed her wrist. The chair beneath her spun violently and she found herself looking at Bob's towering figure above her. The look in his eyes made her remember their New Year's Eve after-party, and her throat twisted so tightly she could hardly breathe.

Chapter 42 – Hockey Tournament

It was bitterly cold in Madison during the long Martin Luther King Jr. Weekend. The Agitators were participating in the traditional January hockey tournament, and the temperatures had dropped well below zero. Players and their parents were staying at a nearby hotel and hurried from their warm cars into freezing cold rinks with concrete riser seating. The majority of hockey fathers stood during games, but the mothers huddled together for conversation as much as for warmth, sitting on fleece hockey blankets from home and on pillows borrowed from hotel rooms.

The team had been humiliated in their first loss, 7–0, by a team whose home ice was less than 15 minutes from their own home rink. After suffering miserably for 80 minutes at the rink, players and parents hobbled to a local pizza joint for cheesy sustenance, liquid courage, and friendly consolation. Chicken wings, mozzarella sticks, and pizzas of all varieties loaded the tables while the hockey players replenished their reserves. The players laughed and joked loudly with each other, while their parents commiserated with beer and shots of spiced liquor.

All the hockey moms in the Respect Dare small group were in attendance. Alma initially thought she wouldn't be able to leave

Marco's side, but at the last minute, Alicia insisted that Alma take a break and go with Mateo and Max to Madison. Alma had been dividing her time between work and the rehabilitation floor of the hospital to be with Marco, who struggled to make progress. Dark circles under her eyes betrayed valiant attempts to conceal the exhaustion that shadowed her, no matter how bright a smile she painted on with lipstick each morning. The boys, who were also having a hard time dealing with the seemingly unending tension and sadness at home, were having fun trading friendly insults and jokes with the other boys.

Seated next to Alma were Anne and Tony, who also brought a sibling along to the tournament. Zach was only a year younger than Pete, so he knew many of the hockey players from school. Farther down the table, Joyce and Jim sat across from each other. Joyce caught herself four times wishing to interrupt her husband and correct something he had said, from the recollection of one of the hockey penalties to the color of the shirt he was wearing. With each near miss, Joyce gritted her teeth and restrained her constant yearning for dominance over her husband.

At the end of the table, Maxine and Samuwel sat with their preschoolers. Occasionally, Maxine glanced a few tables over to check on her daughter, Cynthia, and each time was pleased to see that she had equal voice in the conversations. Samuwel also scoped out the table where his daughter sat, but he was on the lookout for overly friendly advances from Cynthia's adolescent teammates. Samuwel's protective reflexes calmed over time when he observed the respectful and friendly interactions amongst the Agitators.

Mona and Aahil were sitting next to Maxine and Samuwel. The husbands immediately hit it off with a lengthy discussion over software trends. Both felt that social media was having a negative impact on young people and that kids needed to go outside more and play with neighborhood kids, as they both had. Samuwel lamented, "Today, it's all play dates and sleepovers. Everything is scheduled and carefully organized so that the kids are all having a positive experience. If it were up to me, I'd tell the boys to go outside and play a game of tag or hide-and-go-seek. But nobody's ever home—they're at dance class, soccer club, story hour, or a painting workshop. What are you gonna' do?"

Aahil nodded in agreement, "It was the same way when my

son, Samir, was little. Everybody had a tight schedule to keep, so we had to find something to keep him occupied. That's when hockey came into the picture."

Samuwel smiled, "How old was your boy when he started playing?"

Aahil responded, "He was 4 when he started learning to skate, and 5 when he played on his first team." The men continued to talk as pizzas and pitchers of beer were circulated.

Maxine nudged Mona gently and asked in a low voice, "How are things going with you?"

Mona looked at Maxine and realized she was doing more than making small talk. She kept her answers brief and vague, out of fear of being overheard. "I'm okay. Still a little of the same."

Maxine's voice barely made it to Mona's ear, "Have you had a chance to read that book I gave you?"

"The book of John, I think? No. Net yet. I brought it with me on the trip. Maybe I'll have some time to read over this weekend."

"Good. I think you'll find it very helpful as you search for answers." Maxine smiled, and sensing Mona's apprehension turned her focus on the twins, who were starting a small skirmish with the olives and pepperonis they had picked off their slices of pizza. Mona smiled and hoped that Maxine was right. She had been feeling the heavy weight of her betrayal for several days and it was difficult to bear. She wanted relief and if the book might offer a small shred of peace, she would pursue it.

Looking across the room, Mona saw Jessica enter the pizza pub and point to their large, boisterous group. The waitress gestured and led Jessica, Bob, Bobby Jr., and two cranky-looking girls to a separate table adjacent to the long players' table. Mona waved, but Jessica's attention was on the waitress. Jessica was wearing fitted ski pants and a yellow turtleneck with a royal blue team jacket zipped smartly. Her hair was swept up in a sporty ponytail and as she sat down at the table, she removed her dark sunglasses, revealing dark circles similar to Alma's. Mona frowned, but was distracted by Samir who had approached her in search of money for the arcade games and pool table in the back room.

Before she could open her wallet, the coach stood up and

gave his measly version of a pep talk to the players. He issued orders for the families to return to the hotel and make certain that everyone stayed out of the swimming pool, because they had another game at 10:15 that night. After the bar tabs were paid and the leftovers boxed, everybody began to dress for sub-zero temperatures. Mona turned toward Jessica's table, but it was deserted and the family gone.

Chapter 43 — Small Group Meeting Dares #31–33

After the long, cold weekend tournament in Madison, players and parents were tired. Six months, 40+ games, and hundreds of practices were taking their toll on everybody. The players' equipment was showing signs of wear and tear, and no matter how many times the elbow and shoulder pads were washed with ammonia, the sour smell of testosterone and locker rooms would not detach. By the end of January, hockey families eagerly counted down the remaining weeks of the 8-month hockey season.

Several hockey moms trailed their sons who hustled toward the locker room, late for practice. Five of the six women in the Respect Dare small group had assembled and were waiting for Jessica's arrival. Keeping themselves occupied with chitchat, Maxine looked tenderly at Alma, "How are things going with Marco?" At the mention of Alma's husband, the other women quieted and turned their attention toward their friend.

Alma shook her head, "I'm afraid there's been no change since last week. Alicia spent several hours each day with Marco while I was in Madison, but since he is still unable to speak or walk, they had little to occupy their time. The second day, Alicia brought a newspaper into his room, but he seemed to get agitated when she read about the political skirmishes in Chicago. So she began reading Psalms from the Bible to her father. Apparently the prayers of anguish connected with Marco; he listened to her read until her voice grew too tired to continue. After she finished, she took his hand and the two sat together for quite a while before he drifted off to sleep." Alma sniffled and dabbed at her eyes before continuing, "I was worried about Alicia being alone with her dad, especially since he'd been so aloof toward the kids the past few months, but I think maybe their time together was good for her. Perhaps it was healing for them both." Mona, who was sitting next to Alma reached out and took Alma's hand in her own and gave it a gentle squeeze before the two rested their entwined hands on the table.

Maxine spoke up, "I'm glad to hear it, for Alicia's sake. I know how special the relationship is between a father and a daughter. Cynthia was able to connect with Samuwel during the hockey tournament in a way that I don't usually get to see." She tugged at the gold tennis bracelet on her wrist and frowned, "Now that I think about it, I don't really know anything about the relationship between Cynthia and Samuwel. The only time I spend with her is travelling to and from hockey, or a weekend church service, surrounded by a thousand worshippers. I haven't a clue how they interact with each other!" The sudden realization left a worried streak across her face. The volume in her voice rose and anger filled her words. "I spend so much time at work, that I don't really know how any of my family members act with each other." Her frown spread from her lips to her chin. "What the hell am I doing with my life?"

Alma looked directly at Maxine. "Life changes quickly, Maxine. Don't waste a minute. Don't wait for the perfect time to slow down and spend time with your family. That perfect moment may never come." Alma looked down at her fingers encased in Mona's hand and gave it a squeeze. "That goes for all of us."

The room grew still for several moments. Mona jumped when Anne's voice interrupted her thoughts. "Speaking of the perfect moment, I suggest we officially start our meeting, despite Jessica's absence. We're already 23 minutes behind schedule."

After Anne read the group guidelines for a productive meeting, Joyce began. "I had a big revelation in Madison that quite possibly could change everything about my marriage." The women looked at her expectantly. "The last three Dares have got me thinking about how I spend my time with Jim. Even as I read each of the Dares and the stories within the Dares, I was convicted. I nearly choked when I read the Bible verse cautioning wives that it would be better to live on a tiny square on the roof than share a house with a quarrelsome wife (Proverbs 21:9). I mean, sometimes the proverbs are vague and open to interpretation, but this one is pretty straightforward." She looked directly at Alma for affirmation as she quoted the verse from the Bible. "It would be preferable to live on the roof than with a wife that stirs up conflict? Really?" Alma nodded almost imperceptibly, but her smile assured Joyce that she was speaking truth. "In my marriage, I've spent years guiding and steering my husband in a positive direction—or so I thought. While we were in Madison, I paid deliberate attention to the ways I tried to control or correct Jim, and recorded them in my journal. Halfway through our first game, I'd filled an entire page! By the end of our sixth game on Monday afternoon, my journal entries were so numerous and condemning, I considered making a dentist appointment to have my mouth wired shut!"

Joyce held up her journal and angrily swiped page after page, to demonstrate the magnitude of her offences. The women chuckled quietly, but their smiles encouraged her to continue. "I made it through the weekend gritting my teeth and biting my bottom lip to keep me from launching my "helpful" missiles at Jim. Apparently when I eliminate demands, suggestions, and corrections from my speech, nothing is left! I was so quiet that Jim thought I was feeling ill. He kept offering me chicken soup and ginger ale all weekend!" Joyce opened her eyes wide and twisted her lips in a dramatic way that was reminiscent of Lucille Ball, and invited laughter from the women. "Remember last week when I shared my plans for a romantic interlude? Well, I realized that I needed to make some big changes to the way I speak to Jim before I can reignite that spark in the bedroom. No WONDER Jim doesn't make any sexual advances anymore! I've emasculated him to such a degree that he might be afraid I'd order him to wear the lingerie!" The very image of Jim wearing a lacy red teddy was so preposterous to her that she burst into hearty laughter.

"Everything the author has been asking us to do has finally

sunk into my thick skull. The underlying reason for the lack of intimacy in our marriage is that I've been playing Eve to Jim's Adam. That's to say I've been trying to manipulate the things he thinks, says, and does for nearly 40 years." Joyce's voice cracked and her tone shifted dramatically, taking on a somber quality. "I am vowing to you, Ladies, I am going to make some big changes. I need you to hold me accountable. But more importantly, I need your prayers. God has opened my eyes and given me the willingness to change. Pray that it sticks and I don't give up and revert back to Joyce's way." She looked at her friends who were nodding their heads again. "Okay then. We have a plan." She looked around the room and stopped abruptly. "Hey, where's Jessica?"

Mona frowned, "I don't know, but I'm worried about her. She kept to herself when the team went for pizza, then I didn't see her for the rest of the weekend. Did anybody get a chance to talk with her?" The women shook their heads and looked at each other. "Maybe she's sick?" Mona looked around the table and saw her friends shrugging their shoulders, unaware of the reason for Jessica's absence.

Joyce shifted uncomfortably in her seat. From her time alone with Jessica, she suspected it was something more than the sniffles that had kept the young mother away from the others over the weekend, and their small group meeting tonight. Not wishing to gossip or unnecessarily rouse suspicions, she remained silent, but decided to check in on Jessica after her shift at the grocery store tomorrow.

Chapter 44 — Dare #34: Jessica, Mona, Maxine

Get rid of all bitterness, rage, and anger, brawling and slander, along with every form of malice. Be kind and compassionate to one another, forgiving each other, just as in Christ God forgave you.
Ephesians 4: 31–32 NIV

The grocery cart had neatly organized piles of organic produce, free-range beef, cage-free eggs, and almond milk. It rolled steadily around Saturday shoppers who occupied crowded aisles. Mid-way through the gluten-free aisle, the wheels stopped and turned sharply. Completing a U-turn, the cart moved back in the direction from which it came, picked up speed, and careened around the first corner. After nearly colliding with an elderly customer, the wagon rapidly zigzagged around floor displays, stock boys, and sales clerks. It ground to a sudden stop in the warm sweet smells of the bakery section of the store.

Jessica stared blankly at the fresh muffins and wandered idly toward the cakes. The brightly colored frosting poked at the fuzzy edges of her thoughts and her mind drifted to last night's dinner fiasco. It was Kayla's 2nd birthday and Jessica had hosted a party for all of her daughters' friends at the dance academy, where the girls were learning a routine for their first recital.

Since it was Friday, Bob was able to leave the office early and keep the girls from tearing down the pink and purple decorations, while Jessica frantically put the finishing touches on a ballerina birthday cake. She listened to the happy sounds of her giggling toddlers vying for their daddy's attention. Rushing to put pretzel dogs in the oven, Jessica frowned when she heard the doorbell ring, announcing the arrival of the first guest. She was still wearing jeans and a t-shirt, covered by her baking apron, which was layered with swatches of food coloring and flour. The doorbell rang again and Jessica knew she wasn't going to have time to go upstairs and change before all the guests had arrived. Looking into the microwave glass door reflecting her flushed face, she did her best at smoothing down stray hairs and traded her dirty apron for a clean one.

The sounds of guests arriving punctuated her movements with the cake decorator. She had worked on the ballerina cake for hours last night and now her hands were shaking with fatigue as she put the final points of color on the elaborate cake. Bob had instructed her to order a cake and have the entire party catered, but Jessica longed for the simpler birthday celebrations of her youth and wanted to do everything herself, just like her own mother had.

Sounds of excited preschoolers filled the living room, and Jessica wondered how Bob would be able to keep his cool surrounded by squealing little girls. She smiled inwardly as the image of an exasperated Bob stirred secret delight. The pretzel dogs came out of the oven and Jessica arranged them on a tray for the partygoers. The moment she opened the swinging kitchen door Jessica felt a new wave of adrenaline flood her senses. More than 20 spinning girls twirled in ruffled dresses and tried to impress each other with their ability to remember various poses and dance steps.

The mothers had arranged themselves into strategically positioned clusters preventing injuries to both the girls and the stately furnishings in the elegantly decorated home. As Jessica circulated with offers of pretzel dogs, she noticed several of the women in one group eyeing her in a less than friendly manner. Pushing aside feelings of insecurity, Jessica returned to the kitchen to refill the hot dog supply and reapply her lipstick. Hustling between the party and the kitchen, Jessica replenished lemonade, rainbow fruit cups, and the hand-made, dainty tea sandwiches for two hours without a single offer of help from Bob or any of the other women.

Sitting down for the first time that evening, Jessica supervised Kayla in the chaos of opening and recording birthday gifts. Two-, three-, and four-year-old girls swarmed Kayla and inspected every gift. Jessica had to work quickly to prevent kids from grabbing presents and ripping off the paper and ribbons. In the midst of the pandemonium, Jessica caught a glimpse of Bob leaning toward one of the mothers who was attired in an exquisitely tailored yellow dress and expensive heels. He whispered something into her ear. Jessica saw the woman draw back in surprise, but at that very moment, a loud scream yanked her attention back to the gaggle of girls, where one had just burst into tears. Mediating conflict between two preschoolers wasn't easy, but after several minutes of cajoling and comforting the girls, who were fighting over a princess tiara, they ran off to the dining room for cake.

Standing up to follow, Jessica looked over to where she had seen Bob, and realized he was no longer there. Unable to investigate with a dining room of partygoers demanding cake, Jessica led a chorus of the familiar birthday song. Splitting her attention, Jessica scanned the smiling singers who filled the large dining area and felt her stomach drop when she realized that Bob was missing . . . and so was the woman in the yellow dress.

Jessica felt a bump from behind, and realized with a start that she was still standing in the middle of the bakery section of the grocery store. Turning around in a daze, she heard a familiar voice. "Hey, Jessica, I thought it was you. Why didn't you answer me when I called your name?" Joyce searched Jessica's blank face for clues.

"Oh, hi, Joyce. I didn't hear you. My mind was somewhere else."

"You could say that again. You've been standing next to the French bread long enough to make a sandwich!"

Flushing pink, Jessica laughed nervously, "Oh, I'm just tired, Joyce. Yesterday we had a big birthday party for our two-year-old and I overextended myself in preparing the food and organizing the party. I baked and decorated a 3-D ballerina cake all by myself."

Joyce shook her head, "Jessica, you're a great baker, but you've got to learn to take it down a few notches. You're going to burn yourself out before your kids start kindergarten."

With that, Jessica's expression crumpled and she covered her face with both hands. Joyce was astonished to witness her friend's meltdown in such a public place. Jessica's fingers curled into fists and as she pressed them to her forehead, Joyce could see a shadowy bruise wrapped around both wrists. Never one to hold back, Joyce exclaimed, "Jessica! What happened to your wrists? Are you okay?"

Jessica quickly unclenched her fists and lowered her arms, allowing the coat sleeves to cover the place where Bob had constricted her wrists so tightly that her fingers had grown numb. She started to speak, but was unable to grasp the words to convince Joyce nothing was amiss. Instead, she unveiled her shame, "After the party ended last night, things got a little rough."

Joyce's eyebrows arched, "You mean Bob got a little rough."

Jessica's instincts were to protect her husband's reputation. She wanted to defend his actions, but the heavy ache in her chest crushed any ingenious rationalization she could manufacture. Her silence spoke loudly, confirming Joyce's suspicions about Jessica's perfect husband. "Listen, Jessica, I just finished my shift. Let me punch out and you and I can go somewhere for coffee or something."

Jessica bit her lip and taking a deep breath, her shoulders relaxed as if the tension she'd been carrying had been lifted, "I'd like that very much, Joyce. I need to talk with someone I trust."

Mona sipped espresso at the trendy coffee shop located a few blocks from the ice rink, and stared blankly at *The Respect Dare* book in her hands. The current Dare dealt with Jesus' gift of forgiveness, which was still proving to be a stumbling block. She had asked Maxine to meet her during Saturday morning practice so she could get a handle on the concept of mercy and absolution. As a Muslim, Mona believed that Jesus wasn't a deity; rather, He was a messenger, born of the virgin, Mary. He performed various miracles such as healing the sick and raising the dead. Through her studies of the Qur'an, she was taught that the Lord delivered Jesus from crucifixion on a cross, and took Him directly to paradise. This was difficult for her to comprehend—if Jesus was just a messenger who deserved crucifixion, how could He possibly deserve paradise? In her mind, there would be a Day of Judgment when Muslims stand in front of Allah and present all the works they'd ever done. Good deeds would be weighed against the bad deeds on a balance. She knew the heavier side of the scale determined where she would spend eternity in the afterlife—more good deeds and she'd find herself in paradise, but if there were more bad deeds, she would spend eternity in hell.

There was no sure way of being certain of the direction in which the scale would tilt, because nobody is able to keep an accurate account of a lifetime of deeds. Mona accepted that Muslims could increase the weight of their good deeds by leading people to Allah, and reap further benefits based on the amount of good deeds those new believers performed—similar to receiving a sales commission. She was frustrated by the Muslim belief that there was only one guaranteed way of assuring salvation—to shed your blood for the sake of Allah. Because she knew becoming a martyr was an unlikely route for a woman, she spent much of her life trying to make her good-deed side of the balance heavier than the bad, so she could go to heaven.

Mona's sole objective of joining the Respect Dare small group had been to build a support system of women who would encourage her to divorce Aahil. She laid the book down with a deep sigh. Dare #34 challenged her to consider a completely different approach—to push aside the score sheet of Aahil's good versus bad deeds, and forgive him. Could it be as simple as making a decision?

The concept of forgiveness was in sharp contrast with her Islamic beliefs, and she had taken Maxine's suggestion that she research it further in the Bible's book of John. Her confusion and questions had only multiplied after reading about Jesus' pure love for everyone He encountered, even those who were living shameful and sin-filled lives. In one account, a group of teachers of religious law approached Jesus with a woman who had been caught in the act of adultery. They were trying to trap the Son of God into saying something that could be used against Him. According to the law, the woman's punishment was death by stoning and the leaders asked Jesus what He thought they should do with her. Jesus told the group that whoever was without sin should throw the first stone. One by one, the accusers slipped away, unable to carry out the punishment, until only the adulteress remained. *"Jesus straightened up and asked her, 'Woman, where are they? Has no one condemned you?' 'No one, sir,' she said. 'Then neither do I condemn you,' Jesus declared. 'Go now and leave your life of sin'* (John 8:10-11 NIV).

Mona unconsciously tapped her fingers on the journal where she kept her thoughts for small group. If Jesus, who had lived a sinless and miraculous life, could forgive a woman who was guilty of an offense worthy of death, how could she not forgive her husband? Just then, Maxine rushed into the coffee shop, grabbed the latte she had pre-ordered and quickly settled herself into the stuffed chair across from Mona.

Maxine's voice was apologetic, "Sorry I'm late, Mona. I was baking cookies with the twins this morning, and lost track of time." Maxine turned her attention to the steaming cup of frothy coffee in front of her.

"It's okay. It gave me some time to work on Dare #34."

"Thanks, Mona. I've been doing Dare work during my lunch breaks." Mona's arched eyebrow and cynical look prompted Maxine to elaborate, "No, no . . . not like before. I've been blocking off a full hour with no phones, e-mails, or texts to distract me. My poor assistant was completely baffled that first week!" Maxine laughed heartily, carefully balancing her coffee so she didn't spill a drop.

Mona forced a smile, "Poor thing. You have to admit, that's a pretty big change for you." Maxine nodded her head in response. Her New Year's resolution was to establish clear boundaries between her work and family. She still wielded a big sword at the office and made heads roll when necessary, but

Maxine no longer stayed late or worked on weekends. Forty hours of work per week enabled her to keep up with deadlines and still have quality time and energy to spend with her family.

Maxine acknowledged Mona's observation. "You're right. Things have changed drastically, and all for the better, especially with Samuwel."

Mona's head tilted and she prompted her friend, "For example…"

"Well, when I'm talking, no matter how trivial, Samuwel listens. In the past he'd get impatient or interrupt me, but now he really listens. My husband stops whatever he's doing, looks me in the eyes, and doesn't break contact until I finish speaking."

"Amazing."

"I know." Maxine shook her head. "If you had told me five months ago that my marriage would be this sweet, I would have laughed in your face. Who would have thought that this *Respect Dare* would so profoundly affect on my life?" Maxine's smile diminished slightly when she saw Mona's eyes darken and her face tense. "Enough about me. You asked me to meet you here so that we could discuss your questions."

Mona's face relaxed a bit. "Yes. I need some help understanding a few things. I read the book of John last night."

Maxine's eyes opened wide in surprise. "The whole thing?"

Mona nodded her head and explained, "As soon as I started to read about the life of Jesus and His sinless and miraculous life, I couldn't stop. It was morning when I finished."

"Wow, Mona, that's impressive."

"We've been doing *The Respect Dare* since the beginning of September, and from the very start, I've noticed the confidence that you and the other women have in Jesus' forgiveness and salvation." Mona paused, then continued. "In my religion we must do more good deeds than bad deeds in order to earn a ticket to paradise. The problem is, we don't know how much weight each good or bad deed carries. I'm worried that the bad things I've done will outweigh the good." She was quiet for a moment, and then looked tentatively at Maxine, "How do *you* get to heaven? Will your good deeds outweigh the bad ones?"

Maxine took a deep breath and put her latte down on the low table between the two women. "No, Mona. I could never do enough good deeds to cancel out my sins."

A look of anxiety stretched across Mona's eyes. Maxine continued, "If my afterlife was determined by my actions in this life, there is no way I'd be going to heaven. There is only one way to heaven, and that's through Jesus Christ."

"What do you mean 'through Jesus Christ?' Do I have to pass some kind of test or something?"

Maxine smiled. "Here's the good news, Mona. We don't have to *do* anything. Jesus did it all when He was crucified. The blood He shed was the atoning sacrifice for the sins of all believers. His crucifixion and resurrection wiped the slate clean. Jesus covers believers in light, so that when God looks at us, all He sees is Jesus' perfection."

Mona put up her hand to stop her friend. "Wait, Maxine. It can't be that simple."

Maxine's smile returned full force. "Oh, but it is, Mona. God loves us so much, that He made it that simple."

Chapter 45 – Dare #35: Alma, Anne

A fool finds no pleasure in understanding, but delights in airing his own opinions.

Proverbs 18:2 NIV

Alma sat at the kitchen table surrounded by stacks of unpaid bills and unopened letters. She had taken the day off from work to handle important financial matters and tackle the dreaded insurance calls that she needed to make. The hospital was preparing Marco to be released later in the week and she needed to find a long-term rehabilitation center where he could continue treatment and hopefully regain his speech and the ability to walk. In order to do that, she was forced to navigate the snares of different phone extensions, on-hold music, and angry insurance processors who needed convincing that Marco's insurance covered rehabilitation after a stroke.

Alma sighed after getting off the phone with Marco's supervisor at the plant. His tone throughout the entire conversation was defensive. "I don't know how much longer we can cover Marco's insurance. Technically we can drop him after 30 days of not showing up to work. Unfortunately, we can't afford to carry your family, especially given the plant's relocation to Mexico in early spring. Marco's lucky, really. He can get disability now, which is more he would have had without the stroke." She was sure the supervisor had tried to sound encouraging, but the news alarmed her.

Alma's mouth hung open in shock as she listened in stunned silence. She knew that job security was causing Marco an extraordinary amount of stress, but she never thought the threat of losing his job would become a reality. After feebly thanking his superior and hanging up the phone, she considered the uncertain future Marco had been facing at work. She realized he had been quietly shouldering the pressing threat of unemployment alone.

How hard Marco had worked throughout all the years the two had been married! He'd even juggled several jobs at once; doing whatever it took to provide enough income for his family's needs. In addition to a steady income, he secured jobs that provided comprehensive insurance coverage—something that Alma had only recently begun to appreciate. Her husband had faithfully gone to his job every day, and when he came home, rarely complained about the steep problems he was facing at work. He had always paid all their bills, somehow stretching meager paychecks to cover the expenses of his growing and maturing family. Now that he had been in the hospital for almost a month, his income had ceased. The heavy burden shifted, and Alma was not sure how she was going to pay the usual bills, let alone the depressing stack of doctor bills that grew larger each day.

Anne glared at the tall pile of neatly stacked math worksheets that needed to be graded before school tomorrow morning. It was only Monday, but she was already longing for the rest that only a long weekend could offer. She had a doctor appointment after school, and then needed to drive the boys to church, where their youth group was meeting. She rushed through the crowded aisles at the grocery store before going home, and threw dinner in the oven before racing back to pick up the boys. Now their loud music sent sound waves vibrating deeply in her molars, and she knew she needed to start grading papers before she fell asleep on her lesson plan book. Again.

Just as she straightened in her chair and removed the cap from a red pen, Tony bustled in through the garage entrance. "Hi Honey. Sorry I'm late, but things got complicated with a union rep at the job site, and then traffic was awful. Hey, I know this is last minute, but if you haven't eaten yet, maybe you'd like to join me…"

Anne cut him off, "You've got to be kidding me. Are you serious?" Anne pointed to the papers in front of her. "I have a ton of work to do. Do you even know how many things I've done today? After a full day of teaching, I had a doctor appointment, played taxi driver for the kids, went grocery shopping, cooked dinner, and now I've got to grade these papers before I pass out on the floor. Hopefully the boys won't step on my head in their rush to the kitchen for a midnight snack."

Tony looked disappointed, then frustrated, and finally embarrassed. He mumbled, "Okay. No problem, I just thought maybe you could …"

"No, Tony. Whatever it is you're going to ask me, the answer is NO." Anne rubbed her forehead with the heavy force of one who suffers from migraines. "I think I've done enough for one day for this family. I wouldn't go with you if you were offering rides on a unicorn. End of discussion."

With no alternative, Tony, who was still standing in the entryway, turned and walked out the front door.

Chapter 46 – Dare #36: Jessica, Maxine

Those who sow with tears will reap with songs of joy. Those who go out weeping, carrying seed to sow, will return with songs of joy, carrying sheaves with them.

Psalms 126: 5–6 NIV

As Jessica sat in the empty dining room reading Dare #36, she felt a thick wall form in her chest. In this Dare she was taken through a guided imagery, which brought her to the throne of God. Once there, she experienced the warm embrace of the Father of the universe, who called her "daughter." The author told Jessica that she was safe in the arms of God.

When she read those words Jessica couldn't hold back the tears that formed every time she remembered her conversation with Joyce several days earlier. After asking pointed questions, Joyce had gently pointed out that Jessica's husband was not treating her as he was commanded to do. "In the Bible husbands are told to love and treat us as Christ loves the church and gave Himself up for her." Going further, the elder wife assured Jessica that God did not want her to endure any form of abuse, including that which was coming from Bob. In addition to offering wisdom and comfort, Joyce offered Jessica a safe place to stay for her and the girls.

"You can't stay with a man who is hurting you, Jessica."

"But, Joyce, you don't understand. It's not his fault. Compared to the people in Bob's world, I'm a simple girl who makes stupid mistakes. I forget things he's told me to do, and almost always embarrass him when we're in the company of his colleagues."

"Jessica, it doesn't matter *what* you do. It doesn't matter what you forget to do. Bob should *not* be hurting you physically, emotionally, or spiritually—and it seems like he's doing all three."

Jessica began to twist the large diamond ring on her left hand. She was silent for such a long time that Joyce had to sit on her hands as a physical reminder to restrain her tongue from launching like a rocket. After several long minutes, Jessica's wavering voice offered, "I guess you have a point."

Joyce confidently replied, "Jessica, you might not be able to see it right now, but you're in a destructive marriage, and you need to break away from Bob. Maybe he'll change, but that isn't your responsibility. If you can't do it for yourself, do it for your little girls."

At the mention of her daughters, Jessica straightened in her chair and looked Joyce in the eyes. "I know you're right, and I'll think about your offer. Thank you, Joyce." Jessica's phone, which had been vibrating throughout the entire conversation, emitted a ringing sound that made both women jump. She hastily reached for it. "I set an alarm on my phone so I wouldn't lose track of time. I've got to get home, Joyce, but thanks for everything."

Jessica rushed home, prepared to confront her husband and leave with the girls, if need be. When she opened the front door, squeals of laughter and pure delight filled Jessica's ears. She followed the happy sounds coming from the kitchen, and there found Bob dancing around the kitchen making smiley face pancakes for his daughters. When he saw Jessica, he laid down the spatula and approaching her gallantly, bowed, and asked her to dance in a loud stage voice, which prompted boisterous clapping from their youthful fans. Not waiting for her answer, Bob gently removed Jessica's heavy coat, intertwined her arms with his, and twirled her around the island where the girls were seated. As their dance neared its end, Bob whispered apologetic words in Jessica's ears and vowed to change.

Sitting alone at the large, marble dining room table, a battle waged between Jessica's heart and mind. She loved playing the roles of Bob's wife and the mother of their children, but she longed for the secure feeling that came when she imagined reaching up for God and calling Him "Daddy." Another sob pushed up into her throat but Jessica shook her head. She wasn't going to let weakness prevent her daughters from developing a strong relationship with their father, as her own mother had done in South Carolina, when she left Jessica's father.

The lights in Maxine's office were off and she was seated at her desk with eyes closed. She had finished reading the next chapter of *The Respect Dare*, and was trying to imagine herself as a tiny child resting in the comforting embrace of her Father God. She had no trouble envisioning her approach to the throne of God, but allowing herself to be small and childlike was proving to be very challenging. In her mind, every time she stood in front of God, she was a smart and powerful woman who was providing God with a detailed map of her life plans.

Intellectually, she knew that God's plans took precedent over hers, but she also wrestled with the awareness that God gave her phenomenal organizational and planning skills. Therefore, she rationalized, she should apply them to her own life, aiding God with one of His many roles in eternity. Rolling her eyes, she shook her head and spoke aloud, "Come on, Maxine. You're nearing the end of this Dare project and this is something you need to tackle. Now quit being such a big shot, and try again." She prayed, "God, please help me know what You want me to learn."

Taking a deep breath, she tried again. She began by walking toward God, seated on his throne. Again, she asked for help. "God, please let me become the woman You are leading me to be." With that, she let down her guard and allowed God to envelop His strong and gentle arms around her. His low, sweet voice filled her ears, and she felt her body relax until she was able to rest her head against His chest. She felt a soaring joy that was mixed with peace and complete acceptance of herself—just as she was, without fretting over imperfections. She had a sense of lightness, so light that she felt as if she was being pulled upward toward heaven into a bright cloud. In that very moment, Maxine opened her hands and outstretched her arms high to the ceiling as a little child reaches for her father. She uttered one single word. "Daddy."

Chapter 47 – Small Group Meeting Dares #34–36

For the second week in a row, Jessica's seat remained empty as the women begin their small group meeting. Joyce's cell phone made a loud clanging sound, and embarrassed, she searched her purse to turn off the offending appliance. "Sorry, but this was a text from Jessica." Joyce frowned. "She says that everything is fine, but she can't make the meeting today because Bob was stuck in the office and one of her girls is sick." The corners of Joyce's eyes wrinkled as the glare she projected into her phone became visible for all to see.

Anne caught the look on Joyce's face and asked, "What's going on, Joyce? Why are you making that face?"

Joyce shook her head as if to erase the telltale signs of conflict. "Well, Jessica is going through some difficult things at home. I think it would have been good for her to be here to feel our love and support." She considered for a moment, but then decided against revealing Jessica's struggle to the group. "Maybe everybody could remember to pray for her this week?" Heads nodded around the table and Anne took the reins and started the meeting.

When she was finished, Anne took a breath and began.

"I've got to share something and even though we're not supposed to cross talk, I'd like to receive some feedback. These days my brain is so scrambled by pregnancy hormones that I find myself overreacting to even the smallest things. It feels like I'm riding a fast moving train between the lands of laughter and tears." Upon hearing her invitation to break the group rule of 'no cross talk,' Joyce's face blossomed into a toothy grin.

"This weekend, I had to go shopping for maternity clothes. I felt like a big blob of ugly—all of my regular clothes no longer fit, but the maternity clothes all hang on me like my grandmother's muumuus." She shifted uncomfortably in her chair and readjusted her shirt. "I even had to buy new bras and underwear! Do you know how awful it felt to stand in the dressing room, with those garish florescent lights making me look so washed out, and to have a perky 18-year-old fit me for undergarments that make me look like a frumpy old lady?"

With that comment, Joyce's eager grin dissolved into a sarcastic grimace, "No, Anne, tell me what that's like. It must be awful."

Detecting the sarcasm in her friend's voice, Anne backtracked, "See, that's exactly what I'm talking about. My mouth is completely disconnected from my brain and I lose sight of other people's feelings." Turning to Joyce, Anne offered, "I'm sorry, Joyce, I didn't mean to offend you."

The grimace dissolved from Joyce's lips and she assured Anne, "It's okay, Anne. We've all been there. From inconsiderate comments to horrifying dressing-room tales, every one of us has been exactly in your shoes." Anne's face still registered apprehension so Joyce reassured her. "Don't worry, you're among friends."

Somewhat soothed, Anne resumed her share. "So, after a weekend filled with painful shopping adventures, I spent all of Monday racing to catch up with everything I neglected over the weekend—laundry, groceries, grading papers, and even a doctor appointment after a long day of teaching." She paused to catch her breath. "About 7 o'clock Tony walks in the door and starts inviting me out to . . . well, I don't even know where, because I bit his head off before he could even finish his sentence. I whined and complained about all my responsibilities and completely shut him down. In the end, he left the house without another word, and didn't return until nearly 10 o'clock. I was already in bed and too tired to argue. We spent the rest of the week avoiding each other, pretending like nothing happened. I don't even know where he went for those three hours. For all I know, he went to a bar and drank all night." She stopped only for a moment before addressing the group. "So, how can I hold him accountable for his behaviors? With this baby coming, he needs to grow up and share some of the burden of being an adult with me. I can't have four kids to raise by myself—two adolescents, one infant, and a husband!"

Alma looked kindly at Anne and spoke in a confident and smooth manner. "Try not to judge your husband harshly, Anne. It's possible that he's handling many challenging responsibilities without your knowledge." Anne looked at Alma with her head cocked to one side. Alma explained, "Before Marco had his stroke, he'd been more stressed than I'd ever seen him. Although he mentioned challenges at work, I assumed his distracted, moody behaviors at home were because of personal dissatisfaction. Now that I've been handling the bills, insurance, and communicating with his supervisors, I realize what pressure he must have been feeling to provide for us. This month, his plant moves to Mexico, effectively laying off hundreds of workers, and ending all benefits. Marco must have seen this change coming, and in the midst of hockey, our daughter's graduation, and orthodontist visits, he didn't know how we would manage financially." She dabbed the side of her finger at the corner of her eye. "Marco shouldered all of that burden himself. He tried to protect us by sheltering us from the very real threat to our way of life." She reached her hand across the table and laid it gently on Anne's wrist. "Try to slow down and listen carefully to Tony when he talks to you. I wish I had spent more time listening to Marco while I had the chance. Now, even though the therapists at the rehabilitation center are seeing small signs of progress, Marco still can't speak clearly enough to be understood."

Anne blinked a few times and then slowly nodded. "I will, Alma. I'll try to listen more and explode less."

Alma patted Anne's hand. "I know you can do it, Anne. Tony's a good man and worth the effort. Just give him a chance."

Anne smiled and transitioned, "Thanks, Alma. And now

before I burst into another crying jag, who's next?" Her genuine smile pushed aside the tears that threatened to escape their corral.

Joyce sat taller in her chair. "Well, since we're talking about emotional fluctuations and babies, I'd like to share that I spent some of my week taking care of my granddaughter. Janine has been having a bit of trouble with post-partum depression, so I've been helping out whenever I can. The doctors have assured us that Janine will get over this hump, but in the meantime, I'm enjoying every second with my little Sophia Joy." Joyce clapped her hands together and she closed her eyes with a smile.

Opening her eyes and facing the group, Joyce continued, "On a less positive note, I'm having some trouble with refraining from controlling, reprimanding, and/or manipulating my husband. About 50% of the time, I'm a rock star—capable of keeping my mouth closed long enough to fully hear what Jim is trying to say. At other times, I'm a diva, shoving my nose into his business and ordering him around like a stage manager in an opera house." She raised both hands, balled into fists, and shook them slightly in frustration. "I know, I know . . . at least I'm moving in the right direction, but I'm getting impatient with myself. When am I going to get it right all the time?"

Pausing to look at her friends, Joyce rolled her eyes, "Ugh. What you'd all probably like to say is something encouraging about progress, rather than perfection. And you're right. I just wish I had the habit of listening first and waiting to speak." The women continued to look at her mutely. "And yes, I know, this is a humbling process that is growing me closer to the woman God intends for me to be." She lifted her hands in a stop motion toward the ladies. "All right, all right. I'll be gentler with myself while I'm being more obedient to God. I'll keep trying and hope that eventually this respect thing sticks."

She stopped speaking, as if she was finished, but then started again, abruptly, "One more thing . . . I know I'm on the right track, because the other day Jim actually took my hand and held it while we were watching the evening news! And before we went to sleep that night, he kissed me . . . on the lips, instead of the cheek. Yes . . . there's definitely progress here." She folded her arms across her chest and smiled with satisfaction. "That's all for now. I'll keep you posted with any new developments."

The Respect Dare women rewarded Joyce's efforts with generous smiles and Alma even nodded in Joyce's direction. It was during that pause that Mona's unsteady voice floated into the circle of women. "I have something to share." Mona looked at Maxine, who smiled and nodded her head in encouragement. "On Sunday, I attended church with Maxine, and gave my life to your Christ . . . no . . . I mean I gave my life to Christ." With that admission heads whipped in Mona's direction and Joyce let out a loud whoop, while Anne squealed with delight. Alma smiled warmly and Maxine put her arm around Mona's shoulders and gave a tender squeeze.

"Everything happened so fast. I'd been reading the Gospel of John and was really blown away by Jesus' love and kindness. I was particularly impacted by the amount of forgiveness He offered to people while He lived, and for all time because of His sacrifice." She squeezed her eyes shut, and then reopened them. "You know I've been feeling really hesitant to forgive Aahil, and although I don't completely understand the path toward forgiveness, I want to know more. I want to learn about forgiveness, because I want to be forgiven for the secret friendship and kiss that I hid behind my husband's back." Mona wrung her hands and looked up at the ceiling. "I don't know what's going to happen, but I'm going to confess everything to Aahil and hope for the best."

Mona looked at the women seated near her and smiled. Somehow she felt peace, knowing that no matter what Aahil's response would be, everything was going to be all right. In the middle of the group's silence, the door to the party room flung open. Joyce had her back to the door, but swung around quickly, hoping to see Jessica, but instead it was the team's surly coach.

"Just wanted to let you know this was the last practice of the regular season. Playoffs begin this weekend. Here's the schedule." The blunt words tumbled from the unshaven mouth of the coach and he tossed a torn piece of notebook paper onto the table before the mothers. Without another word, he turned and exited the room as abruptly as he had entered.

Anne was the first to recover. "Well, on THAT note, I guess we should wrap up here. Since we won't have practice next Thursday, why don't we take two weeks to finish the final four Dares?" She examined the wrinkled notebook paper left behind by the coach. "It looks like the team's final playoff game is February

14, Valentine's Day. Let's have our final meeting while the team warms up, an hour before the game."

Maxine pulled out her datebook and took the scrap of paper from Anne's outstretched hand. "Sounds like a plan."

Chapter 48 – Dare #37: Alma, Anne

You also, like living stones, are being built into a spiritual house, to be a holy priesthood, offering spiritual sacrifices acceptable to God through Jesus Christ.

1 Peter 2:5 NIV

After a tiring day at work, Alma stepped off the elevator at the new rehabilitation center where Marco would be living for the next few months. As she rounded the corner and headed toward his room, she could hear lively sounds and laughter floating down the hall. Pausing outside his room, Alma quickly recognized the voices of Mateo, Max, and Alicia. The three had paid a surprise visit to their dad and it sounded like they were having a fine time listening to music and telling jokes. Peeking into the room, Alma felt her heart leap when he saw Marco sitting upright in the bed holding hands with Alicia, and reaching out with his other unsteady hand to pat Max's head like he had done a million times in the past.

Alma held her breath as she watched her family interact. Though Marco was still unable to speak coherently, she could see his lips moving and the kids seemed to be communicating with their father. Months of neglect and hurt slipped away as she heard her children tease their father in friendly tones and challenge him to jump out of bed and race them down the hall. Alma's mouth opened in a wide smile when she heard the sound of disjointed laughter rumbling low in her husband's chest. As much as she wanted to join the party, Alma feared her presence would somehow break the spell. She retreated into the family lounge until she heard her rowdy teenagers clumsily skip down the hall and head towards the exit.

After she was certain they were gone, Alma returned to Marco's room and knocked gently on the doorframe, indicating her arrival. When she walked into view, she saw him leaning forward in eager anticipation. Their eyes met, and he slumped back onto the bed and turned his head toward the wall. She felt a heavy sadness push down on her shoulders as she pulled up a chair near the tall stack of pillows that supported his upper body.

Alma didn't reveal her knowledge of the kids' visit, but instead smiled and reached for Marco's hand. As soon as she nestled his limp hand in her strong grasp, she felt a distinct pull and watched sadly as his hand fell back on the bed alongside his leg. She asked a few casual questions about his day and searched his face for some indication that he was happy to see her. Finding none, she was disheartened when she realized that he wasn't even making eye contact with her. His lips weren't moving and there was a tall, cold wall of impenetrable steel between the two.

Trying to cover her disappointment and sadness, Alma described her day at work, and reassured her husband that she was handling everything at home so he wouldn't worry. At the mention of home, Marco shut his eyes and let his head slump to his chest. After several moments of constrained silence, Alma pretended to believe that he was asleep and quietly left the room. Pausing at the door, she looked back and saw that he had lifted his head and his eyes were open and staring out the window. All of the hope and happiness she had felt at the beginning of her visit drained away as strode past the nursing center.

Her tears began to tumble as she exited the lobby and made her way to their rundown car. Once she was safely shut in her car, Alma's cries shook the collection of tools in her glove compartment. Mixed with her tears were shouts. "*Dios Mío*! Why are you doing this to me? This isn't fair! I didn't sign up for this when I got married!" She gasped for air, and continued to wail, "Where are You, God? Why can't I feel Your presence? Please reveal Yourself to me. Help me see that You are still here and that everything is going to be okay." At that Alma sobbed. Her throat grew dry and her yawns outnumbered her cries, until she fell asleep in the parking lot.

It was dark when Alma awoke to the sound of knocking on her window. Peering through the foggy glass, she recognized the security guard from the lobby and opened her window.

"Excuse me, Ma'am, are you okay? Do you need any help?"

It took several moments for Alma to respond. "Yes . . . Yes. I'm okay, and don't need help." She thought a moment and reconsidered, "No, that's not true. I'm NOT okay and I DO need help. My husband is upstairs in the rehab center recovering from a stroke. He can't speak or walk. It's terrible to see him like that, but even worse is that he's completely shut himself off from me. I'm alone. Completely and utterly left alone to face the problems of this life all by myself." Her voice was unsteady but her eyes remained dry. Her tears had been shed and there were none left to fall.

The kind, elderly security guard shifted his weight and then leaned forward so that his face was level with Alma's. The voice that came from his lips was warm and reassuring, "No, Alma, you are not alone. Don't you know? You are never alone. Everything is going to be alright." With that, he straightened, tapped the roof of her car, and walked straight toward the main entrance of the center.

Though he carried a flashlight and wore the jacket of a security guard, Alma was certain that she had just entertained an angel.

Anne had just finished another long Monday filled with the same obligations and activities as the previous week, except today there had been no doctor appointment. She faced another large, seemingly endless stack of math pages that needed grading, and she still hadn't prepared dinner.

It was nearly 7 o'clock when the front door swung open and Tony walked where Anne was sitting, her hands resting on the small bulge that was becoming more and more noticeable every day. Sitting across from her at the table, he patted the stack of papers that lay between them.

"Looks like you've got a mountain of work left to do, huh?"

"Yeah. Nothing new there."

"Um, I was wondering if you . . ."

Anne's back straightened and she interrupted Tony, "If I WHAT?" She heard the sharp tone in her voice and saw the hurt look that registered in her husband's face. Quickly backtracking, she started over. "I'm sorry. Let me try that again." She took a breath and shook her head slightly as if erasing a chalkboard. Speaking gently, she looked directly into his eyes and asked, "What were you wondering, Tony?"

Sensing no sarcasm or impending danger, Tony made a second attempt. "Well, I was wondering if you'd like to join me for a potluck supper and then a Celebrate Recovery meeting at a church not far from the house."

Anne blinked several times while a bunch of rapid-fire questions zipped through her mind and were dangerously close to being spewed like bullets from a machine gun. Instead, she remained silent and waited to see if Tony had anything more to say. He did. "I found the location online and went to my first meeting last Monday. The food isn't bad, and I enjoyed the meeting. The people are really nice, Anne. I was expecting judgment, but everybody was honest and searching for God's healing power."

Anne was blown away when she processed the things Tony was telling her. She wanted to jump up and cheer and ask him a million questions, but she took another deep breath and waited to see if there was more. There was. "I'm not sure how all the steps and principles work yet, but I made it through the whole week without drinking a single beer. What do you say about that, Wifey?" His smile and bright eyes matched the burst of joy she felt springing up in her heart.

Anne took another deep breath and responded in a tone that was warm and filled with acceptance. "Tony, I think that's wonderful. You're wonderful. I would love to join you for dinner and a meeting."

Tony beamed at Anne and they got up from the table. Taking her hand in his, he responded, "Great, but let's get going before all the good desserts are gone. It seems like all those recovering alcoholics really like their sweets!"

Anne laughed, and together they walked toward a new phase in their married lives.

Chapter 49 – Dare #38: Joyce, Jessica

Like newborn babies, crave pure spiritual milk, so that by it you may grow up in your salvation, now that you have tasted that the Lord is good.

1 Peter 2:2–3 NIV

Joyce laughed out loud when she read the title of the chapter for Dare #38—"Initiate." She knew there had to be more about sex than a single reference in a chapter, and perhaps the author had saved the best until the end, but here it was. Dare #38 in the *Respect Dare* book challenged Joyce to initiate lovemaking with Jim.

Over the past several weeks, Joyce had been practicing more respectful patterns of interacting with Jim—particularly refraining from controlling or manipulating his thoughts, words, and/or actions. This bad habit had taken years to develop, and she was reassured by the women at the last small group meeting that it wouldn't be replaced in a couple of weeks. To mark her progress, she kept a tiny notebook record of instances when she was able to restrain the urge to direct Jim, as well as the times when she failed to inhibit her directives. A quick review of her notes revealed that while there was still room for improvement, she was moving in the right direction.

The changes in her behaviors were reaping encouraging rewards. There had been little changes in Jim's actions around Joyce. He had begun to hold doors open for her again, and even surprised her with her favorite flowers last week. This Dare, however, would be taking a large step that was more akin to a leap. Despite her controlling nature, she had never initiated sex in all their years of marriage. She'd always left that to Jim, and because there were so many moving pieces to their busy lives, she didn't much notice the sharp drop of frequency in their lovemaking, until it had reached the point of nonexistence.

Tonight would mark the beginning of a new era. There was no hockey practice or game scheduled, and Jim had offered to drive Justin to Janine's, where he would spend the night under the guise of babysitting Sophia Joy. With minutes until Jim returned, Joyce turned on music and put the finishing touches on her makeup and hair. She rearranged the rebellious body parts that threatened to relocate each time her weight shifted. She could feel a kaleidoscope of nervous butterflies turning her stomach sideways, but was determined to accomplish the mission given to her in this challenging dare. Hearing Jim's car pull in the driveway, she lit the final candle, poured two glasses of wine, and leaned against the wall in the seductive and body-concealing way she'd practiced all afternoon. Taking a large pull from one of the glasses, she steadied herself as she heard the lock slide open and saw her husband standing in the doorway.

A similar stage was set in the home of Jessica and Bob. Soft, romantic music played in the empty dining room, where two candles had burned down to little stubs. Crystal flutes half-full of expensive champagne sat abandoned on the crisp, white tablecloth, surrounded by heavy silver and fine china. Jessica's carefully planned menu lay abandoned on the dining room table. Tastefully arranged plates tempted the eye with Blue Point oysters, tuna tartare, hand-trimmed filet mignons, grilled asparagus, and a delicate spinach and pistachio salad.

A familiar blue glow was emanating from Bob's office computer, where he sat alone with a transfixed stare. Rising from his desk and adjusting the leather belt holding up his fine linen pants, Bob roughly made his way up the stairs to the bedroom, where carefully arranged rose petals marked the way. It had been hours since Jessica had stormed from the table and had locked herself in the bedroom. It made no difference to Bob, who used his key to unlock the door and enter the dimly lit room. Once inside, he locked the door again and made a hasty advance on his sleeping wife.

Downstairs, the last droplets of candle wax dripped onto the stalactite that had formed on the table; leaving only the candlesticks to hear the deplorable sounds of Jessica's cries begging Bob to stop.

Chapter 50 – Dare #39: Maxine, Mona

For if you forgive men when they sin against you, your heavenly Father will also forgive you.

Matthew 6:14 NIV

Maxine and Samuwel sat alone at a desk in the car dealership, where they had negotiated a fine deal for the sleek sedan that Samuwel would be driving in exchange for his practical minivan. Holding hands, the couple was excited to finish the paperwork and see how the vehicle's refined detailing and specialized rims would look in their driveway. While they waited for the business manager to return, they reviewed the events of the hockey season, which was rapidly coming to a close.

Maxine was shaking her head, "I just can't believe that a college scout has been following Cynthia's goal tending this year. Who would have thought that our daughter would be entertaining scholarship offers during her sophomore year of high school?"

Samuwel squeezed Maxine's hand, "I know. Even though it's great, it also makes me realize that our little girl is growing up, and will soon be leaving home for college, and then adulthood. It seems like just yesterday we were buying her first pair of goalie skates. Time has started moving so fast."

"I know what you mean." Maxine nodded. "I can't believe another hockey season has flown by!" She thought a moment then continued, "So much has happened to us this in the last few months. Who would have thought that we would be sitting here after all our bumps in the road this year?"

Samuwel shook his head. "If you'd asked me six months ago where we'd be, I probably would have guessed divorce court."

"Yeah, things were getting pretty strained between us." Maxine admitted.

Samuwel remained quiet and studied the floor for several moments before clearing his throat and beginning. "You probably don't know this, but there was a woman—a mother, really—that was working with me on the preschool's annual fundraiser committee. It wasn't hard work, but it required frequent communication and coordination of a bunch of vendors." He continued to look at the floor. "We kept things professional, but spent an increasing amount of time together as the event drew closer. We worked hard, and the event was a huge success, as you remember." He lifted his eyes and looked at Maxine, who forced a smile affirming his valuation of the event. Inwardly, she felt queasy as she recalled the threat that had haunted her marriage during their dark days of tension and fighting.

"After the fundraiser, we still had tasks to complete—paying the vendors and scheduling a date for next year's event." Maxine felt terror rising in her gut and wondered why Samuwel had waited until this moment to talk about his connection to another woman. She wished he would skip the background information and get to the confession that loomed over her head like the blade of a guillotine. She could no longer hold the fake smile in place and it ran down her chin, like mascara in a rainstorm.

"A couple of days ago we presented our final report to the governing parent group and accepted their invitation to a celebratory lunch. After the meal was over and everyone was getting ready to leave, I went to the restroom, and when I emerged, my co-planner propositioned me—right there in the hallway." Samuwel's attention returned to the floor between them.

Instinctively, Maxine pulled her hand away from Samuwel and clenched the sides of her chair while she waited to sign papers that would financially obligate her for the next 60 months. Samuwel took a deep breath and asked, "Do you want to know what happened?"

Inwardly, Maxine exploded. Every expletive she'd ever known—in multiple languages—waited to drop like heavy cannon balls on Samuwel's head. Her thoughts screamed sarcastically, "No. Please DON'T tell me what happened next. I'd like to torture myself for the next forty years wondering how it felt when you had sex with another woman." Unable to force a single word from her mouth, Maxine nodded feebly.

"Nothing." He looked directly at Maxine. "Nothing happened. For a moment, I was flattered, but then I thought about how much I love you. How much I love our family. I don't ever want to do anything that would jeopardize that and would rather die than hurt you that way." Samuwel's eyebrows were arched and a look of anguish wrinkled deep folds in his forehead. "I don't know what started the change, but when I'm with you, I feel like a man. I know you respect me and that makes me love you more than I ever have before." He reached over and pulled on Maxine's arms until he was able to grasp both of her hands in his. "I am going to spend the rest of my life proving to you that I'm worthy of your respect, and that you will always be the only woman in my life . . . well, other than my mother and our daughter!"

A combination of laughter and a gasp of relief escaped Maxine's lungs and she pulled Samuwel toward her until their foreheads touched. Still holding hands, the two squinted intensely into each other's eyes, confirming what they each felt was true. After a moment, the dealership business manager swept into the room and cleared his throat, embarrassed to have intruded on such an intimate moment. "Well," he boomed, "it looks like we're all going away happy from this deal today."

Mona stood in front of the file cabinets and was nervous to the point of feeling queasy. Aahil had asked her to join him at the office on the biggest football Sunday of the year and organize some of his files while he finished a project. The office was deserted, and she couldn't help but stare at the empty desks, wondering which one housed the wretched Delilah who had twisted Aahil to satisfy her desires. Mona felt the heat rising to her face and more than once felt the urge to search through every desk drawer in the large office, hunting for evidence of deception and betrayal.

Mona had avoided having the forgiveness discussion with Aahil for several days, and the adrenaline that was surging through her veins made her uncomfortable enough to push aside her fear and face her husband. She didn't know how things would turn out, but she was going to shine the light of truth and pray for God's mercy on them both.

When Aahil emerged from his enclosed office into the large cubicle space where she sat, Mona took a deep breath and began. "Aahil, there's something I need to tell you, but this is going to be very hard for me to do. Please just let me talk and don't interrupt me because I might lose my nerve and forget why I'm doing this."

Aahil frowned, but nodded and remained silent. Mona began. "I want a divorce." His heavy eyebrows shot up and his eyes narrowed. She interjected, "No, no, no . . . that's all wrong. Let me start again." She took a deep breath. "I *wanted* a divorce. From the first moment you told me about your affair with one of your co-workers, I wanted to cause you as much pain as I was feeling." Aahil's eyes relaxed a bit and he cocked his head to the side. "For weeks, I was hurting so much that even my body ached. I wanted revenge as much as I needed comfort." Mona rubbed her forehead, remembering the pain that she carried like a lead coffin during the days after learning the truth. "Two things happened. The first was that I discovered an online support group for the victims of cheating spouses. The second thing that happened was that I joined a small group of hockey moms at the rink who wanted to improve their marriages. Each pulled me in opposite directions." Aahil's head tilted the other way as he tried to understand what his wife was telling him.

"In the online support group I learned about the many ways married men and women betray one another. I also learned ways to dig up the truth about your spouse without them knowing about it." Mona looked away, embarrassed to reveal the snooping she had done. "When I was participating in online discussions, I didn't feel so alone—I didn't feel as if I were the only fool in the world who had been deceived by infidelity." At that, she focused on Aahil and took in his sad expression. "The members of the group were supportive and encouraging. Sometimes they were the only motivation I had to get out of bed in the morning." She paused and took a deep breath before resuming her revelation. "After a couple of months of participating in the group, I became friends with one of the members." Aahil smiled at the mention of Mona's ability to forge a friendship during such a difficult time in her life. She continued, "His wife had cheated on him also, and it was helpful for me to see things from the male's point of view." Aahil's smile quickly faded when he realized her new friend was a married man.

"We chatted online for weeks in the chat room, and then when the group started becoming too large, we exchanged e-mail addresses and phone numbers so we could send written messages to each other. Sometime in November, Stephen called me because he was distraught over leaving his wife." Aahil winced at the mention of Stephen's name. "Our conversations began because he was in so much pain, but when things got easier for him, we continued to call each other." She stopped talking and realized that she was drawing out the description of her relationship with Stephen to stall the inevitable revelation of her guilt. Shaking her head, Mona drove straight to the point, "One day we met in the city for lunch and we kissed."

Silence rang loudly in Mona's ears and she stared at Aahil's face while he processed the information she had just delivered. Seeing his lips move, fear rose in her chest. Worried that Aahil would say something terrible before she finished telling him everything, she quickly forged ahead. "The second thing that happened had a completely different effect. I started a friendship with some of the other hockey moms who were committed to improving their marriages. Together we began reading a book and sharing our thoughts and experiences. I listened to the women talk about forgiveness of sins—those of their husbands, and their own bad deeds." One of Aahil's eyebrows shot up again, betraying the suspicion he was feeling.

"After the single kiss—and it was only one kiss—I felt ashamed and afraid of what you'd do. It was about that time that I began to learn about the ways Jesus forgave others and died so that we could be washed clean of all of our sins and guilt. If Jesus, who was perfect, could forgive the most unimaginable sins, then I should be able to forgive you for what you did."

Mona cleared her throat and continued, "Aahil, I forgive you for having an affair. I forgive you, and . . ." Her voice became tangled with a large gulp of air and she concluded weakly, "and I ask forgiveness for betraying your trust in me." Instead of feeling terrified, relief flooded Mona. She had successfully accomplished her mission of forgiving Aahil and confessing her faults to him. She felt a strange peace, despite not knowing how he was going to react.

Aahil slowly folded his arms across his chest, and then deliberately returned them to his sides. Mona saw his fists clench and unclench several times. He took a deep breath, cleared his throat, and after several long moments looked at Mona with serious eyes and said, "Tell me more about this Jesus and His forgiveness.

Chapter 51 — Dare #40: Alma, Joyce, Jessica

The fear of the Lord is the beginning of wisdom; all who follow his precepts have good understanding. To him belongs eternal praise.
Psalm 111:10 NIV

Alma sat quietly in the corner of Marco's room while he worked with a physical therapist downstairs in the PT department. She could hear the therapist's encouraging voice from down the hall as she pushed Marco's wheelchair back toward his room. As they rounded the corner, Alma could see that he was alert and there was a slight smile on his face. However, the moment he saw Alma sitting there, his face fell and he looked away from her.

The therapist also saw Alma and the two exchanged pleasantries. The therapist gave her an overview of the exercises Marco was doing in the center, emphasizing those he should continue once he returned home. While the two women spoke, Marco stared blankly out the window, and made no attempts at communicating with either. The therapist helped him into bed and before leaving the room, reminded him to keep pushing forward.

Alone with her husband, Alma stared at the man who

would not lift his eyes to hers. She felt rejected and alone. She was aware of the fact that Marco's spirits were higher and his connections were stronger with everybody but his wife. Despite the fact that he didn't speak a word, his actions were virtually shouting his desires to remain disconnected from her.

Feeling despair clutching at her heart, Alma recalled the incident with the security guard in the parking lot several days ago. Since that encounter with God's messenger, she had spent many hours in prayer and meditation. She was confident that God would remain with her for the duration of this trial, and that He would equip her with the tools she needed to survive the storm. After many months of searching for God's peace, she once again felt reassurance that God could make beauty from ashes—including the remnants of her marriage.

Alma trusted that, for reasons unknown to her, God had allowed this scenario to unfold in Marco's life, and His plans were always perfect. Sitting in Marco's room while he ignored her was painful and prompted Alma to speak the truth in love. "Marco, I'm your wife and have promised to stay with you in good times and bad, and will see you through sickness and health. I still love you, and I'm not going anywhere, but your attitude toward me is causing me pain. I know you better than anybody in this whole world, and know that you're pulling away from me—just like you've been pulling away from me for the past year."

She took a moment and inhaled slowly to maintain control of her volume and tone. "I don't know why you're hiding, but I have a greater appreciation for all of the financial pressures you've been under at work." She thought she saw his lips twitch, but he made no attempt to communicate further. "I'm doing my best to handle everything with your supervisor, the kids, the bills, and insurance adjusters, but I miss *you*. I don't expect you to jump out of the bed or have a long conversation with me. But it would give me strength and courage if I could see your eyes and you didn't pull your hand out of mine when I sit with you."

Marco made no move to honor Alma's request; instead, he continued to stare at the dreary February sky through the cloudy glass windows. "It's entirely up to you, Marco, but I'm keeping my marriage vow to you—and will do so until the day I die. So you can keep staring out that ugly window, if you want. It won't change things. I'll continue to be the wife that God expects me to be." She stood up, bent over, and planted a soft kiss on his forehead. "Goodbye, Marco. I'll see you tomorrow." Without waiting for a response, or lack of response, she turned and walked out of the room and onto the path that God had prepared for her.

Joyce answered her cell phone on the fourth ring, late Wednesday night. She didn't recognize the number, and was surprised to hear Jessica's voice at the other end.

"Joyce, I think I need your help."

"Jessica? Are you all right? Are the girls safe?"

"Physically we're fine. But I'm so messed up, I can't think straight. It feels like I'm losing my mind." Jessica's voice waivered and took on a higher pitch than normal. Her South Carolina accent was more pronounced than Joyce had ever heard and she wondered about her current state.

"Jessica, where are you? What's going on?"

"I'm at home with the girls. Bob went out of town this morning to visit and inspect a struggling corporation that he might acquire."

Relieved that Jessica was not in immediate danger, Joyce offered, "Would you like me to come over, Jessica? We could talk . . . or not talk." Without seeing Jessica's face, Joyce was having a hard time interpreting the seriousness of the situation.

"No, I don't want to wake the girls. Maybe I shouldn't have called this late."

Joyce reassured Jessica, "Don't worry about it. Jim and I have been staying up quite late these days." At the mention of his name, Jim looked up from the book he was reading and wiggled his eyebrows at her in a suggestive manner. She smiled, but swatted away any romantic thoughts either might be having.

Jessica asked, "Do you remember what we talked about in the bakery section of the grocery store? I tried to overlook some of Bob's flaws. I mean, he's an elder at church and a great father . . . but things seem to be getting worse. He's spending more and more time in front of his computer looking at . . . at . . . pornography."

Joyce could imagine the bright shade of red that characteristically spread across Jessica's face whenever she was embarrassed. Not wishing to steamroll the conversation, she wisely replied, "I see."

"Yes, Joyce. He's spent thousands of dollars on porn and who-knows-what-all he does with other women!" Joyce was thankful that Jessica couldn't see her face, because her eyes were wide and filled with surprise. "He stays up late in front of his computer until the wee hours of the morning. When he finally comes to bed, he wakes me up roughly, suggesting we try something new—usually repulsive.

"Then the next morning he comes down to breakfast and greets me and the girls like nothing happened. He looks as if he stepped right out of court or a church service." Jessica was quiet for a few minutes, and Joyce wondered if someone had entered her room. But Jessica continued, "That confuses me the most—how can he be one man in the bedroom at night, and a completely different man the next morning? He tells me how much he loves me and never had another woman in his life who he trusted enough to experiment the ways I enable him to do." Joyce frowned at the emotional manipulation Jessica was experiencing.

"What am I doing wrong, Joyce? I must be giving off some type of vibe that's encouraging these types of behaviors! Was it because I slept with him before we married? Oh, I'm a terrible person!" While Jessica had been asking those questions, Joyce had heard several short breaks in the line, similar to when another call is coming in on call waiting. "Uh-oh. It's Bob calling. I have to answer this, Joyce. We'll talk more tomorrow at our meeting, okay? B ..." Jessica's final words were chopped in her haste to take the call from her controlling husband.

Joyce's mind was a jumble of thoughts and emotions. Jessica needed help seeing the truth in this tangled and twisted situation—the kind of help that her Christian sisters could readily offer.

Chapter 52 —Final Small Group Meeting

Dares #37—40

It was Valentine's Day and the ice rink was decorated in red hearts with white lacy edges. The Agitators were in the playoffs and about to play their final game. Their record was 7 wins - 38 losses, and they wouldn't be advancing into the championship round. With the coach's poor sportsmanship and complete lack of leadership, the team and their families were limping to the finish line of a very long season.

The only positive accomplishment of which the team could boast was that there were zero concussions, bone fractures, or dislocations in the bunch. Some hockey moms found glory in the injuries—"my son had three concussions, a fractured tibia and a dislocated shoulder," but Alma wasn't one of them. Regardless of the score, she considered it a win whenever Mateo and his teammates skated off the ice without the assistance of crutches, stretchers, or paramedics.

While the team warmed up and had a strategy session in the locker room, the Respect Dare small group met for the last time. There was a sense of finality as the wives entered the party room, but more than that, they felt the deep friendship that bonded them to one another, sharply contrasting with the light-hearted interactions that were typical of hockey families. The hugging and eye contact alone in the glass-walled party room caught the envious attention of several other hockey moms standing in the cold lobby.

Just as the assembled women were taking their seats, Jessica flung open the door and tumbled into the room. Her hair was messy and her clothes were wrinkled. Her face was puffy and there were visible red blotches across her face and neck. All the women looked up when she entered, and somewhat out of breath, her high-pitched voice sounded forced and plastic. "Hi, Ladies. Happy Valentine's Day! Sorry I'm a little late, but Bob is out of town and I had to get the girls to dance by myself. It took me a little longer than I planned to get the pink chocolate ganache hearts on my special chocolate raspberry mousse cups. Surprise! I hope you like them."

Most of the women were delighted by Jessica's offering, but Joyce simply frowned and folded her arms across her chest in silence. While the carrying case of elegant snacks was passed and appreciative "oohs" and "mmms" filled the room, Joyce tried to read Jessica's face for clues to her state of being. It might have been her imagination, Joyce thought, but it seemed that Jessica was looking everywhere except at Joyce. Before she could say anything to catch Jessica's attention, Anne began the meeting.

"Now that we've completed all 40 Dares, and considering today is Valentine's Day, I thought it would be appropriate for each of us to take a look back at the ground we've covered, and share the things that are different in our lives as a result of this process." The women delicately nibbled at their mousse cups and considered Anne's request.

Anne continued, "Maybe I should start, since I had a longer time to think about this prompt." Looking around the table at the nodding heads, Anne rubbed her protruding belly and began. "At the beginning of this journey, I fully believed all my problems were caused by Tony's drinking. I expended all my energy trying to keep everything spinning smoothly—the boys' schoolwork, my classes, our home, Tony's business, and even how we were perceived by others at church."

Several knowing smiles and nodding heads assured Anne that she was not alone. "A couple of weeks ago, I joined Tony at a Celebrate Recovery meeting in a church near our home. Celebrate Recovery is a Christ-centered weekly meeting that helps people overcome addictions, hurts, and hang-ups. I went with Tony, thinking my presence would ensure he stay on the right track and recover from his alcohol dependence."

Anne smiled at the memory of her motivations for attending the first CR meeting. "The men and women at the meeting looked like regular people—not dirty or crazy like I imagined they'd be. There was a teaching that first night about denial—and how people ignore their need for help. After the worship, the men and women separated and shared their thoughts about the lesson. I listened to all different types of women share their experiences of living in an alcoholic home. I was surprised at how bitter and controlling some of them seemed. But there was one woman who smiled a lot and spoke with such peace and confidence."

Anne looked up and rubbed her forehead. "She described different parts of her life—how difficult it had been to live with a husband who drank too much, and then she described how much more difficult life had become when he stopped drinking. I couldn't understand how her life was worse when the problem was removed, and decided he must have been sneaking alcohol behind her back." Anne's hands returned to her belly and she laughed. "The very next thing she said completely blew me away—she admitted that she also had an addiction—something called co-dependency—in which she played an active role in sustaining her husband's addiction. But when he stopped drinking, her co-dependent behaviors became even more pronounced. I'm not quite sure about all of the nuances of co-dependency, but I'm pretty sure I have more than a few symptoms. Instead of "curing" Tony of his addiction to alcohol I have to focus on my own recovery from controlling and manipulating behaviors. I've got a lot to learn, and though this is all foreign to me, I'm looking forward to moving into a healthier way of thinking and living."

Enthusiastic clapping erupted and even a couple of "Congratulations, Anne" were passed along. Maxine, who was sitting next to Anne, patted her on the back and spoke. "My journey in this experience has been filled with extreme highs and depressing lows. When I first offered to lead this group, I only did it because I thought "you all" needed help improving your lives and marriages." Appreciative laughter bounced around the table. "I thought the Dares were simplistic and designed for women who had no other ambitions in life than to be barefoot and pregnant, while making pancakes in their cave." Maxine's ironic smile matched the snorts and laughs.

"I went through the motions of completing the Dares, until they started to paint the picture of a Godly woman that I was afraid to become. That's when I dropped out of the group. I wasn't ready to trust God to lead me into a new pattern of acting in my marriage." Maxine's voice continued in a more serious tone. "Then my marriage imploded. I was in so much pain that I was willing to try a new path, the one that God wanted me to follow. As soon as I began to trust Him and surrender my grand plans and expectations, things dramatically improved with Samuwel. It wasn't always easy, but in my second go-round with the Dares, I did each one fully, no matter how naïve I thought it was." She smiled at the women, who, at different points of their journeys had admitted to similar feelings.

"Now I know why God led me to this Respect Dare experiment—and that it happened at exactly the right moment. There was a landmine in our marriage road that I didn't see, but God saw it. If it weren't for the changes in my habits and actions with Samuwel, I believe the bomb would have exploded and destroyed our lives and our family." Her voice cracked and she took a sip of water from the glass bottle in front of her. "I'm grateful that God led me here to you and this work. I'm blessed by our friendships and am thankful to each and every one of you for encouraging me and joining me on this adventure." When she finished speaking, the women clapped for Maxine's progress as much as her friendship.

Taking the initiative, Mona's voice stood out from the receding applause. "Well, it looks like we're going around the circle tonight, so I guess it's my turn." She put her right arm around Maxine's shoulders. "My friend Maxine has been instrumental in helping me understand forgiveness. When you invited me to join your group last fall, I was filled with hatred for my husband, and only agreed to participate in order to build a cheering squad that would support my decision to get a divorce."

This was the first time she verbalized her initial motivation for joining the small group, and it felt like a dark secret had been lifted from her conscience. "I knew it was wrong, but I was so filled with loathing that I couldn't see any other way out of my personal prison." Mona patted Maxine's shoulder. "But then I started to get to know you girls. The more I observed your hope in the middle of terrible situations, the more curious I became about your love of God and faith in Jesus' saving sacrifice. Over time, I felt conflicted between the teachings of Allah and the living Spirit I saw working in you and your marriages. I was most impressed by the fact that you didn't constantly carry the weight of your sins and faults, as I'd felt condemned to do for the rest of my life. At the time I didn't know what it was, but today I know and call myself a Christian."

A whistle, a hoot, and a loud cheer rose up from Mona's sisters around the table. Maxine stood and lifted her hands to heaven, shouting, "Praise to you, Jesus!"

Mona giggled nervously. "And as a baby Christian, I wanted to start with a clean slate, so last week, I confessed my secret relationship with Stephen to my husband. I even told Aahil about the kiss." The room fell silent. "Before I finished, I described the power of forgiveness, and told him that I forgave him for his infidelity. I also asked him to forgive me."

She paused and observed the dramatically eager faces of the women around her. "Well, he didn't forgive me outright, but asked me to tell him more about Jesus and the plan of forgiveness. I'm not sure if I said the right things, but Aahil, Samir, and I joined Maxine's family at church the following Sunday." Mona smiled sheepishly before confessing, "I don't think Aahil enjoyed the service, but who knows where this will go? All I know is that I'm not afraid to take the next steps because God is directing my feet." She looked at the soft faces of her friends. "Thank you, sisters, for your patience with me, and accepting me just as I was. If it weren't for you, I'm sure my life wouldn't be the same." When she indicated she had finished speaking with her signature shoulder shrug, all of the women moved to hug her in a large group hug, resembling hockey players after a goal. The only difference was that Mona's goal had eternal implications.

Joyce spoke above the celebration, "Mona, I'm delighted that you're part of our family in Christ! It's always a celebration when a new member is admitted to the Kingdom of God." The women nodded as they made their way back around the table. "Well, Gals, it looks as if it's my turn to reveal the fruits of my efforts with these Dares. My story, as I now understand it, is quite straightforward, really. After being married to me for almost 40 years, Jim had his masculinity beat out of him by my constant nagging and manipulating. I learned that it was my behaviors that were pushing him into a corner, which made authentic intimacy nearly impossible. Truly, I've learned so much during my time with you wonderful ladies. On a side note, Anne, I think your Celebrate Recovery group is something that might help me stay on the right track. Can you give me the meeting information before we leave?" Anne nodded her head and smiled knowingly.

Joyce returned to her original thought, "Basically I was losing the battle of Eve's curse. I wanted to control the things Jim said and did, so that things would run, as they should—or at least how *I* thought they should go. The more I minded my own business and less of Jim's, the closer he was able to get to me. And since I'm a girl that doesn't like to kiss and tell, I'll only say that the completion of the 40 Dares has brought a very satisfying element back into our lives." While the room swelled with catcalls and whistles, Joyce finally caught Jessica's eye, only to lose it when she turned quickly to search for something in her purse.

Joyce happily accepted everyone's affirmations and turned her attention to Alma, who had hugged Joyce more fiercely than any of the other wives. Alma cleared her throat and then began in a calm and peaceful voice. "I'm so happy for you, Joyce. I'm glad that you and Jim have rediscovered one of the greatest blessings of marriage." She grew quiet, then smiled. "I'm at a point in my life that I accept the way things are. I wouldn't have chosen this road for our family and my marriage, but here we are, and God is with us. Marco and I still have giant walls to hurdle, and I have faith that God will give us the humility and courage to do just that." Her smile had softened into a wistful, longing expression.

"I miss the relationship I once had with my husband—the emotional connection and the physical closeness. But this test is teaching me an important lesson. No person—not a husband, or a child, or a parent, or a sibling—was designed to meet and satisfy all of our needs. There is only one that can fill the hole inside my heart, and that is God. It has always been God. I think I made my relationship with Marco and the kids a higher priority than my relationship with God for many years. Today my focus is on my Heavenly Father, with my family running a close second place."

Alma's confidence returned and her voice was strong. "Like Mona, I don't know what the future holds for me and Marco, but no matter what happens I will stay obedient to God's will for my life. I'll keep my marriage vows and get a little closer to being the woman God made me to be. I'm grateful for the women God has brought in my life to remind me that He is the Creator and Master of all things—and I love you all." While the women again rose from their seats to surround Alma with hugs and kind words, Joyce noticed that Jessica had moved to a corner of the room and was whispering into her phone. She chewed on her bottom lip and a frown rippled the smooth skin on her forehead.

Jessica got off the phone just as the women were returning to their chairs, so only Joyce had noticed the interruption. She watched Jessica stash her phone in the designer purse and smooth her hair and apply a coat of lipstick in preparation for her turn to share. Clearing her throat loudly and formally, Jessica began to speak, "Hi All. I hope you enjoyed your dessert cups. They're a traditional Valentine's Day treat in my home. The girls just love them." Jessica's voice was flat and Joyce thought she saw Anne frown.

"These Dares have just been a transformational journey for me." Joyce thought Jessica's voice now resembled a princess in a make-believe fairy tale. "This work has taught me how important it is to establish positive patterns early in married life so you don't end up in miserable relationships . . . and I have you all to thank for that." Joyce processed Jessica's insult, disguised as a statement of gratitude. She definitely saw Mona frown because her lips were pressed together so tightly she looked as if she were repressing an unruly belch.

"I have also learned how important it is to keep Jesus at the center of my life every single day. I have every confidence that He will lead me through dark valleys and beside quiet waters." As

Jessica droned on quoting various motivational quotes mixed with Bible verses, the women grew impatient. Joyce shifted uncomfortably in her chair, and she could have sworn that Maxine rolled her eyes.

Jessica rapidly continued, "Over the past few months, Bob and I have grown closer as a couple. We communicate more, and we . . . we . . ." The words stopped flowing from Jessica's mouth and her face crumpled like a paper mask. She looked up at the women staring at her and could feel their disbelief and irritation. Blinking several times in fast succession Jessica snarled, "Oh, who do I think I'm fooling? If my Mama were here she'd say, 'cut the crap, Jessica!'" She looked around the room wildly mumbling random words like "reputation" and "church elder" and "financially ruined." Her eyes were wide and darted around the room before halting at Joyce. Jessica froze. She was motionless except for her eyes, which shifted back and forth. The women sat in stunned silence, staring at the pretty young wife who had just come undone.

Joyce rose and dragged her chair to the empty space next to Jessica. Turning her friend's chair so the two women faced each other, Joyce took Jessica's hands and stared intently into her eyes. "Jessica, look at me." Being ignored, Joyce repeated the command a little more sternly. "Jessica, look at me." Slowly, Jessica relaxed and focused on her friend.

"Good. That's good, Jessica. Take a deep breath." Looking at the women Joyce called out, "Can someone get Jessica a little water?"

Alma exited the room and returned with a paper cup filled with water. Jessica drank the water while Alma, who realized the young woman wasn't much older than her own daughter, was suddenly filled with compassion and a fiercely protective instinct. She stroked Jessica's hair and asked, "Jessica, what's wrong?"

Jessica looked at Joyce, who nodded her head encouragingly. Jessica turned to face the group. "My marriage is in shambles. Everything is a mess. It's like I'm stuck in a toilet that swirls me in circles and keeps me off-balance." Jessica raked her fingers through her hair and with desperation in her voice turned back to Joyce, "I don't even know where to begin or how to sort this out. You tell them, Joyce. I can't do it. I'm too ashamed." She pushed her hands through her hair a final time and pulled them down so they covered her face.

Joyce looked around the table, saw Maxine nod, and began. "It seems like Jessica's husband has some type of addiction to pornography. It's been escalating over the past few months and has gotten to the point that Jessica no longer feels safe." Jessica took a few deep breaths and sensing the security around her, visibly relaxed. Joyce continued, "She called me last night asking for help, but had to get off the phone because Bob was calling from out of town. I suspect he made a bunch promises he won't keep. Things are getting bad and Jessica needs our help. She and the girls need to get away from Bob and go someplace where his influence and money can't find them."

Now the eyes of the other women grew wide and Jessica perceived their surprise. She backtracked. "That might be a little extreme, I think." She frowned and appealed to Joyce with her sweetest voice, "It's not that bad . . . really. He went a little too far just a couple of times. I don't need to leave him. Um . . . maybe he could just get some counseling or something . . ."

The mama bear in Alma rose up and in a firm voice she objected. "No, Jessica. Your instinct last night was right. You need help separating the truth from fantasy."

When Alma stopped talking, Anne touched Jessica's shoulder, and assured the young woman. "Jessica, I've heard there are lots men and women—even church leaders—who develop addictions to pornography. Many of their situations end badly." Having Jessica's full attention, Anne pleaded, "Right now, you need to put a safe distance between you and Bob. It would be wonderful if he goes to counseling and breaks the chains of seduction, but it won't happen overnight. Until it does, you need to be protected. You need to find a stable and secure place where you can regain your footing." Jessica listened to every word Anne spoke, never breaking eye contact, and heard the other women quietly agree with Anne's position.

"She's right."

"You can stay with me, Jessica"

"Listen to her, Honey."

Just then the buzzer sounded in the main rink, marking the start of the first period. The women refused to move, but Jessica was eager to escape the frank orations of the women who cared about her too much to back away from the truth. To break the spell she stood self-consciously and made it clear to the other women that the conversation was closed. "I hear what you're all saying and I know you're right. Thank you for your offers, but I'm going to have to figure this out for myself, or I'll never be able to stand on my own two feet without depending on someone else." She buttoned her coat in preparation for the cold temperatures in the rink. "I've got this. I promise." She put her hand on her heart and smiled bravely. Gently pulling Alma's arm upward, Jessica took a deep breath and shouted with false enthusiasm, "Now let's go lose another one!"

The women numbly followed Jessica out of the party room and toward the rink. Joyce looked back into the dark room and wished it could be that easy.

Chapter 53 – A New Season

Therefore, if anyone is in Christ, he is a new creation. The old has passed away; behold the new has come.

2 Corinthians 5:17 ESV

Alma slammed the trunk closed and hustled into the large Park District building with its silver dome reflecting the hot August sunshine. As soon as she entered the chilly ice arena she regretted her selection of shorts, t-shirt, and sandals almost as much as she regretted her promise to bring Marco to the ice rink to watch Mateo's first practice of a new hockey season.

Pushing the cumbersome wheelchair through the rink's lobby, Alma wistfully looked at the dark party room where she had spent many hours learning, growing, and loving. Shaking away the memories, she was thankful for Alicia's presence as together they maneuvered the wheelchair's heavy rubber wheels over the threshold and into the cold rink. Wheeling Marco into a special section reserved for the handicapped, Alma felt a chill ripple across her shoulders. She pulled the stadium blanket out of her hockey mom bag and draped it over his torso and legs. She fastened the Velcro on his wool coat and placed an Agitator ski cap on her husband's head.

"Marco, I'm going to say hello to some of my friends sitting over there." She pointed to the cement bleachers several rows higher and toward center ice. "Is it okay if I left you with Alicia for just a little while?" He nodded almost imperceptibly and she leaned forward and placed a tender kiss on his cheek. Alma climbed the stairs and shuffled over to where her Respect Dare sisters were sitting. When she looked back at Marco she smiled at the picture of Alicia sweetly holding hands with her father.

Approaching the group, Alma immediately saw Anne bouncing a baby on her knee. The little girl was dressed in clothing that celebrated Chicago's favorite hockey team. The familiar profile of an Indian chief was emblazoned on her red and black jogging suit, hand-knitted hat, and hockey slippers. The zooming, colorful figures of skaters on the ice below fascinated the infant.

Alma laughed with delight, "Ah, I see we have a new hockey fan! How old is she now, Anne?"

"She turned three months yesterday. She's finally starting to sleep through the night—just in time for me to go back to school!"

Alma was surprised and asked, "You're going back to work?"

Anne smiled. "Not full time. I couldn't bear to leave Emma with a nanny all day. I've volunteered to tutor struggling readers two afternoons a week. I love being a mother and spending all my time with the baby, but to be honest, devoting the entire summer to the boys and Emma began to turn my brain into a soggy sponge." The women laughed with recollections of when it took all day to get out of their pajamas. "How are you, Alma?"

Alma smiled, "A little melancholy, I think. Alicia started college this week. Without Marco's income, things have been really tight. Despite her full scholarship, Alicia made the decision to remain at home and get a full-time job. Instead of going away to school and living on campus, she enrolled at a university downtown and commutes every day."

Maxine asked, "How are things with Marco?"

Alma's smile faded slightly. "He's making progress, but things are going slowly. He's able to say simple words—enough for us to play 20 questions so I can figure out what he needs. But his leg function hasn't returned the way his doctors had hoped. We do exercises every night at home to keep things moving, but his muscles have atrophied to such a degree, there isn't much hope."

Joyce, who was listening quietly, laid her hand on Alma's shoulder and interjected, "Never give up hope, Alma. Our God is mighty. Nothing is impossible for Him."

Alma patted Joyce's hand, and noticed the stylish haircut and highlights that framed Joyce's face. "Thanks for that reminder, Friend. Some days I get so caught up in the practical that I forget about the supernatural. God is good."

"All the time." Joyce replied.

"What about you, Joyce? How are things with you and Jim?"

"Well, the fire is still crackling, if that's what you mean!" The women laughed so loudly, several of the team members looked up from the ice. Joyce lowered her voice. "Things are going well with us. I started going to Celebrate Recovery where Anne and Tony go, and have been uncovering the underlying reasons I spend so much time and energy trying to make everything go my way. Some of the work is tough, I'm not going to lie, but like the Respect Dares, God is in the middle of it and revealing His great blessings." Joyce lifted her purse and shuffled through its contents, removing a 3x5-inch baby album. "This, Ladies, is called a Brag Book, and prepare yourselves, because not only do I have pictures of the most beautiful granddaughter in the world, there's also a few photos from our second honeymoon in Jamaica!" The women started to whistle and hoot again and this time more players looked up from the ice. "Oh great, now Justin is going to complain that I embarrassed him during practice." Joyce stood up and dramatically waved at her son on the ice and called out in a falsetto voice, "Hi, Sweetie," before Maxine and Mona pulled her back down.

Maxine scolded, "Joyce, you know this is going to be a moment he relays to a therapist someday, right?" Joyce nodded and smiled a toothy grin. Maxine countered, "Cynthia tells me if I ever call out to her from the stands, she'll quit playing hockey forever. " Maxine nudged Joyce with her elbow. "I know you're all wondering how Samuwel and I are. Well, things have been a little bumpy, I'll admit. This past spring, I was passed over for a big promotion. It was something that I'd been working for years to attain, but it went to a female executive with no kids or husband to slow her down. I was pretty resentful for a while, but then a close friend reminded me of my priorities." Maxine leaned into Mona's shoulder, indicating she was the friend to whom Maxine was referring. "I realized that the promotion would have taken me out of the home again and potentially back into bad patterns. I'm coming to terms with the fact that I'm not going to be the top executive at the company, but I am taking away a bigger benefit than a larger 401K—a tremendous husband and remarkable kids."

Maxine's smile was genuine and affirmed that her words were true. "Speaking of kids, I'd better check on the twins. They're in the small rink taking a learn-to-skate class with Samuwel. The boys have been to so many of Cynthia's games that they want to become hockey players. Just when I thought I was nearing the end of the hockey mom road, they pull me back in!" The women laughed and hugged Maxine before she jogged down the steep steps and out of the rink.

Mona was the last of the women to share. "Things are getting back to the way they were before Aahil . . ." Mona shook her head and began again, "I mean, our marriage is even stronger than it was before." The women could see Mona was nervous sharing such personal information with women she hadn't seen in six months. Anne extended the baby to Mona who reached out and snuggled Emma in a loving embrace. Giving her eyes somewhere to look and her hands something to do, she was more comfortable sharing. "Aahil and I have gotten over the infidelity and are closer than we were before. I don't know if it was because of the marriage counseling—which I couldn't believe he agreed to—or our time together reading the Bible."

She cradled a drowsy Emma and traced her delicate hands with a finger. "We've been attending a community Bible church near our home where there are several former Muslim families who have also converted to Christianity. We go to a Bible study on Tuesday nights and read from the Bible every morning before Aahil goes to work. Samir even attends the youth group and the church and has been talking about getting baptized." She leaned forward slightly and smelled sleeping Emma's forehead. "Mmmm. I love the smell of babies' heads." Sitting up straight, Mona declared. "You women changed my marriage and my whole life. I'm so blessed that God brought you all into my life."

"We feel exactly the same about you too, Mona." Anne smiled at her friend and the two women leaned their shoulders against each other. In the distance, Anne saw a girl in overalls heading in their direction. What Anne though was one of the young figure skaters turned out to be Jessica with her hair in a ponytail and a baseball cap tilted on her head. As she neared the cluster of women, they could see paint smears across the legs of her pants and the bridge of her nose. Under the dirty nose, was a familiar smile with sparkling white teeth.

"Hey, y'all! It's me, Jessica!" The women were surprised to see Jessica and greeted her warmly with hugs. "Aww . . . look at your little baby, Anne! She's beautiful."

"Thanks, Jessica. You're looking pretty good yourself."

Jessica's face turned a slight pink, "Aw . . . quit teasin' me, Anne. I must look a sight." Alma noticed a more pronounced southern twang in Jessica's speech. "I just ran into Maxine at the little rink. She told me y'all were up here."

While the women chatted amiably with Jessica and gave her updates, Joyce frowned. If Jessica was here, it was because she had brought her stepson, Bobby Jr. to practice, which meant she hadn't left Bob. It made Joyce shudder to think of the life that Jessica must be living with Bob. At their final meeting, Joyce vowed to stay connected to Jessica, but days later when Joyce called she got a message that the phone had been disconnected. She figured that Jessica had Joyce's number and would call if she needed help, and left it alone.

"Hello, Joyce? Earth calling Joyce?" Jessica had leaned over and was trying to catch Joyce's attention.

"Huh? Oh. Sorry. What?"

"I was asking everyone how early their kids started skating on the ice. When did Justin first learn to skate?"

"Oh, um . . . I think he was five or six. Why?"

"Well, I signed the girls up for skating lessons and was wondering if there was a difference in the start age between hockey players and figure skaters."

Joyce pondered Jessica's question and then asked, "Are you planning on putting the girls on a hockey team so you can juggle Bobby Jr.'s hockey games with theirs?" While Joyce's words indicated an interest in Jessica's daughters, what Joyce really wanted to know was if Jessica was still with Bob.

Jessica didn't shrink at Joyce's question. Instead she shook her head firmly. "After our last meeting, I thought a lot about the things y'all said to me. Up until that moment, I couldn't get a handle on which was the right thing to do. When something terrible would go down with Bob, I planned to leave. But then he would come home the next day and be so apologetic and vulnerable. He told me that he needed me to help him do better, and that he didn't know what would happen to him if I left. My mind switched from go to stay almost on a daily basis. I was starting to think that I was going insane."

She adjusted the baseball cap on her head. "When I called my mama in South Carolina, she told me she couldn't take us in because her new trailer park was only for folks who were 55 and older. When I called my sister she was being evicted from her apartment because her boyfriend had gambled their rent money for two months in a row. I felt stuck. I didn't have enough cash to afford even the cheapest of apartments in an ugly neighborhood." Jessica began to pull at a hole in her overalls.

"I spent a lot of time praying at church and it was there I learned about a safe haven for women and children in abusive situations. Bob came home from his business trip and the next day while he was at work, I packed a few things for the girls and we left." A look of admiration crossed the faces of Jessica's friends. "We lived at the secret house for six months before I had established a solid foundation—a job, childcare, and housing. We moved into our tiny apartment a couple of weeks ago, and even though it's cramped and a little dingy, I'm happier in that cheap apartment than I ever was in Bob's glamorous mansion filled with expensive things." Jessica rolled her eyes and made her friends smile at her courage.

"Today I've been painting the kitchen, but had to take a break to bring the girls to their skating lesson. I was worried that I would run into Bob, but I shouldn't have, because Bobby Jr. turned 16 over the summer and probably drove an Italian sports car to practice." Jessica looked at her phone and jumped. "Oh man, I've gotta' run. The girls' skating class ends in five minutes, and I want to take a couple of pictures with my second-hand phone. Jessica gave the women her number before dashing off to watch the final minutes of the girls tumbling on the ice.

Thinking about Jessica's baby girls on the ice made Alma contemplate life's lessons. She hoped that Jessica would learn how to protect her boundaries in the future, long before escape was the only option. Maybe it's better to fall down when you're young, Alma thought. It's easier to learn from your mistakes. Plus, you're closer to the ground and it's easier to bounce back up.

Alma stood and stretched the cold from her knees and hips. "Well, I'd better get back to Marco. Alicia has class this evening and has to get going. I'll see you at practice on Thursday?" The women responded with large smiles and nods, and several thumbs went up.

Alma smiled and carefully traced her path across the bleachers, and then down a few steep rows to where she had left her husband and daughter. Standing at her mother's approach, Alicia apologized, "Sorry, Mamá. I have to leave for class."

Alma hugged her daughter. "It's okay, Mija. Thank you for coming with us." Alicia kissed her mother on the cheek and bent over to kiss Marco on his forehead, before dashing out of the rink.

Sitting next to Marco's chair, Alma asked, "Marco, do you want me to put some gloves on your hands?" She looked into his face and watched his lips twitch while he head shook side to side. She reached down to feel the temperature of his hands. "But your hands are getting cold. I don't want you to catch a draft." She began to reach for the hockey bag where she kept enough layers to withstand temperatures that dropped below zero, but felt his grasp on her hand tighten.

"Okay, I hear you." She turned slightly to watch the team skate one of many drills they would repeat a thousand times during the next season. Instead of releasing her hand as he had so many times before, Alma felt Marco's grip tighten. And together they sat. Together.

ABOUT THE AUTHOR

Tammy Oberg De La Garza is an Associate Professor at Roosevelt University in Chicago, Illinois. She is the lead author of *Salsa Dancing in Gym Shoes*, and has been involved in educating children and adults for more than 25 years. Tammy's countless hours in women's ministries, small groups, marriage ministry, and step studies have helped her understand the vital importance of developing healthy relationships with women of varying ages. Her hope is that women will experience strength in sisterhood and unlock the power of faith, healing, growth, and acceptance. Tammy is married to the love of her life, Rey, is familiar with playing the role of a hockey mom to their son Alex, and delights in the long "girl-talk-sessions" with their daughter, Sierra.

www.TammyDeLaGarza.com

Made in the USA
Middletown, DE
03 August 2016